S0-ASI-636

"Don't you have any sense, Audrey?"

"What?" she asked Gray, baffled.

"Talk about a lamb among wolves. Don't trust anybody."

"But, if you—"

"Don't…trust…anybody." He stood, bracing his hands on the table, and loomed over her, his posture filled with the same tension she had sensed before. His gaze traveled over her face, lingered a fraction on her mouth.

"Not even you?" she asked, intensely aware of his scrutiny.

"Especially not me."

Dear Reader,

I'm always getting letters telling me how much you love miniseries, and this month we've got three great ones for you. Linda Turner starts the new family-based miniseries, THOSE MARRYING McBRIDES! with *The Lady's Man*. The McBrides have always been unlucky in love—until now. And it's wedding-wary Zeke who's the first to take the plunge. Marie Ferrarella also starts a new miniseries this month. CHILDFINDERS, INC. is a detective agency specializing in finding missing kids, and they've never failed to find one yet. So is it any wonder desperate Savannah King turns to investigator Sam Walters when her daughter disappears in *A Hero for All Seasons?* And don't miss *Rodeo Dad*, the continuation of Carla Cassidy's wonderful Western miniseries, MUSTANG, MONTANA.

Of course, that's not all we've got in store. Paula Detmer Riggs is famous for her ability to explore emotion and create characters who live in readers' minds long after the last page is turned. In *Once More a Family* she creates a reunion romance to haunt you. Sharon Mignerey is back with her second book, *His Tender Touch*, a suspenseful story of a woman on the run and her unwilling protector—who soon turns into her willing lover. Finally, welcome new author Candace Irvin, who debuts with a military romance called *For His Eyes Only*. I think you'll be as glad as we are that Candace has joined the Intimate Moments ranks.

Enjoy—and come back next month, when we once again bring you the best and most exciting romantic reading around.

Yours,

Leslie J. Wainger
Executive Senior Editor

Please address questions and book requests to:
Silhouette Reader Service
U.S.: 3010 Walden Ave., P.O. Box 1325, Buffalo, NY 14269
Canadian: P.O. Box 609, Fort Erie, Ont. L2A 5X3

HIS TENDER TOUCH

SHARON MIGNEREY

Silhouette® INTIMATE™ MOMENTS®

Published by Silhouette Books

America's Publisher of Contemporary Romance

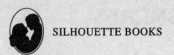 SILHOUETTE BOOKS

ISBN 0-373-07935-4

HIS TENDER TOUCH

Copyright © 1999 by Sharon Mignerey

This edition published by arrangement with Harlequin Books S.A.

® and TM are trademarks of Harlequin Books S.A., used under license.
Trademarks indicated with ® are registered in the United States Patent
and Trademark Office, the Canadian Trade Marks Office and in other
countries.

Look us up on-line at: http://www.romance.net

Printed in U.S.A.

SHARON MIGNEREY

lives in Colorado, with her husband and two dogs, Angel and Squirt. From the time she figured out that spelling words could be turned into stories, she knew being a writer was how she wanted to spend her life. She won RWA's Golden Heart Award in 1995, validation that she was on the right path.

When she's not writing, she loves puttering around in her garden, walking her dogs along the South Platte River and spending time at the family cabin in Colorado's four corners region.

She loves hearing from readers, and you can write to her in care of Silhouette Books, 300 East 42nd Street, 6th floor, New York, NY 10017.

For my mother, Thelma, who shared the marvelous gift
of stories
For my daughters, Yvette and Celeste, who are a joy to
me always
For my granddaughter, Gillian, who teaches me that love
is a continuing circle

In memory of Carol Henry
A little romance, a little mystery, and DJ, too.
I miss you every day, my friend.
This one is for you.

Chapter 1

Gray Murdoch reined his horse to a stop at the edge of the ridge. Below him spread a valley—lonely, wild, forbidding—as curtains of cold spring rain dropped from menacing, gunmetal-dark clouds. The day suited his edgy mood perfectly.

The storm separated him from the ranch. Even so, he lingered a moment, inhaling deeply. He settled deeper into his shearling jacket, a frigid gust reminding him this was a March storm, every bit as likely to spit out sleet or snow as rain. Beneath him, the horse stamped restlessly.

"Easy, boy." Gray patted the gelding's neck in reassurance, then touched the animal's flanks lightly with his boots. As they descended the steep slope, he could almost sense the horse's anxiety to be back in the barn. At the bottom, the horse broke into a ground-eating lope. Gray leaned forward, absorbing the horse's movements beneath him.

The rain billowed within the wind, alternately hiding and revealing the foothills of the San Juan Mountains to the west. Out of one of the curtains of rain, a band of horsemen appeared, riding toward him. In the next instant, they were hidden by the rain. Gray didn't recognize them and wondered who they were.

Wind whistled around him, bitterly cold.

A woman's anguished scream ripped through the sound of the storm and his horse's rhythmic gait. He pulled on the reins, instinctively reaching for his service revolver.

It, of course, wasn't there. Hadn't been for the past seven months.

His heart pounding, he leaned over the saddle horn and scanned the empty valley. Rabbit brush, a few yucca and broad expanses of sand met his gaze. Beyond, the wall of rain would reach him in a matter of minutes.

He didn't see a woman anywhere.

No band of horsemen, either.

He urged the horse into a walk. The animal sidestepped, his ears laid flat against his head.

Another shout echoed around him, deeper this time, and more guttural.

She screamed again.

Gray recognized terror.

Though he could not see her, he turned toward the sound, the need to help pouring through him. The veil of rain wavered, and the first sprinkles splashed on the dry ground around him. Nothing accounted for a man's shout or a woman's scream. Nothing.

The storm blew closer, the air rippling with the sound of the falling torrent. A bolt of lightning flashed. A half-dozen fingers of brilliant white light blistered the ground. A clap of thunder reverberated, deep, primal, as much felt as heard.

From within the mist, a woman appeared and dashed toward him. Her hair streamed behind her in a dark cloud. She clutched a cradle board against her breast. Dressed in a buckskin tunic and moccasins, she ran as though chased by the devil himself.

Her face blanched. She ran faster, her movements jerky. Her face pinched with fear, she looked right through him.

Gray urged the horse into a run and called out. He couldn't make himself heard over the roar of the rain and another rumble of thunder.

She turned her head and looked over her shoulder.

Four riders burst out of the storm. They wore hats pulled low, and dark capes flapped around them. They raced after her.

She cried out. Gray didn't understand the words, but he felt her desperation. As she came toward him, he leaned far down, intending to lift her onto the saddle behind him.

Braced for the instant he'd lift her weight, he reached for her.

And touched nothing.

She ran past him.

Carried by his own momentum, he fell from the saddle and hit the ground. Instinctively he rolled, taking the brunt of the fall on his shoulder in a bone-jarring impact.

He stood and faced the oncoming riders, wishing he had his weapon. Waving his arms, he shouted at them.

They bore down on him without altering their course and without slowing.

A spotted pony and its rider leaped over him. The other riders thundered past as though he weren't even there.

He turned around.

The valley was empty.

No woman.

No mustangs ridden by dark men wearing dark, flapping coats.

Another jagged bolt of lightning ripped across the sky, casting eerie light over the empty plain. Deafening thunder rumbled toward him as a drenching, cold rain poured from the sky.

Audrey Sussman arrived at the guest ranch in the middle of a storm about an hour after day slid into murky night.

It was a fitting end to a miserable drive.

The compound of buildings illuminated by the headlights from her car looked ancient as a legend. Puma's Lair. The name conjured images of a wild, secluded hideaway. Apt, she decided. The guest ranch was miles from nowhere.

Not even a yard light was on. She peered through the windshield at the water-soaked adobe walls that looked as though they had bled.

The moment she turned off the headlights and killed the engine, the patter of rain against the car became more intense. For all the activity she saw, it might have been midnight instead of a few minutes past seven.

She was late arriving because she had spent an unplanned couple of hours in Fort Garland getting her car repaired, every one of the problems small and irritating. She would have thought the repairman was out to gouge a poor, unsuspecting tourist if the whole bill hadn't been under fifty dollars. Unfortunately, the repairs hadn't been good enough—her car had coughed and sputtered the last forty miles, making her wonder if she would ever arrive. She hadn't stopped, hadn't wanted to be stranded on a lonely stretch of highway.

She should have figured the guest ranch would look this…inhospitable and forbidding.

Taking a deep breath, she opened the door and stepped into the shockingly cold deluge. She dashed through the opening in the wall, up a flagstone walk to an old-fashioned arched door. The scent of wood smoke hung in the air. Cozying up to a fireplace after being out in this weather would be great, she thought, feeling an icy trickle of water soak through her hair to her scalp.

She knocked on the door. A crack of lightning split open the sky, and white light bathed the compound.

There, in the middle of the yard, a woman stood. Her arms were wrapped protectively around a…cradle board.

"Hi," Audrey called.

In the darkness that followed the lightning, the woman vanished.

Audrey peered into the black gloom, doubting what she had just seen. She *was* alone. Shaking her head at the vivid conjuring of her imagination, she knocked on the door again. Thunder rumbled toward her, bone deep and oppressive.

"C'mon, Richard," she urged the ranch manager, a man she was acquainted with only by phone. Shivering, she wrapped her arms around herself and listened for the sounds of someone—anyone—approaching.

One last time, she pounded on the door.

It swung open on the creak of ancient hinges.

Sudden light spilled from the room, until it was blocked by a large man who filled the doorway.

She lifted her head, unable to see the man's expression. Another flash of lightning momentarily cast white, eerie light on his features. His mostly gray hair fell in long braids down each shoulder. Weather and long years had carved deep lines in his face.

"Richard, I'm Audrey Sussman." She met his scowl and forced a smile she didn't feel. "I know I'm late, but the storm—"

"He isn't here."

That at least explained why this man didn't look as she had imagined Richard Emmanuel looking. He didn't move out of the doorway, a reinforcement of his you're-not-welcome-here stance.

"The place is closed," he said, confirming what she already knew. "It won't be open for another two weeks."

"I know that," she said with more patience than she felt.

He nodded and started to shut the door. Audrey extended her arm and put a foot in the threshold. "I'm expected. When will Mr. Emmanuel be back?"

"I don't know."

"Invite the lady out of the rain, Hawk," another deep voice commanded, this one with a hint of a drawl.

Hawk hesitated an instant, then stepped out of the doorway. Audrey followed him into the building. Puma's Lair. The name echoed through her mind, accompanied by her own assessment of the ranch's isolation. She gave herself a mental shake. She was expected, she reminded herself.

Even so, she wasn't ready to confess that she doubted her car would make it back to the nearest town.

As her eyes adjusted to the lighting, she discovered the room wasn't as bright as she had thought while standing outside. A kerosene lamp cast a golden glow in one corner, and a fire burned in a small pueblo-style fireplace in another.

A man, larger even than Hawk, lounged against a doorjamb on the opposite side of the room. Behind him, a dark hallway stretched, dimly illuminated by a faint, flickering light.

"Hi," she said.

"Hi," he returned.

Hawk closed the door. "What do you want?"

Without the draft from outside, the room instantly felt more comfortable. Audrey moved toward the inviting warmth of the fireplace. Automatically, she adjusted the pair of broad silver bracelets she always wore on her right arm.

"I'm here to do the audit," she said, the fire's heat feeling good to her. Putting Hawk's name to the payroll records she had spent the past week reviewing, she presumed this must be the caretaker and handyman. "You're Jacob Hawk, is that right?"

He nodded curtly.

"Jacob...Jake—"

"I am called Hawk."

"Hawk, then," she agreed. "Will Richard be here tomorrow?"

He shrugged. "Who knows?"

Or cares, Audrey mentally added. "Do you have a phone?"

"On the desk," the second man said. "Unfortunately, it hasn't been working all night."

He moved toward her, his expression filled with intense concentration, the color of his eyes indistinguishable in the dimness. He was many years younger than Hawk, and she might have thought he was Richard except that his voice was far deeper. She had the oddest feeling she should know him, but from where she couldn't have said.

"Like the electricity?" she asked, noting the electric fixtures on the ceiling and dark lamps throughout the room.

The corner of his mouth lifted, and he nodded. "Like the electricity."

Glad the tension in his gaze had lessened somewhat, she extended her hand. "I'm Audrey Sussman."

The beat of a second passed before he took her hand and answered. "Gray."

"Is that a first name or a last name?" His hand was large—much larger than hers—warm and callused. Inviting.

He didn't smile, but something in his expression eased a bit more. "Grayson Murdoch." He released her hand, but his gaze didn't leave her face.

She wondered what he was looking for. Her appearance was ordinary by any standards—brown hair, brown eyes, average height and the requisite curves. Nothing about her warranted so earnest a stare. Not even being soaked to the skin. Which was too bad, because he was the sort of man to whom she would give a second glance—a long, long second glance.

Gray's height was eight or nine inches above hers, and she angled her head to maintain contact with his gaze. Tall as he was, his shoulders were almost too broad for his height. He wore a warm-looking corduroy shirt the same faded shade as his jeans layered over a gray knit prairie shirt. Shaggy dark hair framed his face, which was all angles and planes. Except for his mouth.

Wide with a full lower lip, it was made for smiling. She looked back at his eyes and had the feeling this man didn't smile nearly enough.

Grayson Murdoch's name hadn't been on the payroll records. In spite of that, she had the feeling he belonged here as much as Hawk.

His attention remained focused wholly on her.

"Have we met?" she asked, sure she would have remembered if they had.

He studied her as though trying to fathom some private mystery. "No. Is your car locked?"

"No." She answered automatically, his question seeming to come out of left field, surprising her.

"I thought I'd get your bags and bring them in." He glanced toward Hawk. "What room do you want her in?"

Unlike Hawk, Gray seemed to assume she would be staying. He waited for Hawk's answer with the assurance he would get the response he expected.

"The one on the far north end, I guess."

"I'll meet you there." Gray pulled a nubby wool sweater over his head and snagged a clear slicker off a row of pegs next to the entryway, slipped it on, opened the door and stepped outside. Audrey envied his layers of warm-looking clothes. She shivered once more and turned her back to the fire's heat, grateful for the warmth that reached through her soaked garments.

She glanced around the room, her experienced eye finding about what she had expected of a guest-ranch lobby. The original Southwestern decor was minus the trendy colors touted in the best decorating magazines. The dark-stained pine floors gleamed, and the faint scent of old-fashioned floor wax tickled her nose. It conjured images of home and hearth, at once filling her with the ache of loss and a vague notion of anticipation. Lately, she'd begun to dream of her own home, unsure whether the urge was the beginning of a ticking biological clock or her deep loneliness since her mother's death.

Hawk, muttering under his breath, retrieved a key out of the desk.

"This is some storm," Audrey said, inserting a cheerful, conversational note into her voice that usually made people open up.

"Yep."

"The rain surprised me." She gave a rueful chuckle. "I didn't exactly come prepared."

He didn't answer.

So much for the weather, she thought, searching for something new to talk about.

He headed toward the dark hallway, then paused. She understood he was waiting for her. Reluctantly, she left the fire's heat and followed him down the corridor.

"How many guests can Puma's Lair accommodate?" she asked, merely to make conversation. Based on the records, she knew thirty-five guests were the most that had ever been here. Small, compared to the other resorts owned by Lambert Enterprises.

"Don't know. Never thought about it."

"I'll bet you'll be glad to see spring come."

"The season makes no difference to me," he answered.

"Does it often rain like this?"

"No."

Audrey sighed and gave up trying to lure Hawk into conversation. A couple of sconces held flickering candles that cast undulating light. First kerosene lanterns and now candles, she thought, feeling as though she had stepped into a hundred-year-old time warp. A chilly draft skittered through the hall, and a forlorn whisper of wind whistled through a crack somewhere.

If Richard had planned to be gone, why hadn't he said

so when they had set the date for her to come from Denver? And who was Grayson Murdoch of the intent eyes?

"Does Gray live close by?" She hadn't noticed any other cars parked in front.

"Uh."

Did that "uh" mean yes or no? Audrey wondered with a trace of irritation.

They took a couple of turns that left Audrey disoriented about where they were in relationship to the lobby. On one side of the hallway was an expanse of glass, and cold crept through the windows. For a moment, lightning illuminated the hall. At last Hawk stopped in front of one of the doors and inserted a key. The door swung inward on a creak of hinges badly in need of oil.

"I forgot to bring a lantern," Hawk said. He handed Audrey the key and brushed past her. "I'll be back in a minute."

She watched him disappear down the dark passage, then peered into the black room. Not even the outline of a window was visible. She swallowed and wished Hawk, however taciturn he was, would hurry back. Of all the stupid fears to have left over from childhood, being afraid of the dark had to top the list.

Years—a whole lifetime—had passed since she had been trapped in the dark, smelling the smoke from a fire.

"Years," she murmured, wishing the vague alarm stealing through her would go away. She forced herself to step inside. There's nothing to be afraid of, she silently scolded. Even so, coiled in the pit of her stomach was a primal fear as intense as when she had been five. She waited just over the threshold for her eyes to adjust to the darkness. Finally, making out the dim outline of the bed and dresser and a window on the opposite side of the room, she crossed the room and pulled open the drape. The night beyond was as black as the inside of the room.

She whirled around, needing to see the light in the hallway, needing the reassurance she wasn't trapped. Another lightning strike flashed beyond the hallway windows, silhouetting the large form of a man at the doorway.

Audrey sucked in her breath on an audible gasp.

"It's just me," Gray Murdoch said.

"My word, but you scared me," she said, pressing a hand against her breast.

"Didn't mean to. If you want to see what's out there, I'll have to go open the shutters on the outside of the building. And, frankly, I'd rather not. Sometimes those old hinges stick."

"That's okay," she murmured. The man must be around a lot to know such a thing.

He moved silently into the room. She couldn't see him so much as feel the disturbance of the air as it shifted around her.

"It's still raining like a son of a gun out there. Where's Hawk?"

"He went back to get a lantern. Thanks for going out to get my things. Has the electricity been off long?"

Gray brushed past her, carrying the scent of rain and damp wool. "All night. I didn't bring in everything in the trunk. Just the suitcase and a smaller one that matched."

"That's fine," she said. "I thought the ranch had a generator."

"That hasn't worked in years. You left your keys in the ignition," he said, handing them to her.

"Thanks," she replied. Gray had an easy familiarity with the ranch, one that provoked questions in Audrey's mind that she gave voice to. "Do you spend a lot of time here?"

"If that's a roundabout way of asking if I live here, the answer is yes."

"But you're not an employee."

"You're the one doing the audit, Ms. Sussman—"

"Audrey."

"Audrey." A pause followed. "I rent one of the cabins

out back. The roof has a leak, so I've temporarily moved down here.''

"Ah."

A wavering light preceded footsteps down the hallway, and a moment later Hawk appeared. He came into the room and set the lantern down on the dresser.

"The bath is two doors down that way." Hawk's gaze lit on Audrey, then slid to Gray. "Is there anything else you want?"

Room service, she thought. And a nice steaming bowl of soup. "I suppose it's too late for something to eat. I'd be happy to ma—"

"Like I said, we're closed. Ain't nothing much in the kitchen."

So much for Western hospitality, Audrey thought. "So long as there is hot water and I can take a shower, I'll be fine." She didn't like it, but there was no point in complaining.

"Hot water we have plenty of, thanks to a propane heater and an artesian well," Gray said. He looked at Hawk, opened his mouth as if to say something. Some silent communication passed between the two men, and Gray shrugged. He glanced at Audrey, then followed Hawk into the hallway and closed the door.

Audrey stared at the closed door a moment, then at her watch. It was barely seven-thirty. She felt like a little kid who had been ushered off to bed. She dug through her purse and found a crumpled package containing a pair of crushed crackers and a couple of green-apple hard candies. Unwrapping one of the candies, she popped it in her mouth. Audrey looked around. The exterior shutters may have protected the windows, but they didn't keep away the sound of the storm. A wayward branch—she hoped it was a branch—brushed against the window in an uneven pattern, feeding her all too active imagination.

The room was chilly. An empty fireplace in the corner

about three feet off the pine floor appeared to be the only source of heat. But not a single stick of wood filled the tiled cubbyhole next to the fireplace. Above the cubbyhole was a pine panel, cut into an intricate design and stained the same dark shade as the floor. The area behind the panel was obviously hollow. She tried opening the panel like a cupboard door. It didn't budge.

She stood on tiptoe, struggling to see into the dark cavern behind the panel, needing to dispel her impression of being watched.

"This is stupid," she muttered under her breath. Obviously, it was storage for books or knickknacks or something. Too small for a person to hide back there. "Get a grip, girl!"

She opened her suitcase and fished through it for her bathrobe and nightgown. A year ago, she would have loved to have a rainy night all to herself with nothing to do except read a good book—in fact, she had prayed for this kind of retreat. She loved mysteries, the dark, scary kind. The book in her suitcase, which had been so appealing when she bought it, held absolutely no allure now.

Spurred into action by her undisciplined thoughts, she picked up her cosmetic case and headed for the bathroom. The shower warmed her, but failed to soothe her whirling thoughts. Her arrival had been nothing like she expected, but then nothing about this trip had made sense from the beginning.

She still had no clear idea of what she was doing here. Without notice or explanation, her boss, Howard Lambert, pulled her off another project and told her he wanted her to audit Puma's Lair.

She had worked for Lambert Enterprises long enough to recognize Howard's eccentric requests. This one topped the list, especially since Puma's Lair was his baby. He personally oversaw every detail.

"Business isn't quite right," he had told her. "Money is disappearing that shouldn't. Go do an audit."

She had seen no evidence to support his suspicions. If money was disappearing, he needed his CPA, not her. He had told her he trusted only her to find any irregularities. "What irregularities?" she had asked him. He hadn't known.

The shower lived up to Gray's promise. There was plenty of hot water—enough to get her warm. If she could just solve the hunger pangs, things would be hunky-dory all around. She returned to her room, her stomach growling and her imagination focused on food.

She unlocked the door and pushed it open. A savory aroma wafted through the air. A small fire crackled cheerfully in the hearth, chasing away the room's chill. A covered tray sat on the small table. She set down her cosmetic case and lifted the cover. A bowl of steaming chili and hot tortillas met her gaze. Her mouth watered, and she smiled.

Unable to imagine the laconic Jacob Hawk having a change of heart, she decided her benefactor was probably Gray. Grateful, she sat down to eat. The chili tasted as good as it smelled.

The sound of men arguing brought Audrey wide awake some hours later. She lay with her head pressed against the pillow, listening, her heart pounding. An instant of disorientation was replaced with her realization that she was at Puma's Lair.

The eerie whisper of wind in the hallway ebbed and flowed, masking the words. She sat up in bed and listened more intently. She slipped out of bed and opened the door a crack.

"Just calm down. Everything is under control." She thought the voice sounded like Richard. Relief flowed through her so suddenly she had to admit she had been worried when he hadn't been here when she arrived.

"We had a deal," Hawk said.

"Nothing has changed there." It was Richard's voice. There was no mistaking his Southwestern drawl.

Anxious to talk to someone she knew, she put on the navy silk robe on the end of her bed, opened the door and stepped into the hallway.

It was empty. Only the dancing shadows from the flickering candle met her gaze. Beyond the wall-to-wall windows, the night was utterly black. An odd movement caught her eye, and she realized she was looking through another window at the end of the courtyard. Two men were walking down the hallway.

Doubting they would have heard her if she called, she padded to the end of the passage, where it turned onto another corridor. The undulating shadows seemed to have a life of their own. A prickle of unease raised the hair on the back of her neck. More than ever, she needed to talk to someone familiar. Richard was a telephone acquaintance only, but for now, he would do.

The adjoining hallway was empty, but their voices were more distinct once again.

"It's got to," Hawk was saying. "We can't let Lambert walk away with everything."

Lambert? Audrey mentally echoed. Walk away with what? A draft lifted the hem of her robe, and she shivered, wishing she had packed velour and flannel instead of silk.

The voices faded again, and Audrey hurried to catch up. She came to yet another corner where the hallway took off in several different directions. She cocked her head, listening, trying to determine which of the empty corridors they had taken.

A moment later, she heard them talking again, and she followed their voices along another expanse of floor-to-ceiling windows. The candles flickered wildly as a draft brushed down the hall. The floor tiles felt unbelievably cold against the soles of her feet, and she added slippers to the things she wished she had packed.

She turned another corner, and the voices seemed to be coming toward her.

"...need is anyone snooping around." The voice was Hawk's.

"Lambert wouldn't—"

"You've told me a dozen times that he'd sell his own mother to get what he wants."

"And he'd have to be suspicious to send someone to..."

"Spy?"

"He insists this is a routine audit."

Suddenly, Audrey felt someone behind her. She glanced over her shoulder just as a pair of arms came around her. A lurch of raw panic clawed through her, and she opened her mouth to cry out.

A hand clamped over her mouth. In her ear, a nearly silent voice commanded, "Shh!"

Chapter 2

Be quiet? She would not! "Let go of me, you—"

She pulled at the hand held against her mouth, furious, angry tears burning at her eyes. The arm around her waist tightened, and as though she weighed nothing, she felt herself lifted off her feet.

"Shut up!"

She recognized Gray's voice as he backed into a niche that was even darker than the hallway, bringing her with him. His hand still pressed against her lips, he turned her toward the wall—a door, its texture smooth.

Incensed at being manhandled, she jabbed backward with her elbow. With frightening ease, he captured both of her hands with one of his, using his weight to press her against the wall.

"Be quiet," he whispered in her ear. "When you're snoopy, you hear things that you really don't want to know about. You should have stayed in your room, Audrey."

His calling her by name accomplished what force hadn't.

She stopped struggling, though to stop trembling would have been impossible.

Against her, his body radiated heat, making her feel warm, except for her feet. His posture was intent, and she had the sense he was listening. As her body relaxed slightly, he loosened his hold on her. "Shh," he whispered again.

In the next instant, she heard Richard's voice.

"She'll do the audit for Lambert and she'll leave," he said. "I've talked to her numerous times. Doubt she'd know a potted plant from a corral."

"And you're going to do nothing!"

"If she gets in the way, I'll handle it."

"We don't need this kind of scrutiny. Not now."

"She'll find nothing out of the ordinary." Richard's voice sounded mere feet away. "And lower your voice. It's not like we're alone."

Enveloped by Gray's heat, Audrey's heart pounded. Tension radiated from him, mirroring the sense of danger that thrummed through her.

They passed by, Hawk still complaining. Evidently, the man could say more than three words at a time when he chose. The outright threats—directed toward her, for Pete's sake—shocked her. And for some reason, Gray had protected her. She could have blithely interrupted, or worse yet, let them see her eavesdropping. What were they talking about? It—whatever *it* was—validated Howard Lambert's suspicion something was wrong.

Gray's hands held her hidden against the wall with no more force than necessary to keep her from moving. His head was bent, his cheek pressed against her hair. The feeling of danger faded, and she sighed as Gray's arms now felt protective rather than confining.

Never had she been so aware of another person. His heat. The pressure of his body along the length of her back. The scent of soap on his hands. Swallowing, she forced herself to think. Gray had been right—this was something she didn't want to know about. But now that she did, what next?

He removed his hand from her mouth. Against her ear, he whispered, "If I ask you to stay here and be quiet, will you do it?"

"Why?" she asked, not sure at all what she was asking.

Gray pressed his finger against her mouth, leaving behind a band of warmth. "I want to see where they've gone so we can get you safely back to your room."

Without looking at him, she struggled to compose her thoughts. Instead, her awareness centered on him. Finally, she nodded.

Gray slipped down the hall after Richard and Hawk.

She peeked around the corner and watched him a moment, realizing she couldn't hear him at all. He moved as silently as a shadow. Earlier, she hadn't known he was even close to her until the instant he grabbed her. Now she sank against the wall at the rear of the vestibule and leaned her head back.

She wrapped her arms around herself, cold once again. Slipping into the ordered mode of thinking that was automatic for her, she tried to make sense of what she had just heard. Business was business, separate from her personal life. Except this had become personal, and darned if she understood why.

Richard evidently didn't think much of her, which surprised her. Their infrequent conversations had been friendly enough. Threats were the last thing she would have expected. An occasional power outage was as sinister as things got in her life. Until now.

Audrey heard soft footfalls from the end of the hall. Gray, at last. She peeked out of the vestibule. Hawk strode toward her, his face devoid of expression, his black eyes riveted on her. She remembered too late that Gray's footsteps were soundless.

"I was right," Hawk said. "You were here."

"I'm looking for the kitchen," she stated, striving for a confident, calm tone. "I wanted to make a cup of tea."

"I smelled you when I came past here a minute ago." He came to a stop in front of her, so close that he was crowding her.

If she had been in the office back in Denver, she would have pushed her way past him. Instead, she found herself backing into the vestibule, annoyed with her lack of assertiveness. A silk nightgown and robe that left her shivering with cold weren't exactly a power suit.

"You might as well start talking."

"About what?" That much was true. She had no idea what to say.

"Leave it to Lambert to send a woman to do his dirty work."

"Dirty work?" She looked Hawk up and down. He glowered right back. "Sometimes it does take a woman to clean up. Such as recommending that staff be dismissed for being rude and uncooperative. Right now, though, I'm more interested in finding the kitchen so I can make a cup of tea."

"What's going on here?" Gray interrupted conversationally from behind Hawk.

Gray's uncanny silence again startled Audrey. She noticed that Hawk didn't so much as flinch.

"She says she's looking for the kitchen."

"And why wouldn't she be?" Gray responded. "I imagine she's hungry after being sent off to her room without any dinner." He brushed past Hawk and Audrey, then pushed open the door at the rear of the vestibule. "I thought I'd have a piece of that chocolate cake Mary Maktima baked this afternoon. Anyone care to join me?"

Astounded the kitchen was close enough to give substance to her lie, Audrey nodded. "That sounds good."

"You're a fool," Hawk said to Gray. "I know you're Richard's cousin, but—"

"Cousins?" Audrey's gaze slid from Hawk to Gray.

"Yeah," Gray confirmed, his expression unreadable. "My mom and Richard's are sisters." He moved into the room, struck a match and put it to the wick of a kerosene lantern that sat on an old-fashioned butcher-block table.

The room was large. An array of pots and pans hung over a center worktable. Two oversize refrigerators stood side by side on the opposite wall, flanked by a stove on one wall and a set of big stainless-steel sinks on the other. With the ease of a man familiar with his surroundings, Gray found the cake and set it on the table. Audrey turned around and discovered that Hawk was gone. She faced Gray without moving into the kitchen.

Cousins. And she had been so sure he was protecting her when he pulled her out of the hall. For all she knew, he had been protecting Richard or—

"Were you serious about wanting some tea?" Gray asked.

Or what? Surely Gray was the one who had brought her dinner. She eased her fingers into her hair and pressed the heel of her palm against her temple.

"Headache?" he asked.

"Some." She left the doorway, paused uncertainly next to the worktable, then perched on a stool. Her visits to Howard Lambert's various resorts were never like this. People were pleasant to her, treated her with courtesy and cooperation. Not as though she was the enemy. The thought made her shake her head in complete bewilderment. "None of this makes a bit of sense."

"How's that?" He filled a teakettle with water and turned on a flame at one of the burners.

"From the minute I got here, Hawk acted like he couldn't stand me." She propped her elbows on the table and watched Gray cut two large pieces of cake. "At least now I know why."

"He's not as hard-nosed as he comes across."

"And you're no better," she added. "Who were you protecting out there? Was it that you didn't want Richard to see me? Or that you didn't want me to see Richard?"

Gray almost smiled. "Is there a difference in that?"

"You know what I mean. And you're the one who brought me dinner, aren't you?"

He slid the cake in front of her and followed it a second later with a steaming cup of water accompanied by a small basket of assorted teas. "Is there a point to all your questions?"

"I've...I thought Richard was..." She shook her head in frustration. "I don't know what I think."

Gray sat down on a stool across the table from her, cut off a big piece of cake with his fork and put it in his mouth. Audrey watched as he slowly chewed, obviously savoring the flavor. He followed the bite with a long swallow of milk. Her gaze fastened on the bob of his Adam's apple and, a couple of inches lower, the fascinating fringe of dark hair that extended above the top button of his shirt. His sleeves were rolled partway up. The revealed skin was tanned, and the veins on the backs of his hands and tendons of his arms were pronounced.

She shivered as she recalled the sensation of his hand against her mouth. He had smelled of soap, but mostly she remembered his warmth. Her palms grew damp, and a feather of yearning wound through her belly.

She was losing her mind. Hormones. An awakening libido. That's all it was. After all, she had been thinking about *that* lately, wondering how to step into the dating scene. As an adult, it seemed a lot more difficult than it had as a teenager. Had she known then that she'd make it to nearly thirty and still be a virgin, she would have sown a lot more wild oats.

She ought to have been frightened of Gray, she decided. She had been scared, but not of him. She hadn't liked being manhandled, but she admitted to herself she liked the feeling of his arms around her.

Oh, yes.

Pulling the tea bag out of the mug, she squeezed out the excess water and set it inside her spoon, then took a cautious sip, watching him over the rim of her cup.

"I think," Gray said, "you're wondering what the hell you stumbled into."

She met his gaze. His dark eyes studied her with that intent way he had.

"I think you've probably never heard yourself talked about before, not like that, anyway. Hawk is the obvious bad guy. He was sullen when you arrived, and as you've figured out by now, he's not real thrilled to have you here." Gray took another bite of his cake. "How am I doin' so far?"

He had been on the money. To confess that she liked almost everyone she'd ever met and that she got along well with almost anyone didn't seem believable in the present circumstance. Everything that had happened since her arrival was so out of her experience, she kept thinking this was a dream from which she would soon awaken. In fact, she hoped so.

Gray must have read something of her agreement in her expression because he nodded and continued. "Richard wasn't here when he said he would be, so you must be wondering."

"I am," she admitted.

"And there's me," he continued. "And you're probably thinking, what was I doing in the hall?" Gray swallowed the last of his cake. "I'm Richard's cousin. That's true. If I were you, I'd be saying to myself, who do I trust? Richard's apparently up to something, Hawk can't wait for you to leave and I've got ties to Richard that could put me in cahoots with him.''

She hadn't gotten so far as putting all that together. ''You sound like a detective or something.''

''Or something,'' he muttered.

She took a bite of the cake and, as Gray had, savored the flavor of chocolate and, surprisingly, cinnamon.

''A piece of advice, Audrey.'' He nudged away his empty plate and leaned toward her. ''Do your audit and leave.''

''Howard knows something is going on. That's why he sent me.''

Gray's jaw clinched. ''Don't admit that to me, woman. Damn! Don't you have any sense?''

''What?'' she asked, baffled.

''Just because I lay this all out for you nice and neat—that doesn't mean anything. Talk about a lamb among wolves. Don't trust anybody.''

''But if you—''

''Don't…trust…anybody.'' He stood, bracing his hands on the table, and loomed over her, filled with the same tension she had sensed before. His gaze traveled over her face, lingered a fraction on her mouth. She licked away a crumb of cake, intensely aware of his scrutiny.

''Not even you?''

''Especially not me.''

''Even though you're warning me to—''

''You're a woman who does what she wants. Just don't be stupid about it.'' His expression became shuttered.

''I'm—''

''And don't go snooping around. The scent from your shampoo and your bath—I noticed that, too.''

She swallowed, remembering again how close he had been to her, remembering she had been able to smell him, too. Clean. Masculine. Faintly musky. Being so close was better than she had ever dared imagine. Tiny electric brushes of sensation curled through her.

"When I checked a little while ago, Richard had locked himself in his quarters. I'll make sure Hawk has gone back to his cabin. So you don't need to worry."

"Even though I'm not supposed to trust anybody, even you."

A bare flicker of humor lit his eyes.

"The lady is learning." He straightened and headed for the door. "Can you find your way back to your room?"

She nodded, not sure at all she could, but unwilling to make the admission to him.

"See you in the morning, then."

She watched him close the door behind him. With his departure, the kitchen seemed enormous, and she felt very alone.

Sipping her tea, she centered her thoughts on Gray's precise summation of the situation. She would never have analyzed this evening the way he did. Never. She would have still been wondering if she had really heard the threats and been trying to convince herself she had misunderstood.

She gathered the few dishes they had used, washed them at one of the giant sinks, dried them and put them away. All the while, his warning echoed through her mind. *Don't trust anyone.* She faced life presuming most people were honest, and so far, they had been. She wasn't stupid, though. She locked her house, hid her Christmas shopping in the trunk of her car and never gave out her credit-card number over the phone. But not to trust anyone? She couldn't live like that.

When she left the kitchen, though, she did so warily with Gray's warning in the back of her mind and her own apprehension of Hawk. At this point, she wasn't looking forward to meeting Richard, either.

By the time she got back to her room, she felt chilled again from walking barefoot on the cold floor. The door was slightly ajar, and she remembered she hadn't locked it when she left. She pushed open the door and glanced around the room before entering, even as she cursed Gray for his warning.

The elusive phantom that brought her dinner had been back. Recalling how silently Gray moved, she decided her image of phantom fit—no cheerful leprechaun, but a shadow-spirit that recognized her wishes.

More wood had been stacked in the cubbyhole, and some had been added to the fire, which banished the chill. A quilt with geometric squares of blue, cream and terra-cotta covered the bed, as though someone—she was convinced it was Gray—knew she had been cold.

She glanced at the intricately carved wood panel and again had the sensation of being watched. She picked up the shirt she had worn earlier and draped it in front of the panel. The makeshift curtain was no protection from her imagination, but she felt reassured.

After making sure she had locked the door, she climbed into bed without taking off her robe and made one last discovery from her phantom. A warm stone wrapped in flannel was at the bottom of her bed, which had wonderfully heated the sheets. She rested her feet on the stone and gratefully soaked up the warmth. She yawned, vaguely surprised she felt drowsy at all.

Don't trust anybody.

Not even Gray.

Not possible, she thought. He was exactly the kind of man a person would trust…with her life, even.

Hours later, she thought she heard whispered warnings swirl around her and she could have sworn she heard her name. She opened her eyes and stared at the glowing embers in the fireplace. The coals seemed like evil eyes, watching, ever watching. With a mutter of disgust at her own childish fears, she tossed the covers back and got out of bed to add more wood to the fire. Climbing back in bed, she pulled the covers to her chin and watched the shadows rippling on the ceiling.

Faint sounds slithered through the room, a draft, she told herself. She listened a moment longer, then closed her eyes. Again the forlorn sounds became hushed voices that carried veiled words she could almost understand.

Sleep, when it came, was fitful, filled with dire warnings she couldn't make sense of and the reassuring presence of a large man with intent eyes.

The following morning, Audrey dressed, more than a little disgusted with her choice of wardrobe. She had not packed anything that would sufficiently keep away the chill of the wet, gloomy day that met her gaze when she opened the drapes. She remembered Gray telling her the outside shutters were closed last night. This morning, they had been opened, and the world beyond the window looked bleak.

She finally layered a blue calico print shirt over a red sleeveless sweater and jeans. She thrust her bare feet into a pair of deck shoes, wishing for socks.

When she had asked Howard what Puma's Lair was like, he had told her the climate was similar to another resort he owned outside of Scottsdale, Arizona, but the atmosphere was more casual. "Think warm," he had urged her. At the time, she had thought he was talking about the weather, but concluded he had been talking about clothes.

She ventured from her room, discovering that the glass hall faced a courtyard with an adobe wall on the opposite side and more windowed hallways on the other two sides. Doors at either end of the corridor provided access to the yard. In fair weather, it would be a pleasant place to sit.

The aroma of bacon and cooking onions grew stronger as Audrey approached the kitchen. She heard the murmur of voices—Gray's and a woman's.

Audrey's stomach tightened, and she momentarily slowed her steps. As she straightened the collar on her shirt and adjusted the silver bracelets on her wrist, the memory of being held in his arms washed over her.

"Can Mr. Lambert really sell off the mineral and water rights?" the woman in the kitchen asked.

Mineral rights? Water rights? Audrey cocked her head to the side. How very odd. Howard hadn't said a thing about mineral or water rights for Puma's Lair. Yet she had been investigating the sale of water rights for another property he owned in southern Colorado. The money raised would leave him short of the amount he needed for his newest resort, but he would be a whole lot closer.

"He owns it, so he can do pretty much what he wants," Gray answered.

The woman made an unhappy sound, then said, "Richard should stop it."

"That takes money—lots of it, which Richard doesn't have. And even if he did, the ranch doesn't belong to him."

Nothing more was said, so Audrey went to the doorway and looked inside.

Gray sat on one of the stools at the big worktable. In daylight, gloomy as it was, his hair was a golden brown, lighter than Audrey had imagined last night. It was a color she envied, thinking her own hair the color of mud in comparison. His hair curled over the collar of his shirt, a hunter green plaid flannel that looked warm.

Audrey forced her attention beyond the man. A plump Indian woman hovered over the stove, her back to the door. A pair of skylights made the room brighter, and several lit kerosene lanterns provided a cheery glow.

"Hi," Audrey said from the doorway.

"Good morning," Gray said, standing up. He pulled out the stool next to his and motioned toward it. "How'd you sleep?"

"As well as could be expected."

"For thunderstorms, an unfamiliar bed and being cold."

The knot of awareness in Audrey's stomach gave another tug. "Yeah."

"Mary, this is Audrey Sussman," Gray said. "Audrey, Mary Maktima."

She wiped her hands on her apron, a tentative smile on her face, and came toward Audrey. "I'm happy to meet you, Miss Sussman."

"Please call me Audrey. Last night, I had a piece of cake you baked. Delicious."

"But now you're ready for breakfast."

"As a matter of fact, I'm starved. I don't know what you're cooking, but it smells great."

"Green chilies," Gray said. "Her favorite ingredient."

Mary smiled over her shoulder at him, her smile warmer than the polite one she had given Audrey. "I have not seen you complain." She came back to the table carrying a pot of coffee and another cup. She filled it and handed it to Audrey, then filled the cup in front of Gray as he sat back down. "Now tell me about your drive. Did you come from Denver?"

"Yes," Audrey answered. "I thought I was leaving winter behind, coming to New Mexico."

"Ah, Mr. Lambert, he forgot to tell you about the rain."

"He forgot to tell me a lot of things," Audrey murmured.

"When you didn't get here yesterday, I was worried you had problems of some kind—car trouble or something."

"I did," Audrey said. Somehow, in the light of day, confessing that the car had given her trouble was much easier—safer. "In fact, my car still isn't working right."

Mary patted Gray's arm as she came by. "You should talk to this man, then. If it has an engine, he can fix it."

"What's wrong with it?" Gray asked.

"I'm not sure," Audrey said. "It runs, but the engine isn't smooth, and if I give it too much gas, it dies."

"Richard was worried when you were late," Mary said.

"He fussed all morning, hoping you'd arrive before he left for Albuquerque."

"That's odd," Audrey responded. "I'm pretty sure I told him I wouldn't be getting away from Denver until about noon. He even warned me to watch out for the deer after it got dark."

Mary set plates of steaming food in front of her and Gray.

"This looks great." Audrey picked up her fork, taking a bite of the hash browns, which were liberally spiced with green chilies.

"Mr. Lambert, when he comes, often brings his son. I thought perhaps you'd bring your family with you. Gray says you came alone."

Audrey nodded without speaking, wondering how much of Mary's inquisitiveness came from genuine concern or from suspicion. Under other circumstances, Audrey would have easily responded that her only living relative was her brother, a Navy SEAL, whom she hadn't heard from since shortly after he came home for their mother's funeral eight months ago. But it was no surprise. She normally heard from him only once or twice a year. Gray's warning to trust no one kept her from volunteering even that tidbit about herself.

"Are you married?" Mary asked, her glance shifting from Audrey to Gray.

Audrey's gaze fell to her plate as she wondered why Mary had asked. "No. No husband. No children. No—"

"Unmarried cohabital unit?" Gray interrupted, his voice teasing.

"No. Not one of those, either." Some of her tension dissolved, and she laughed. Her laughter hid a carefully constructed facade. Her mother's death had left a yawning hole bigger even than her long illness had created. Audrey spent years—eight to be exact—watching her mother fade from the vibrant woman she had once been. She glanced at Gray. "And you?"

"I don't have one of those, either."

That didn't exactly tell her whether the man was married or significantly involved. Since she'd be here only a day or two, it didn't really matter. Even so, she was attracted to him, wishing she had the experience and the self-confidence to act on it.

"Do you live here on the ranch, Mary?" Audrey asked, forcing her attention away from Gray.

Mary nodded. "For as long as I can remember, my family has lived here."

"I don't understand." Audrey had the impression the ranch had been abandoned for years before Howard Lambert bought it at a tax auction.

"My people have lived on this land since the time before the beginning."

Time before the beginning, Audrey mentally echoed, liking the cadence of the words. She smiled. "You're from one of the pueblos, then. Taos?"

"Taos is only one of many. Once, there were many more." Mary extended her arm in a graceful gesture that encompassed the entire room. "Before the Spanish came, we were here. And after the Spanish came, we stayed."

"Where?" Audrey asked.

"Here."

"There is a pueblo on the ranch property?" Audrey asked.

"That's not the way they see it," Gray explained. "The ranch, once part of the Delgado Spanish land grant, is on the land of the pueblo—La Huerta."

"Ah." Audrey had seen a reference to a Spanish land grant, which had been huge in comparison to the present-day size of the ranch. "La Huerta, what does it mean?"

"'Orchard,' named so by the Spaniards," Mary said.

"Orchards!" Audrey had known the pueblo people were

farmers and traders, but she hadn't imagined orchards. "What kind of fruit?"

Mary smiled. "Peaches." In the next instant, her smile faded. "Named by Spaniards and destroyed by them, as well. Our heritage, our very way of life stolen. Then, and now."

"I don't understand."

"The Spaniards burned the orchards, killed many of our people, put many more into slavery in search of gold and forbade the practice of our religion." Her dark eyes no longer held any warmth when she met Audrey's. "What little that we have left will be gone when Mr. Lambert sells the water."

Audrey shook her head.

"We know—" Mary thumped a hand to the middle of her chest "—I know that is why you are here."

"I see." Audrey glanced at Gray. Don't trust anyone, he had said. It ought to be easy advice since no one seemed to trust her, either.

Chapter 3

"I came because Howard asked me to," Audrey said, summoning a smile. "That's all. He doesn't need to come here, or send me, to sell the land or its mineral rights."

"Then why did he send you?" Mary asked.

"To audit the books," Audrey answered.

"No one's ever come before."

"All the more reason for me to be here, then."

Mary stared at her a moment. "Where do you live?"

"In an apartment," Audrey answered evenly, though the change in subject surprised her.

"A place without any roots, any connection to the land. A place you could leave at a moment's whim." Mary snapped her fingers.

"I've lived there many years." Audrey lifted her chin. In the long months since her mother's death, the apartment had seemed more prison than home. She spent less and less time there, the memories too close, too painful. Lately, she had dreamed of a house in a small town, filled with a husband and a child or two. "Your point is...?"

"Simply that you would not understand the connection we have to the land. For us, it is not simply real estate on which to build a dwelling. It is the Mother."

The vehemence in her voice left no doubt as to how Mary felt. It was a view Audrey understood, though obviously any agreement or sympathy she expressed would be met with disbelief.

"Morning, Mom," came a feminine voice from the doorway.

Audrey turned to see another woman sweep into the room. Her short black hair was cut into a spiked, chic style, which complemented her fragile bone structure. Dressed in jeans and a velveteen tunic, she looked as though she might have stepped out of one of the boutiques in Santa Fe. Her smile grew even wider when she saw Gray, and the deep lines around her eyes suggested she was twenty years older than she appeared on first glance.

"Hi, big guy." She dropped a kiss on his cheek on her way to giving Mary a hug. "How's the whittling?"

"Same old, same old," Gray said. He didn't smile, but for an instant, Audrey thought he would and wondered what they referred to.

"I'm here for the supply order, Mom," the woman said. In the next instant, she extended her hand to Audrey, her smile warm. "Hi, I'm Francie. You must be Audrey."

"Yes."

"Hawk told me that you had arrived last night."

"You know Hawk?" As soon as the question was out, Audrey wanted to retract it. Of course she knew him, since she'd talked with him.

Francie laughed. "Yeah. Kinda. He's my husband. You're here for the week?"

"A few days at least. Depends on how long things take." Audrey couldn't imagine this vibrant woman married to Hawk.

"I hope you have a chance to look around while you're

here," she said. None of Hawk's animosity toward her nor Mary's suspicion of her was evident in Francie's open expression. "Our small pueblo has its own charm, though it's not as big as some."

"I'd love to see it," Audrey responded, genuinely interested.

Without saying a word, Mary handed Francie a sheet of paper, which Francie scanned briefly. "Okay, I'm off. If you run into Hawk, tell him I shouldn't be more than a couple of hours." She paused at the doorway. "Oh, and Audrey, it was nice to meet you. If you don't have anything else planned for tonight, why don't you have dinner with us? Say, about six-thirty?"

The invitation was completely unexpected, and Audrey sensed Mary fairly bristling with disapproval.

"Thanks," Audrey returned. "That sounds nice. I'd love to." At the moment, she couldn't imagine sharing a meal with Hawk, but Francie's was the sort of hospitality that she'd been expecting.

"You, too, Gray. You'll show her the way?"

"Depends," he returned, his tone teasing. "Who's cooking? You or Hawk?"

"Hawk, of course." She waved. "See you later."

Thinking that mother and daughter couldn't have been more different, Audrey pushed away her plate and stood up. "It's time for me to get to work." A fraction of Francie's friendliness in Mary or Hawk would have been welcome. Glancing at Gray, Audrey asked, "Have you seen Richard this morning?"

"Not yet," he responded.

"Time for me to go find him, then." She paused at the doorway and looked back at Mary. "Breakfast really was delicious. Thank you."

Mary met her glance for an instant, then nodded.

Gray found himself following her into the hallway. If he believed his cousin, Hawk and Mary, this woman was up to no good. No woman had ever looked less like a villain, however. Not from the first instant he saw her yesterday.

"Francie is really Hawk's wife?" Audrey asked as the kitchen door closed behind them. Two people couldn't have been more different.

"Yep." Gray fell into step beside her. "She helps Mary out when she's not at the clinic in town." At her questioning glance, he added, "She's a nurse. Told me once that it was a good profession to have, following a career army man around. She could always count on a job."

Audrey shook her head. "Hard to imagine Hawk in the army."

"No harder than imagining you as an auditor," Gray returned. She was too soft, too pretty and too innocent looking. Her face was an open book, reflecting every nuance of emotion.

"Really?" She arched a brow. "And just what do auditors look like?"

"They're squinty eyed and suspicious," he said.

She narrowed her eyes an instant before grinning. "Maybe that's because I don't usually do audits."

"What do you usually do, then?"

"Analysis," she responded. "All the background information to determine if a resort is a good buy or not, if it's being run profitably or not."

"Sounds boring."

She grinned. "Sometimes it is. Sometimes I'd chuck it all in to be a chef, preparing fabulous food for appreciative guests."

"So why don't you?"

"I don't know how to cook," she responded. "I'm strictly a microwave kind of gal."

He raised an eyebrow. "And the man in your life thinks that's okay?"

"Probably not—if there were a man."

"Ah." He gave her another of his intense glances. "At least the mystery of why you're not suspicious is solved."

"I'd hate living my life like that."

The simple statement confirmed her genuine bewilderment and hurt at being so openly disliked. Her behavior had been characterized by unfailing good manners when she had every right to bristle at Hawk last night and at Mary this morning. She had warmed right up to Francie, had been more than willing to meet her halfway despite the way Hawk and Mary had treated her.

What would it take to see her lose her cool? Gray wondered. If her mission was as simple as she stated, why were Richard and Hawk tied up in knots? Everyone else seemed to think the water rights were being sold, so why didn't she? None of it added up. If she was as innocent as she seemed, she could be in a hell of a lot of trouble.

If so, she was exactly the kind of woman he couldn't walk away from. Exactly the kind of woman he had sworn to stay away from.

If he had a lick of sense, he'd go his own way right now and ignore her until she left.

She turned toward the front of the building, then paused when the hallway ended and split off in different directions.

"I'll show you where Richard's office is," he said, indicating she should turn right.

"Sure I can trust you to lead me there?" The teasing note was back in her voice.

"I warned you."

She sighed, and her steps slowed. "Yeah, you did. Not trusting anyone, though. I don't have to like it. So what do you think?"

"About what?"

The glance she slanted him was filled with disbelief. "Am I here to help Howard sell off the water rights?"

"Probably." It wasn't the answer he wanted to give her, wasn't even the answer he believed.

She wrapped her arms around herself and stopped walking, her gaze focused on the courtyard outside.

"Well, at least I know where I stand. The sooner I get to work, the sooner I can do what I'm paid to do—which will prove all of you wrong, by the way—and go back to Denver." She glanced at him. "I guess I should thank you."

"For what?" That unfailing courtesy again, and he didn't deserve it.

She faced him, and ticked off on her fingers. "Bringing in my luggage last night when it was raining. Bringing me dinner. Keeping me out of trouble when Richard and Hawk were talking. Bringing me an extra blanket and building a fire." Her smile slipped. "And warning me I shouldn't trust anyone." She swallowed. "That's quite a lot."

"It's nothing." And in his mind, it *was* nothing. He had long ago accepted his own fate—he was a man who could not turn his back on a woman in trouble. Equally, he was a man with a violent past whom no woman should trust.

"I really would have liked to have heard more about Mary's pueblo, La Huerta."

"For the right audience, she's quite a storyteller, all right. Old legends and ghost stories. She sees meaning and symbolism in everything. If she's at Francie's tonight, you may have a chance to know her better."

"Ghost stories? This place has a ghost?" Audrey glanced at him, her eyes wide, looking so much like she had yesterday that his throat closed. Mary had told him the story months ago, but he hadn't really believed it until he had seen for himself.

"Yeah." He cleared his throat. "There's a particular one about a Comanche woman who lived on the pueblo."

"What happened to her?"

"Legend has it that she escaped from one of Kit

Carson's camps during the time the Indians call the Scorched Earth. She was accused of stealing.''

''Gold?'' Audrey asked.

He shook his head. ''Only white men valued gold. The Indians believe the pueblo's owner gave her a deed that she was to take to Sante Fe. They believe it would have returned the land to them. Except she was captured and then later disappeared.''

''And the deed was never found,'' Audrey said.

''No, it never was.'' He stared down at her. ''And now she's seen sometimes when it storms.''

Audrey swallowed. ''Does she carry a cradle board?''

''Yes. How do you know?''

''I think I saw her last night.'' Audrey waved toward the outside. ''There was a flash of lightning, and she was standing there, looking so real that I spoke to her.'' She caught his gaze. ''Have you seen her?''

Gray nodded, searching her face. ''And she looks enough like you to be your twin.''

''Who looked like whose twin?'' came Richard's voice from the end of the hallway.

Stunned that she might have seen a ghost herself, much less one that looked like her, Audrey turned to face the man striding toward her and Gray.

Richard still wasn't as she had imagined him.

His silver hair must have once been dark brown like his eyebrows. His features were smooth and patrician, looking the way royalty should and seldom did. Audrey would bet a month's pay his pressed jeans had a designer label on the back pocket and that his Tony Lama boots had never been near a horse. She would have pegged him as a manager for one of Howard's more ritzy resorts around Santa Fe or Scottsdale.

Maybe that had been the source of his bitterness last night, she thought.

His nearly black eyes fastened on her.

"Audrey, I presume." The smile he gave her stopped at those dark eyes.

She offered her hand. "Richard Emmanuel?" she asked lightly, matching his tone.

He laughed. "Please accept my apologies for not being here last night. I trust you got settled in all right."

"For being sent to bed without any supper, I did fine," she answered.

An instant of startled silence followed before he laughed again. "You're joking, of course."

"Actually not." Audrey's gaze slid to Gray. He didn't look anything like his cousin, even down to the eyes. In the daylight, she could see Gray's eyes were hazel—a shade that absorbed more light than they reflected, a warmer, more inviting color than Richard's. In fact, she much preferred Gray's more rugged, less pretty face to Richard's.

Abruptly, Gray's warning echoed through her mind. *Don't trust anyone...especially not me.* But trust him she did, warnings or not.

With effort, she retrieved her train of thought. "I was saved by a generous and elusive phantom, though, who first brought me dinner and firewood to heat my room."

"First?" Richard asked, raising an eyebrow.

Audrey's gaze didn't leave Gray's face. "And an extra blanket later, which I appreciated." She rubbed her arms up and down her arms. "I didn't come prepared for this kind of weather."

Again Richard laughed. Audrey, to her surprise, found herself disliking it and him, a feeling she hadn't experienced since Mary Lou Jones had teased her about her breasts during gym class in junior high school.

"Who is ever prepared for spring weather?" Richard asked. Spreading his hands wide, he added, "I'm afraid your trip may have been for nothing, however. The power is still not on, which will make running the computer most difficult.''

Audrey smiled. ''I brought my own, Richard. A laptop. And extra battery packs. Even if the electricity stays off a couple of days, I can still get the job done.''

''I'm glad to hear it,'' Richard said. ''You're ready to get to work, then.''

''The sooner the better.'' She touched Gray's arm. ''Thanks for everything.''

''No problem. I'll take a look at your car if you want.''

''I'd appreciate that. Thanks.''

''I'll be by in a few minutes to get your keys,'' he said. She turned around to look at him and smiled.

He held her attention with another of his intense looks. ''I'm going horseback riding later. You're welcome to join me if you like.''

''I haven't ridden in years, but if the weather clears—''

''Weather or not,'' Richard interrupted, ''my cousin is not the head of the hospitality department. And I'm sure you have too much to do.''

He was right. She did have a lot to do, but darned if she was going to let him dictate her schedule.

''Riding sounds like fun,'' she said to Gray. ''Just give me a half hour's warning when you're ready.''

''Sure,'' Gray agreed.

She wondered what it took to make the man smile. Given her reaction to him, she would probably melt into a puddle at his feet if he did.

''What's the matter with your car?'' Richard asked.

''I wish I knew.''

''This audit really is a waste of time,'' he said, unlocking the door to his office. Once inside, he struck a match, lit another of the ever present kerosene lamps and adjusted the wick until it was brighter.

''Maybe,'' Audrey murmured, following him into the

small room. Heavy drapes were drawn across the window. "You know how Howard is."

Richard frowned. "Unfortunately." His eyes glittered when he met her gaze. "Just how well do you know Lambert?"

"Well enough to know that when he says 'Jump,' I'd better ask, 'How high?'" She smiled to take the sting out of her words and expected Richard's expression to lighten somewhat. It did not. "This shouldn't be a big deal, Richard. What I told you on the phone the other day still holds. I've got about three other items on my desk in Denver that are more urgent than this audit. Just point me in the direction of the records for the past three years."

"Why the hell does he want you to go back three years?" Richard asked.

"You'll have to ask him."

Richard scowled. "I'll be away for most of the day," he said. "And don't bother trying to call me on my cell phone," he added, waving toward the old-fashioned black phone on the credenza. "When it rains like this, the service is on and off like a yo-yo."

"Then I'll have to make do." She assumed Richard's rudeness had nothing to do with her personally, but she didn't like being on the receiving end of it. "You can cooperate with me or not, Richard. It's your choice."

"Are you laying down all your cards?" he asked. "Or throwing down a gauntlet?"

"I'm not challenging you, if that's what you're asking. As for laying down my cards, my reason for being here is obvious."

"Lambert thinks I'm stealing from him."

"He believes things are not quite right—yes."

"Spare me the euphemisms!" Richard spat. "He sent you here to make sure I'm not stealing the ranch from him."

"Are you?" It was the sort of direct, unexpected question that sometimes got to the heart of things quicker than more subtle methods. Stealing? Of course, she had considered that. Stealing the ranch, though, hadn't occurred to her. Odd. How could he steal the ranch?

Richard snorted, a harsh, vile sound she hadn't expected from a man so good-looking. "You tell the bastard that he made a bargain with me and I've lived up to my end of the agreement."

"What agreement?" she asked, baffled by his anger.

Richard waved an arm. "This is half-mine. Did you know that? Or at least it will be."

She shook her head.

He laughed. "You don't think I would have agreed to manage this place for the measly salary I'm paid without getting something else, do you?" He shook his head. "I've done my part for the last three years, and in another month, it's half-mine. Hell will freeze over before he cheats me out of it."

Richard slapped the middle drawer of the file cabinet. "Everything you want is in here. Tell Lambert one more thing. If he double-crosses me, he'll live to regret it." Four strides carried him around the desk and to the door, where he turned around. "You're not wanted here."

"I noticed." She replied without breaking eye contact with him, unreasonably hurt at being so actively disliked.

Richard stormed out of the office. She watched him cross the lobby and disappear down the hallway. She had never seen an agreement that gave Richard half of the ranch. His voice had the conviction of truth, though. If it weren't true, why would he have said the ranch was his? This, on top of Howard's bizarre behavior when he sent her down here. She'd give a lot to be able to talk to her boss, to ask him directly if Richard's claim was true, to find out why he had really sent her here.

As if in answer to her silent request, the telephone behind her jangled suddenly, the jarring sound making her jump.

Audrey turned to the credenza beneath the window and answered the phone.

"Puma's Lair," she answered, the old-fashioned black telephone receiver feeling heavy in her hand.

"Where's Rich?" a gruff male voice asked.

"He's just left the office. Can I take a message?"

"I'll call back." A click ended the conversation.

Audrey hung up, thinking the conversation peculiar. She picked the receiver back up, expecting the phone to again be dead. It wasn't, so she dialed the number for Lambert Enterprises in Denver.

When the line was answered on the other end, she said, "Hi, Laurie. It's Audrey. Is the boss in?"

"No, he took off for Scottsdale last night. Said he wouldn't be back until the end of the week."

"Problems?" Audrey asked, surprised he was not in the office. Before she left for Puma's Lair he had told her he would be in Denver all week.

"I don't honestly know," Laurie answered, static blurring her voice. "You know how he gets sometimes."

"Yeah." Unfortunately, she did. Eccentric, hardheaded, and demanding. Had he not also paid her very well, Audrey would have changed employers years ago. "Thanks, Laurie. I'll give him a call there."

"Want me to leave a message?"

"That's probably a good idea in case I miss him. Ask him if there is a written agreement between him and Richard Emmanuel that gives Richard half of Puma's Lair."

"Got it," Laurie answered.

When the connection was broken, Audrey called the resort in Scottsdale. The manager's secretary told Audrey that Howard wasn't there, was not expected, in fact.

Static interrupted the conversation, then the line went dead. Intermittent service, just as Richard had said. Wishing she had brought one of the office's cellular telephones with her, Audrey drummed her fingers on the desk. Where was Howard? Not in the office, and not in Scottsdale. Just like him to be suddenly unavailable when he expected everyone else to be at his beck and call.

A knock on the wall next to the open door made her look up. Gray stood in the doorway. Her heart gave a little jump of pleasure and anticipation.

"Hi," she said.

"I'm here for the keys to your car."

Fishing them out of her pocket, she said, "You don't know how much I appreciate this." Her fingers brushed Gray's as he took the keys from her. "Thank you."

"You already thanked me. Let's see what the problem is first. Maybe I can't even fix it."

"Well, at least you'll be able to help me sound intelligent if I have to call a mechanic. They always make me feel like I'm mentally deficient and emotionally disturbed when I talk to them." She smiled. "And by the time we get done, at least one of those is usually true."

"You said something earlier about having had car trouble all day?"

"Yeah." Audrey chuckled ruefully. "I was late last night because I stopped in Fort Garland when I noticed the engine getting hot. Turned out I had a slow leak in the radiator hose, which needed to be fixed. And I was also leaking oil. Evidently, the oil filter didn't get put back on tight the last time I had the oil changed. Then, the last fifty or sixty miles, it didn't have much power, and it sounded funny."

He held up the keys. "Let me take a look, and I'll be back in a while."

"Take your time. I'm not going anywhere." After he left, she opened the top drawer on the file cabinet. The labels on the files were blurry, reminding her she needed her reading glasses.

"You'd forget your nose if it weren't attached to the middle of your face," she muttered to herself. She left the office, making her way through the maze of hallways back to her room, waving at Mary as she passed the kitchen.

When Audrey opened the door to her room, she was surprised to find the bed had been made and the room straightened. That was service she hadn't expected, and she made a mental note to thank Mary—or at least find out whom she should thank.

The ever present draft shifted through the room, making Audrey shiver. She rubbed her hands up and down on her arms, remembering and envying the warm shirts that Gray wore. Opening one of the drawers of the dresser, she found her purse and took out her glasses.

The draft's whispered sounds seemed to take on the form of words again, reminding Audrey she had awakened during the night sure someone...something...had been calling her name. She paused at the door to listen. The sounds shifted around her, beckoning, making her scalp crawl. Closing her eyes, she tried to pinpoint what bothered her so much. Nothing within the sounds was unusual...and yet...

Abruptly, she left the room and shut the door firmly behind her, making sure it was locked. "Get a grip," she said to herself. "It's just the wind in this drafty old building." And her vivid imagination, now anticipating a ghost in every corner. She gave herself another mental shake. She didn't believe in ghosts. She wasn't sure what she had seen last night, or even what Gray had seen, but that wasn't it. Facts. Figures. Tangible things. Those were real. Ghosts and whispered drafts calling her name weren't. Simple as that.

Back in the office, she tried hard to keep her attention on the books. Everything was in order, with nothing to account for her boss's suspicion that things weren't quite right. Not for the first time, she suspected she had been sent on a wild-goose chase.

A storm squall moved through, beating rain against the window, but without the dramatic lightning from last night's storm. The draft she had noticed earlier intensified, bringing not just cold air swirling around her, but more slithering, whispering sounds that made the hair on the back of her neck stand on end.

The kerosene lamp flickered. Just as she had in her room, she could have sworn she heard her own name.

She forced herself to focus on invoices for repairs to the ranch. But within seconds, the hushed sounds of the draft returned, breaking her concentration.

"This is ridiculous," she said, throwing her pencil down on the desk. She didn't want to believe it, but she couldn't dislodge the notion that the sounds were aimed at her. It was yet another of the strange things here at Puma's Lair. First there were threats made in the middle of the night. Then talk of ghosts. Why, those two things alone would give anyone the willies. Now this...

She pushed her chair away from the desk and turned to face the window. A brief ray of sunshine broke through the clouds and sent a stream of light through the window, across her desk. Cheerful as the day looked, the whispers swirled around her, casting a spell of dismal gloom. And within them was a summons, soft, nearly imperceptible, persistent. *Audrey. Come to me.*

What she needed, she decided, was someone to tell her this was her imagination. Someone she could believe. Someone she could trust. Gray was the one she wanted to go to, and not just because she wanted reassurance. Richard, Hawk, Mary—any one of them would probably tell her she was about to be possessed and her only hope was to leave.

She glanced through the window to her car. Gray was

nowhere in sight. Which made sense, Audrey decided, since it had been raining again. The man wouldn't be standing around in the rain trying to figure out why her car didn't run.

Audrey left the office and went to the kitchen, hoping Mary could tell her where she could find Gray. Mary wasn't anywhere to be seen, and Audrey tried to remember if Gray had said where he was spending the day. Last night, he'd said something about renting one of the cabins, so maybe that's where she'd find him.

She headed outside, where the rain had slowed to intermittent sprinkles. The air was crisp, but the temperature wasn't as chilly as she had expected. Normally, she loved the scent of the rain in the air. Today, it reminded her she was unprepared for the weather and that she wasn't welcome here. Even so, she lifted her face and inhaled deeply, then lingered over a flower bed filled with old-fashioned grape hyacinths, crocuses and daffodils.

Audrey turned around to look at the lodge. The building almost seemed suspended in time. She found it impossible to determine which part of the compound was the original structure. From here, it looked almost as though it had once been a fort, few windows facing the outside. From the inside, she knew the glass-faced hallways led to interior courtyards. Old-style shutters framed all the windows, most closed over the glass as they had been in her room last night.

She found yet another stone pathway. It followed a line of cottonwood trees that stretched their bare limbs toward the sky, the leaf buds swollen with a promise of spring. At the end of the path, a half-dozen adobe cabins were scattered on a shallow slope.

Drawn by a longing within herself, she followed the path. Yes, she wanted answers to the sounds within the draft, and Gray was the logical person to turn to. She admitted to herself that was merely the surface reason. This man, some-how, felt...right. She had wondered if a love like the one she remembered between her parents would ever be hers. Gray Murdoch most probably wasn't the man, but he still drew her as no other ever had.

A grove of piñon trees hid a big four-wheel-drive Blazer, her only indication she was still in the twentieth century. Beyond the piñons, she saw a shed. Light shone through the window, and the sound of classical music spilled from the building.

She headed toward the building, hoping she had found Gray. If so, the music surprised her. She would have thought country and western would be more his preference than Beethoven or Mozart.

A mangy-looking tiger-striped cat sat on the stoop, giving itself a bath. At Audrey's approach, the cat watched her with unblinking amber eyes. Its expression was made more intent from one eye being slightly more dilated than the other and the ragged edge of an ear that flopped over. The blue door behind the cat was slightly ajar. Audrey stepped onto the stoop and knocked lightly. No one answered.

The cat nudged the door farther open with its nose and let itself in, its tail waving in the air like a regal flag.

"Hello," Audrey called.

The cat meowed, as if in summons.

Audrey pushed the door open farther and let herself into the shed. The pungent aroma of freshly cut wood assailed her. A wall directly in front of the door was divided into irregular shelves that were filled with an assortment of tools, blocks of wood, cans of stain and finish. She trailed her hand over the items on one of the shelves, stopping when she reached an intricate carving of the cat that had led her into the building.

The paw was curved toward the cat's face as though in

another moment it would brush across the cheek where the hair was ruffled from the last swipe. She picked up the small figure, found it surprisingly heavy for a piece of wood and traced the lines with her fingertips.

"Curiosity killed the cat, you know," Gray said from behind her.

Chapter 4

Audrey's heart leaped, and she dropped the sculpture.

With deceptive quickness, Gray snatched it from midair.

She met his gaze and swallowed. "You've just scared another year off my life."

"A whole year, hmm?" He put the figurine back on the shelf.

"Maybe you should wear a bell."

"Like Horace here?"

"Horace?"

"The cat."

She glanced down, but the cat was nowhere to be seen. "Funny name for a cat."

"He's a funny cat. Not to mention a little hoarse."

She grinned. "Ah. Hor-ace. As in 'He has a sore throat' or as in 'He's not really a cat, but a horse'?"

"After you hear his purr, you'll understand." He reached for her hand. "I gather you're here for the tour."

"Which tour is that?" she asked, allowing herself to be

led. For the moment, she had what she had wanted—another chance to be with him.

The entry hall opened onto a large space. Floor-to-ceiling windows filled the north side of the room. Light, bright, despite the overcast day. A captivating life-size figure of a mountain lion leaping toward the sky dominated the room. Piles of wood shavings surrounded a base that kept the cat grounded. Even there, its toes were flexed as though in the next instant it would jump.

Shivers chased down her spine, making Gray's hand around hers feel all the more warm.

"The tour of a world-famous sculptor's studio, I gather," she said.

"Famous? Not even close." He turned down the volume on the stereo as they passed it.

He let go of her hand as she approached the sculpture. She touched one of the extended paws, feeling the cat's strength and grace, expecting its warmth. "Puma," she breathed.

Beneath her hands, the wood felt almost alive. The cat's face was even with her own, its expression as intense as the man who carved it. She traced the outline of its eyes, down to its nose, the feel of the wood against her fingers smooth, vibrant. She glanced up and found Gray watching her, his arms folded over his broad chest, his expression unreadable.

"There is no point in telling you this is wonderful," she said. "You already know."

"Yes."

The tiger-striped cat—Horace—brushed against his legs.

"Why *do* you do this?" she asked. She hadn't anticipated this aspect of him, another facet of the man that fascinated her as much as his isolation and his self-confidence did. "And why wood?"

He picked up the cat. "It makes great kindling if I don't like the results."

"I can't imagine that happening," she murmured. "So this is the whittling that Francie asked you about."

He shrugged without answering, continuing to scratch the cat's ears. The cat closed his eyes and kneaded Gray's shirtsleeve, his purr loud and satisfied. And hoarse, just as Gray had said. Gray's eyes met hers, and the memory of being in his arms washed over her. Unable to bear the intensity of his gaze, she glanced away, returning her attention to the life-size sculpture in the middle of the room. Last night, she would have never guessed he was a sculptor. She didn't know what she thought, but she hadn't expected this.

"What led you to sculpting?" she asked.

He crossed the room and picked up a chisel with a deadly-looking blade. "I've always whittled."

She gave the puma another long look. "I think you're being too modest."

"It's merely a way of spending time until..."

The music reached a crescendo.

"Until?" she prompted when the music settled to a softer volume.

He shook his head. "It's not important."

It was very important, she thought, wishing she knew what he had been about to say. He circled around the figure, and she wondered if he saw the perfection she did or the flaws of creation.

"Were you always a sculptor?"

"Were you always an accountant?"

"Financial analyst," she corrected. "And no, I wasn't. What does that have to do with your being a sculptor?"

"Nothing," he admitted. "I just wanted to know how you saw yourself." He stopped circling the puma and moved toward her.

She swallowed as he touched her jawline with his finger and tipped it up. His gaze lingered over her face with the same expression he had when he circled the mountain lion.

Again, she wondered what he saw and didn't realize she had asked the question out loud until his eyes met hers.

"A lovely, desirable woman," he said simply. "With fine, soft skin. Luminous clear eyes shades darker than brandy." He traced the line of her eyebrows. "You make me wish I were a painter."

She had always thought she was ordinary, average. She wanted to tell him so. In this instant, though, beneath his scrutiny, she felt the way he described her. Desirable and desired. Beautiful.

Most of the time, she felt confident, together—an extension of her persona at work. Just now, she was reminded of how sheltered her life had been these past years and how inexperienced she really was. And she wished she wasn't. Oh, what she would give to have the confidence to ask this man to show her how it really was between a man and a woman.

As though he had all the time in the world, he brushed his fingertips over the contours of her face. Chills feathered over her scalp. Her breath hitched, and she held it. His tactile exploration of her face was intimate, more so than any other caress she had ever experienced.

"I'm glad you're not," she murmured.

"Not what?" His breath whispered over her face.

"A painter." She swallowed again, tearing her gaze from his intense scrutiny. "Painters are visual."

"Ah." He traced the sides of her face and her jawline, then the shell of her ears. He stepped closer, heat radiating from his body. "Audrey, look at me," he whispered.

She glanced up, found his face mere inches from hers, so close that the colors of life reflected in his hazel eyes were distinct. He bent closer, brushed his cheek against hers, then waited for her to tilt her head up.

She lifted her face, and his lips skimmed hers with no more pressure than his whisper. Like the rest of him, his lips were warm. She relaxed against him. His hands slid into her hair, cupping her head, holding her still as his gaze fastened on her mouth.

The refrain telling her this man was the right one echoed through her heart. She leaned into him.

His lips brushed hers again, then claimed them completely, surrounding her with his heat. He kissed her as though he sensed she didn't want it to end. She wrapped her arms around his waist and gave in to the sensations that she had kept bottled inside forever. On a sigh, she touched his lips with the tip of her tongue, her caress far more shy than she intended. His own breath caught, and h'- arms came around her in a rush.

He returned her tentative touch in kind, then trapped her in a storm of sensation when his tongue swept over hers, claiming what she had already given.

If she had ever dared dream of a perfect kiss, this would have been it. Longing poured through her and ignited passion beyond anything she had ever experienced. The texture of his mouth, the aroma of his skin, the blazing heat of his hard body—nothing had ever felt so…right.

When the kiss ended, Gray rested his jaw against her temple and stared through the window toward the approaching storm.

She clung to him, and her quick breath kept pace with his. Gray's arms tightened around her even more. Her body felt soft against him in all the ways a woman was supposed to be. He had wanted to hug her like this last night. He had gone to bed thinking about her, sure he would never be able to hold her.

Gray sure as hell hadn't expected this.

One moment she had been shy, and he had been ready to end the kiss. Then she had leaned into him and became fire in his arms. If a woman had ever responded more, he couldn't remember it.

He tipped his head to the side, trying to see her expression. When she finally lifted her head and looked at him, her cheeks were pink. A trace of uncertainty flitted across her face.

"I just met you," she said, her tone bewildered.

He wondered what that had to do with anything.

She loosened her arms from around his waist and stepped away from him. Her fingertips trailed across the statue of the puma, and she glanced at Gray over her shoulder. "I wasn't sure..."

"Of what?"

She became even more pink. "If I was the only one who felt—"

"You're not the only one," he confirmed. Her obvious embarrassment suggested that she didn't normally feel a pull this intensely. Or if she did, she didn't normally act on it. And yet, she had been on fire for him.

He hadn't intended to do a thing about the attraction he felt for her. She'd given him none of the usual come-on signs, and he had been positive what he felt was one-sided. His eyes narrowed as he watched her gather herself. She hadn't struck him as the kind of woman who would be interested in a short fling.

Maybe he was wrong.

He hoped so.

His cardinal rule with women was to keep it short and keep it simple. No long-term relationships. Ever. Maybe that was part of her allure—she would be here for a day or two, then gone. That thought gave him an unexpected pang of remorse.

She cleared her throat. "Actually, I came to ask another favor."

"What?" he asked.

She glanced at him and became, if anything, even more pink.

He crossed the room and tipped her face toward him. Without touching her otherwise, he gave her another lingering kiss. "Whatever you want," he murmured against her mouth, "consider it done." He kissed her again, savoring the softness of her mouth.

She dropped her forehead against his chest. "When you do that, I can't even think."

"Good." He touched her hair. "What do you need, Audrey?"

"Hmm?"

"That favor..."

"Oh...that." She stepped away from him. "I think I'm hearing things," she said, trailing her fingertips over one of the puma's outstretched paws.

Gray wished she would look at him. "What things?"

"Strange...tones...in the draft." She glanced at him. "I know it sounds stupid, but I keep thinking I'm hearing my name in the currents of air. It woke me up last night, and I heard it again this morning. In my room, and in the office."

"I hear moans in the hallways all the time," Gray responded, shaving off a curl of wood on the puma's haunch. He smoothed his fingers over the wood, and pulled another thin slice off the sculpture.

"I could almost swear that I heard my name." She ducked her head and wrapped her hands around her waist. "I can't believe how stupid..."

Slipping the butt of the chisel in his back pocket, he closed the distance between them. "You thought if someone else listened they could either tell you they didn't hear anything unusual or confirm that you're hearing...things. Right?"

She nodded.

"Let's go, then." He held out his hand to her, and she took it. Something about her made him think of walking with her like this in ten years or twenty. On the walk down the slope to the lodge, he reminded himself he was no Boy Scout who could be trusted. As easily as she seemed to give her trust, he wanted it, craved it, in fact. His need for

her trust, however, didn't change the essential fact. He was
the last man she should give her trust to.

He deliberately counted his reminders that he wasn't the
man for any woman, not long-term. The beatings his father
regularly, unpredictably gave his mother. The jail time his
oldest brother had served for beating his wife. The restraining order against his middle brother for the same reason.
Their flaw, and his.

At her room, she unlocked the door, and they went inside. The first thing Gray noticed was that the scent he
associated with her was more pronounced, soft, feminine,
elusive.

"Listen," Audrey said, almost in a whisper. "It's as
though it knows I'm here. After I'm in here a minute or
two, then I hear it. At first, I thought it was just—" She
laughed, her voice brittle. "Just my imagination."

Gray sat down on the edge of the bed, and after a scant
moment, Audrey sat down, as well, leaving a two-foot
space between them.

Then he heard them. They ebbed, then flowed, hushed,
whispery moans much like the ones he heard nightly. Suddenly, Audrey grasped his hand and glanced at him, her
eyes wide.

Come. The summons was nearly lost within the mournful
draft. *Audrey. Come to me.*

The hair rose on the back of Gray's neck, and he touched
Audrey's cheek in reassurance. "I hear it."

He stood and moved across the room, looking for the
source of the whispered moans, which seemed to be coming
from the fireplace. Since the damper on the chimney was
open, that made certain sense, but if any cold air brushed
over the ashes in the fireplace, he couldn't feel it.

"What's behind the panel?" Audrey asked.

Gray raised his eyes to the ornate carved panel above
the fireplace. "If it's like most of the others, only storage,"
he said. "Many of the original rooms of the hacienda had

them. According to Richard, some used to lead to hidden passageways.'' Gray glanced over his shoulder at her. ''A way to spy on guests and wives suspected of being unfaithful.''

''Lovely,'' she murmured. ''I kept feeling like I was being watched. What's happened to the passageways?''

''I don't know. Some might still be around.'' He grasped the panel door. ''This one is a cubbyhole for storage, though, if it's like the one in my room.''

He pulled, expecting the panel to swing open. It did not. With sensitive fingertips, he traced the face of the panel. An instant later, he discovered it had been nailed shut.

Taking the chisel out of his back pocket, he gently pried the panel away from the wall. With the nails loosened, the panel swung open on its hinges.

A square speaker about three inches wide sat on the bottom shelf. Gray swore.

''What is it?'' Audrey asked from his side.

He moved to let her look even as he took note of the tiny, neat hole drilled in the back of the wall. Through it ran a black wire connected to the speaker. Confirming his hunch, the whispered summons came out of the speaker.

''Audrey. Come.''

She remained silent a long moment before she cleared her throat and looked at him.

''If somebody is trying to scare me,'' she said, ''they're doing a dandy job.''

She began to pace, and Gray recognized the onset of an adrenaline rush in her.

''This had to be planned, you know. And last night, Hawk didn't act like he even knew where I was supposed to stay.'' She pointed at the speaker. ''That thing called my name, so this room is where I was supposed to be, isn't it?'' She went back to the cubbyhole and yanked on the cord connected to the back of the speaker. ''Where does this lead to, anyway?''

"My room," Gray said.

Audrey's face lost all expression, and Gray watched her, waiting for her to jump to the obvious conclusion.

"Well," she finally said, "if you had known we were going to find something that implicated you, you wouldn't have been so eager to help me figure out where the whispers were coming from."

He hadn't been the recipient of that kind of faith in a long, long time. It felt good. And the sooner she realized her trust was misplaced, the better.

"Or maybe it's a ruse to make you think you can trust me," he responded.

She smiled faintly. "After you told me not to trust anyone, not even you? If you want me to think you're not trustworthy, you shouldn't have offered to see if you can figure out what's the matter with my car and you shouldn't have agreed to listen to these sounds that have been driving me crazy." Or kissed me so sweetly, she silently added. She nodded toward the wall. "Let's go find out what's on the other end of this wire."

They left her room and entered Gray's.

Audrey noted the decor was much like that of the room she was staying in. Men's toiletries were scattered over the dresser, but the room was otherwise neat. Gray opened the closet door, pushed aside the clothes and peered inside. He snagged a flashlight off the nightstand next to the bed, pushed on the switch and aimed the beam of light inside the closet.

As she had suspected it would, the wire trailed up to the ceiling, where it disappeared through another hole. "At least I know there is a reason for hearing things. What next?"

"We can climb into the attic and see where the wire goes, or we can take our best guess."

"I don't suppose we're talking grandma's attic, complete with steamer trunks and ancient treasures."

"Were talking tight, dark, dusty and full of mice."

She shuddered. "Lovely. So, now we take our best guess and search the lodge, right?"

"Sure you want to do this?" Gray asked, thinking the stakes had been raised. His cousin's careless threats no longer seemed so casual.

Audrey glanced at Gray, then nodded. "I deal in facts and figures. I need to make sense of this."

Gray caught her hand. "You might not like what you find out."

"Are you trying to scare me?"

"Maybe," he admitted. "For your own good."

She nodded. "Even though I'm not supposed to trust you."

He stared at her a moment without answering.

"I'm not a quitter," she said. "Let's find out where this wire goes."

Gray studied her a moment, all his instincts on full alert. He wanted to find the transmitter without involving her. He wanted her where he knew she'd be safe. Which was nowhere on the ranch.

"How about I look for you?"

"How about we do it together?" she countered. "C'mon, what's the worst that could happen?"

She couldn't imagine, Gray thought, or she wouldn't have asked.

"There's a big key ring in the lap drawer of Richard's desk," she said. "Do you suppose it would have the keys we need?"

"To everything except his quarters."

"I'll go get them."

She slipped out of the room before he could stop her. Gray followed her down the hall, listening to the patter of her quick footfalls as she turned the corner and vanished. Seconds later, she appeared in the hallway and held up the keys.

They methodically searched, working their way up the hall toward the center of the lodge. A half hour later, they had nothing to show for their efforts.

"Where next?" Audrey asked where the halls intersected.

"Laundry room and linen closet are that way," Gray answered, pointing. "Richard's quarters down there. Let's assume for a minute that Richard put the speaker in your room."

"He's my favorite suspect," she murmured dryly.

"He wouldn't want someone else to stumble across the transmitter."

"That eliminates the laundry room and linen closet."

"Except it's a direct shot, and nobody's around except Hawk and Mary. Since the lodge is closed..."

"Then let's take a look."

Gray opened the laundry room, and again their search was futile. They moved on to the linen closet, which was unlike any Audrey had ever seen. The room was an odd shape. Two sides were shelves copiously filled with bedding and towels. An ornate carved panel similar to the one in Audrey's room was at the far end. However, this one was door-size, held shut by a crossbar. Audrey removed the crossbar, pulled open the door, the hinges nearly silent.

"Looks like no one has been in there in a hundred years," Gray said from behind her.

"Places like this are my worst nightmare," Audrey said. Cobwebs hung from the ceiling, and dust covered the floor. She shivered. With the lights off, the opening would be darker than a tomb. Gray touched her, and she started.

"You really don't like this, do you?" he asked, brushing his hand over her back in a gesture of reassurance. With his other hand, he aimed the beam from the flashlight into the vestibule.

She pushed the door shut. "The idea of being..." She took a deep breath. "When I was four or five, I was trapped in the cellar of a burning building. It was pitch-black. Terrifying.''

''I can imagine,'' Gray said.

Audrey forced a chuckle. ''I still sleep with a night-light on.''

''Can't say I blame you.''

''The worst part is I don't really remember any of it,'' she continued. ''Only what my mother told me about it.'' Turning away from the carved door, she surveyed the shelf in front of her, which was filled with towels.

''Sometimes that's just as well.'' Gray began searching the shelves, pulling neatly folded stacks of sheets away from the wall. ''Sometimes it's better if you can't remember.''

She heard footsteps down the hall, and an instant later, Richard appeared in the doorway.

''Did you lose something?'' he inquired. ''Or is this a physical inventory to accompany your audit, Audrey?''

Audrey straightened a pile of towels and gave him a level stare. ''Actually, we're looking for a transmitter or a tape player.''

''A transmitter to what?'' He raised a dark eyebrow.

''One attached to the speaker in my room,'' Audrey explained.

''You must be talking about the intercom,'' Richard said.

Audrey shook her head. ''I don't think so.''

Richard smiled, an expression of indulgence. ''If you want to waste your time like this... How did she manage to suck you into this game, Gray?'' He shrugged, then turned his glance back to her. ''My cousin always did have a soft spot for anything in a skirt.''

She made a point of glancing at her jeans. ''That lets me out then.''

''Have fun on your wild-goose chase.'' He gave them both a final, raking glance, then walked away.

"Damn," Gray muttered. "Why'd you tell him what we're looking for?"

"Most people return truth with truth."

"That's a nice fairy tale, Audrey. Most people cover their butt." He ushered her out of the closet and pulled the door shut behind them.

Audrey caught up with Gray as he stalked down the hall. "Let's suppose you're right—"

"I know I'm right."

"Okay." She touched his arm, hoping he'd stop and face her. He did not, so she followed him, his posture rigid.

He didn't stop until they reached Richard's office. Inside, he returned the keys to the lap drawer, which he slammed shut. He turned to face her, his expression stony.

Hoping to defuse his irritation, she smiled at him. "C'mon, so what if Richard knows? This was obviously a ploy to make me leave. And since Richard knows I'm on to him, I shouldn't have any more trouble. Problem solved."

"Just like that?"

"I'm hoping so. Maybe Richard's the kind of guy who expresses his frustrations a little forcefully. Howard's like that. He threatens to kill his wife when she bounces a check. You know?"

"I know," Gray muttered.

"He never has," Audrey said. "Killed his wife, I mean. I'm just trying to make the point that he…overstates things. Maybe a little like Richard."

He folded his arms over his chest. "I'm glad you've figured out everything."

"You don't sound glad."

"Believe me, I hope you're right."

Relieved that his anger seemed to have faded, she smiled. "Now, who else was I gonna call? Ghostbusters?"

He almost smiled. "Back to work for a while?"

"Yeah," she agreed, wondering what it took to make the

man smile. "Though I think yours is a whole lot more interesting than mine."

"If you don't like it, why keep doing it?"

"A question I've asked myself a lot lately," she said.

"Are you going to be okay in here?"

"Sure," she said.

He glanced outside. "Since it's stopped raining, I'll take a look at your car."

After Gray left, Audrey sat back down at the desk and stared blindly at the pages in the open folder.

If you don't like this, why keep doing it? Gray's question was one she had asked herself a lot over the past several months.

With effort, she forced her attention back to the work at hand.

"I'm glad to see you back at work instead of chasing phantoms," Richard said from the doorway a few minutes later.

Audrey glanced up and met his gaze. "I don't chase phantoms or figments of my imagination, Richard."

"You seem to have made quite an impression on my cousin."

"He's been very kind to me since I arrived."

"You don't strike me as the kind of woman who would go for rough stuff," Richard said, leaning against the doorjamb and crossing his feet.

"Get to the point, if you have one."

He smiled. "I wouldn't be trusting him, if I were you. He can be quite…violent. He killed a man, you know."

"And just how would I know such a thing?" she countered, tightening her fingers around a pencil. Gray kill a man? She couldn't imagine it. "Goodbye, Richard."

She sensed him watching her a moment longer before he left. His telling her that Gray had killed a man sounded like a kid bragging that his father was bigger, tougher, meaner than any of the other fathers. Audrey admitted she didn't know Gray, but she was certain he couldn't be a killer. Could he?

That question never completely escaped her thoughts as she continued to work. Within another half hour, she needed to compare the data stored in her computer to Richard's files. Through the window, she could see that the hood of her car was open. If Gray had unlocked the car, she could use the trunk latch inside it to retrieve her computer.

She went outside, noticing the air felt cooler than it had when she had gone to find him earlier. A storm squall on the other side of the valley hid the foothills behind them, and the smell of rain was in the air again.

Gray was nowhere in sight as she approached the car, though she noticed he had left some tools lying on a quilted cover next to the engine. His cat, Horace, sat on the courtyard wall, watching her approach.

Audrey came to a stop and held out her hand. The cat gave her a delicate sniff, then butted his head against her hand in a demand to be petted. She complied, grinning when his hoarse purr rumbled from his chest.

"We could do this all day, I bet," she said, giving Horace a final pat. "But that doesn't get the work done."

As she had hoped, the car was unlocked, and she popped open the trunk with the latch inside the car. Coming around to the back of the car, she reached inside for the black nylon case that held her laptop computer.

An odor rose from the trunk. She frowned. Nothing looked out of the ordinary. But the smell—it was a familiar and unpleasant one she couldn't quite place.

She set the laptop case on the ground. A bundle of clear, thin plastic was wadded up near the front of the trunk. She moved it aside.

It dripped, and she realized the odor was of blood.

Audrey turned the plastic wrapping over.

A bloody mess of fur and paws and goo from some poor creature slid onto the floor of the trunk.

Chapter 5

At first, she stared in puzzlement, some fragment of her mind denying what she saw. Realization came, and she whimpered.

Unable to take her eyes away, she wrapped her arms around herself. Another cry clawed up her throat. She stared a moment longer, then turned away. The awful image burned through her head even when she closed her eyes against it.

"Audrey?"

She opened her eyes and watched Gray stride toward her, carrying a battered toolbox.

"What's the matter?" Gray asked.

"I came out to get...my computer." She glanced back at the mess in the trunk of her car. Her chin quivered and she whimpered.

Gray peered into the trunk, then swore. Abruptly, he set down the toolbox and steered her toward the log next to the path, then pushed her down.

"Put your head between your knees," he ordered, his

voice gruff, his hands at the back of her neck, "before you faint."

A dozen questions without a single obvious answer raced through Gray's mind as he divided his attention between Audrey and her car. Old habits surfaced without his giving them conscious thought, and his gaze strayed back to the car, searching for clues.

He left Audrey long enough to examine the trunk and the ground behind it. There sure as hell hadn't been anything other than her luggage and the box of files in the trunk last night. He would have felt better if he had seen some evidence of a forced entry.

He sat back down next to Audrey and caressed her nape. "Are you okay?"

Audrey opened her eyes and found herself looking at damp earth—gravel and blades of grass. "Why would anyone do that?"

"Don't think about it." Gray touched her chin, urging her to sit up, bringing her face toward him. "Let's get you inside."

Afraid she might keel over, Gray kept his hand on her elbow as she stood up.

"My laptop," she murmured, waving toward the back of her car.

"I'll get it." He left her standing in the middle of the path, retrieved the black case from the ground behind her car. Inside, he led her through the maze of hallways until they reached her room. He tried the door and discovered it was locked.

"Key?" he asked, holding out his hand.

"Key?" she repeated. "What key?"

"Your room key, Audrey." Gray's eyes narrowed. She didn't sound anything like herself, and she stood drunkenly, further convincing him she would fall over if he let her go. "Where is it?"

She gave him a glassy smile and shrugged.

"In your pocket?"

"That's a good idea." Her hands were trembling so badly as she searched, Gray doubted she could have found a huge padlock in her pockets, much less a room key.

He touched the pockets on her fanny, didn't feel any keys there, then searched through her front pockets.

She shivered.

Gray looked sharply at her. "It's just the adrenaline, Audrey." He called her by name with effort. Endearments he had never in his life used sprang to mind. Honey. Babe. Love.

Tears appeared in her eyes, tears she must not have wanted, he thought, because she swiped angrily at them.

"I hate feeling like this."

"I know."

Her face had about as much color as salt. He hated her expression right now—beaten, cowed, cornered. Like too many of the women he had encountered almost weekly on his beat. Like his mother and his two sisters-in-law. Women who were at the mercy of men bigger and stronger than they were.

Gray found the key in one of the front pockets of her jeans, unlocked the door and swung it open. He pushed her into the room, then directed her into the chair by the window. Gray set the computer down on the table, then knelt in front of her.

Her gaze held a hint of panic when it met his. He took both of her hands within his.

"You're going to be okay," he murmured. "It's just the roller-coaster ride from the adrenaline. The rubbery legs, the tight feeling in your chest, the urge to cry."

"For a sculptor, you know a lot about adrenaline."

She still sounded drunk to him.

"I wasn't always a sculptor," he said.

"No?"

"No."

"What were you?"

"A cop."

"Oh." Her eyes widened, and he could see her pupils were dilated, even accounting for the dim light in the room.

"Cop. Sculptor. Mechanic."

"Jack-of-all-trades, all right. Are you gonna be okay for a minute, ba— Audrey? I want to get you a glass of water and some aspirin." He stood up.

She reached out suddenly and clutched his hand. "Please," she whispered. She straightened and swallowed as though she realized she was begging. With effort, she stopped the trembling of her chin. She released his fingers and gripped her hands tightly together. "I'm fine."

Gray knew she was anything but. "I'll be right back. I promise." He strode out of the room.

Audrey Sussman was in a hell of a lot of trouble, he thought, inventorying what he had found wrong with her car. Someone had stripped the insulation off the wires leading to the distributor, which had shorted out when they got wet. By itself, he might have thought it was normal wear and tear. In combination with a slow leak on her radiator hose and the loose oil filter that she had told him about, he didn't think so.

The repairs had been easy to make, and he'd given the rest of the engine a once-over, looking for anything else that could cause her problems. Someone hadn't wanted her to get here, someone who didn't particularly care if she had been stranded or not.

Someone. Damned if he could think of anyone besides Richard who had a reason for wanting her gone.

And now this dead animal. That was a hell of a lot more threatening. Not Richard's style, but certainly effective. Gray's hand clenched into a fist. The sooner he convinced Audrey to leave, the better.

Audrey sat straight in the chair after Gray left. She took a deep, shuddering breath and tried to empty her mind. She was stronger than this, for heaven's sake. It wasn't as though she hadn't seen dead animals before. But to deliberately put one in the trunk of her car... The act was calculated to frighten her.

It succeeded.

She wanted to run from here as fast as she could.

She pressed the heels of her hands against her eyes as though she could force away the images. This was worse than last night. This felt evil.

"No." Unable to wait passively a moment longer, she lurched to her feet and ran from the room. Gray's room was, after all, only a few feet away.

In the hallway, she collided with a large man. Even before she looked into his face, she knew he was not Gray.

Hawk gripped her arms.

"Let go of me!" Unreasonable panic rose in her. The final tenuous thread of her control broke. She struggled against him, pushing her hands against his chest, kicking at him. His grip on her arms, if anything, tightened.

"For God's sake, what's the matter with you?"

"Let me go. Please."

"Take your hands off her," she heard Gray say.

The grip on her arms loosened instantly.

"Audrey?" Gray questioned. "What happened?"

She turned to his concerned voice sure as a compass needle to magnetic north. His arms closed around her, and she burrowed against him.

"What's going on?" Hawk demanded.

"Somebody put a dead animal in the trunk of her car," Gray said, noting she looked even more frightened than she had when he left her.

"No way."

Gray shook his head.

"I don't like this."

"That makes two of us."

"Need a hand with anything?"

Gray tossed him the keys. "Do you mind cleaning up her trunk?"

"No problem." Hawk cocked his head toward Audrey. "Is she leaving?"

"Yeah." Gray stared at Hawk. He hadn't figured Hawk would be the type to mutilate an animal, either, but the man had made it plain from the first that he didn't want Audrey here.

Absently running his hand in a soothing caress up and down her back, Gray watched Hawk walk away, wondering if trusting Hawk in this was a mistake. Audrey shuddered in his arms, and he glanced down at her.

"Are you okay?" Gray asked.

"I'm not," Audrey whispered. "Oh, God, I'm not."

Remembered threats, whispering scary voices and the images of the dead creature became suddenly more vivid. Feeling her stomach churn, she broke away from Gray and ran toward the bathroom. Inside, she barely had time to kneel over the commode before she was violently ill.

Moments later, Gray knocked on the door of the bathroom, then pushed it open. Audrey was sitting on the closed lid of the toilet. She obviously had been sick, and recalling the skinned, decapitated mess in her trunk, he couldn't blame her.

He took a washcloth from the towel rack, wet it with cool water, then washed her face. He filled a cup with water, instructed her to rinse her mouth out and noticed she turned beet-red when she spit into the sink.

He handed her mouthwash. Turning his back to her, he made a production out of folding up the washcloth while she finished rinsing her mouth. Then he handed her the aspirin he had gone to his room to retrieve.

Gray's mind raced, assessing possibilities. The dead animal was meant to be a warning. But from whom? And more importantly, why? Despite Richard's threats, Gray couldn't imagine his doing anything like this. He would bet Hawk hadn't done this, either. If not Hawk or Richard, then who? Damn it, who?

Gray squatted down next to her. "Audrey?"

"What was it?" she asked.

He didn't have to ask what *it* was.

"It wasn't a cat, was it?"

"No." He shook his head. Prairie dog, most likely, but he kept that to himself. Whatever it had been, she didn't need to know.

"Promise?" She met his gaze, and he brushed her hair away from her face.

"I'm sure." He cupped her cheek. "It wasn't somebody's pet."

She nodded once, her eyes very bright. "This is stupid," she finally said. "I don't even know why Howard sent me down here. This whole thing is stupid. I have more important things to be doing, but instead, he yells and I trot down here. And for what?"

"Going home may be the best thing."

A long moment of silence passed. She finally nodded and lifted her gaze to his. "But I feel like I'm quitting."

"You're being smart." Gray stood and offered his hand. Without a word, she came to him, placing her hand in his. The ease with which she trusted him hit him in the gut, and his fingers tightened reflexively around hers.

Damn, but being trusted felt good. He glanced down at her, and as though she sensed his gaze, she looked up at him. Her eyes were still red and swollen from crying. Abruptly, another woman's face took the place of Audrey's. Instead of trust, hers was filled with a certain weariness and resignation. And fear. That most of all.

With a silent oath, Gray reminded himself that trust was the last thing he had to offer a woman. The absolute dead last. Wake up and smell the roses, he told himself. She's not for you.

Together they went back to Audrey's room, where Gray opened her suitcase and laid it across the bed. She began transferring clothes from the dresser drawer.

"Threats in the middle of the night," she muttered. "Ghosts, legends, mutilated animals, and things that go bump in the night. Never mind they had a little help from modern technology. I feel like I'm losing my mind. Howard will think I'm off my rocker."

"No, he won't," Gray assured her. "He'll think you're smart to leave."

She gripped the sides of the suitcase, then glanced over her shoulder. "What about you?"

"I think you're being smart," Gray replied evenly.

"You told me not to trust you."

His Adam's apple bobbed. "And you shouldn't."

"But I do." She straightened and moved toward him. "And I don't want to leave without—"

Gray shook his head. "Don't say it. Please, don't say it." He wanted to reach for her, gather her close and assure her everything would be okay. The intensity of his need made him clench his fists.

This went far beyond the need to enjoy her soft body and lose himself in the intense pleasure he would find there. Needing to touch her body, and heaven knew he wanted to, paled in comparison to claiming her as his.

She was his. Perhaps even before he saw her for the first time last night, she was his.

The realization scared the hell out of him.

The need to protect competed with the need to possess. He knew the demons that waited if he chose possession, had seen firsthand those demons in his father and his brothers. Audrey deserved his protection, and by God, she would get it.

She watched him with wide eyes as he moved away from her. He went to the closet and stripped a pair of slacks from a hanger, handing them to her. She folded them and laid them in the suitcase. Without talking, they packed the rest of her clothes and toiletries.

With a last glance around the room, Audrey decided she had everything. She looked at Gray, who met her glance briefly before looking away. At last, here was a man who had felt so right. And she was positive that when she drove away from the ranch, she'd never see him again.

His expression was hard as a granite mask as he glanced around the room. "Looks like you've got everything."

"Yes," she said, her attention still on him. "I'm sorry," she added.

"What the hell for?" His eyes glittered. "Don't *ever* say you're sorry when someone else—"

"For the trouble I've put you to," she interrupted.

"It's no trouble." Gray picked up the suitcase and computer and led the way down the hall.

Carrying the smaller case, Audrey watched Gray's broad back. His posture was stiff, and he acted as though he couldn't wait to be rid of her. The thought she might never see him again tore at her. Why did this one man draw her so?

Outside it was raining again, almost as hard as it had been last night when she arrived. Audrey glanced at her watch. It wasn't yet noon. Even so, she felt as though she had been here days instead of hours.

"Wait here," Gray said at the door, grabbing the ever present rain poncho off the hook next to the door and pulling it over his head. Carrying her bags, he sprinted out to the car, which was mostly hidden by the adobe wall surrounding the courtyard. He disappeared a moment when he bent over. When he stood, Hawk stood with him, which startled Audrey. She had forgotten about Hawk. Gray unlocked her trunk and put the two cases inside. They huddled together, talking.

She watched the two men a moment longer before deciding that she was being ridiculous to wait for Gray to come back. She stepped over the threshold and dashed through the rain to her car.

Gray glanced up when he saw her coming. He was frowning, and an even deeper one marred his features as he watched her run toward him. He took the case from her and set it in the trunk as Hawk opened the door for her. Audrey slid in behind the wheel.

"I'm sorry you're the one who found the animal," Hawk said. For the first time, his tone sounded something other than hostile. Not quite friendly, but not as if she were the enemy.

Ignoring the rain, Gray squatted down next to her, his eyes level with hers, bracing himself between the seat and the open car door.

"Are you going clear back to Denver tonight?" he asked.

She hadn't thought about it. "I don't know."

She had the urge to brush a wet lock of his hair away from his face, and to keep from touching him, she clasped her hands together in her lap.

"When you get back to town, Audrey, call someone you trust and let them know where you are and where you're headed. Okay?"

She swallowed. "I'm leaving. Isn't that enough? You don't have to keep scaring me like this."

"I'm not trying to scare you," he responded, his voice once again gruff. "It's just sensible, all right?" Suddenly, he ducked his head and leaned inside. Audrey caught a whiff of the scent that was indefinably him, and her stomach lurched. He settled his mouth over hers in a warm kiss. "Be safe, Audrey Sussman," he whispered, then pressed the keys into her hands and straightened.

He closed the door, and Audrey stared at him through the window. He lifted his hand in a brief salute, and she wrenched her gaze away and tried twice before she was able to stick the key in the ignition.

She backed her car away from the parking area. After she had turned around, in her rearview mirror, she watched Gray run through the rain to join Hawk at the lodge entrance.

She firmed her chin and drove away from Puma's Lair. Keen disappointment settled in her chest; she would never know where the pull of attraction might have led. They had been acquainted mere hours, after all.

She had gone less than a mile when she met an oncoming car. Behind the wheel was Francie, who smiled and waved when she recognized Audrey. She brought her vehicle to a stop and rolled down her window.

Following suit, Audrey added to her list of regrets, remembering Francie's invitation to dinner.

"If I'd known you wanted to go to town," Francie said by way of greeting, "I would have offered to take you. The road is really treacherous."

"I'm not on my way to town," Audrey responded. Between them, the rain began to fall harder, splashing through the open window into the car. "I'm leaving."

Surprise chased across Francie's face. "Already?"

She managed a smile. "Already. Can I take a rain check on that dinner invitation?"

"But of course. I'll hold you to it." She smiled and began rolling up her window. "Take good care," she called.

Audrey nodded, rolled up her own window and put the car back into gear. Although last night she had thought the two-mile-long road between Puma's Lair and the highway was treacherous, today it was even worse. Her progress was much slower now. Monster-size puddles filled the road, and she knew she would be in big trouble if any of them were as deep as she feared. The muddy road alternately grabbed and repelled the wheels, making her progress down the narrow track slow. The slipping and sliding made the drive seem endless.

With the confusing events of the past day swirling through her mind, Audrey pressed a little harder on the accelerator. The rear of her car fishtailed, and with a muttered curse, she immediately let up on the gas. At this rate, she would be lucky to keep the car on the road.

Mud splattered across the windshield, smearing into a film she could not see through when the blade wiped it aside. The next swipe didn't improve her visibility any, and Audrey stopped the car. The pouring rain and several more swipes cleared the mud away. Next to the road, a few head of cattle huddled together.

She stepped on the gas once again, and negotiated the twists and turns in the road with care. Finally, she rounded the last curve before the bridge. Water gushed over the bank a little above it, turning the field next to the road into a shallow pond.

Audrey remembered thinking the bridge had looked none too sturdy last night. In daylight, the pair of logs with the boards attached looked even less substantial than they had in the dark. Only knowing that she had crossed the bridge last night reassured her she could safely cross again.

Another splatter of mud covered the windshield. For an instant, she could see nothing, and she turned the windshield wipers to a faster speed. When she could see once again, an immense bull stood in the middle of the road a few feet in front of her.

She slammed on the brakes.

The car slid to the edge of the road where it came to a halt. Once more, mud obliterated her view. When she could see again, she watched the animal meander across the road as though it had all the time in the world.

An immense crest of water surged over the bridge. Suddenly it gave way. Almost in slow motion, it turned over and floated down the river.

Had she not swerved to avoid the bull, she would have

been on the bridge. She cried out and gripped the steering wheel as though it were a lifeline.

Between Audrey's car and the far bank, the creek swelled. A couple of logs floated by. She almost laughed. *Floated* was too tame a word. They charged down the river, carried on the back of the water, rolling and twisting, like monstrous snapping beasts.

"Oh, God," she breathed as realization poured through her. She could have washed downstream, too.

She hated the idea of going back to Puma's Lair, but there was no choice now. So far as she knew, this was the only road in and out of the ranch. She put the car into reverse, and stepped on the gas.

The wheels spun, but the car didn't move. She put the car into low gear, but the wheels spun in that direction, as well. She rocked the vehicle, hoping to ease it out of the mud.

Outside, the rain still fell in torrents, and she knew this time she had no choice but to wait until the rain stopped. The walk back to the ranch was a couple of miles, which was going to be miserable in the mud, downright foolish in the rain.

She stared through the windshield, waves of fatigue washing over her. She'd sit here where it was warm and wait for the rain to stop. Then she would walk back to the ranch.

Yawning, she settled her head against the headrest. Yes. That's what she'd do.

And her eyelids drifted shut on a final thought. She'd see Gray again.

Worry rode Gray like a toothache almost as soon as Audrey's car disappeared around the bend in the road. There were too many "coincidences," and someone had gone to a lot of trouble to scare her. In his experience, there was a limited number of reasons for someone to go to all that trouble. Greed and revenge were almost always at the top of the list.

Gray went into the lodge, hoping to find Hawk or Richard and get answers to his questions. He didn't find them. He couldn't imagine either one doing the mutilation. But the whispered threats over the speakers seemed exactly the sort of thing Richard might do.

Gray strode through the hallways, making a mental list. The speaker in Audrey's room, the mutilated animal, her car trouble, Richard's absence last night, his threats after he returned. What the hell was going on? Gray's list of questions was long, and his answers were nonexistent.

He silently let himself into the room Audrey had used, then closed the door behind him. Her scent was still present, reminding him how she had responded to his kisses. The speaker was still on the shelf, and Gray sat down on the bed, wondering what activated it. Whatever it was, it had to be battery operated since the power had been off all night.

Remembering that Audrey had been certain the ''voice'' sensed her presence, Gray began checking for bugs. He didn't find any, but felt no relief to the worry that nagged him.

He kept feeling that he had overlooked something important.

He wondered if Audrey's drive through the mud back to the highway had been okay. Taking his car keys out of his pocket, he climbed into his Blazer. It couldn't hurt to check, and he would be a lot happier knowing she was all right.

The road was worse than Gray ever remembered it being, and he put his vehicle into four-wheel drive after he rounded the first curve. The mud sucking at his tires convinced him that she couldn't have made it back to the highway. He kept looking for signs of her tracks in the road. By the time he reached the last stretch before the highway, he had slowed his pace to a crawl to keep the Blazer on the road. At each turn, he expected to find Audrey's car. At each turn, he hoped he would not.

Relief that she had made it this far competed with disappointment he wouldn't be seeing her again. Childish, he decided. He would breathe easier once he knew she had made it to the highway without mishap.

As he approached the bridge, the road became even more treacherous, and he fought to keep going in the right direction. The next instant, he spotted her car.

All his worry bunched into a seething knot in the pit of his stomach.

Her car had evidently slid off the road as she came down the slope, and it was stuck in inches of mud. Without a winch, he wouldn't be able to free it. He didn't see her inside the car, and his imagination fastened on a dozen hellacious possibilities. Where was she?

As Gray navigated the final yards of road, he spared a glance ahead to the bridge—or where the bridge should have been. Cursing under his breath, he brought his own vehicle to a stop. Except for the roadbed that disappeared into the flowing water and reappeared on the other side, there was no evidence a bridge had ever spanned the creek.

Returning his attention to Audrey's car, he saw her silhouette behind the driver's seat. She didn't notice his approach, and his relief was short-lived. His imagination conjured a new set of worrying possibilities. He got out of his truck and slogged through the mud. The windows were steamed up. Even so, he could see that her arms were wrapped loosely over the top of her steering wheel, and her head was drooped over it.

His first thought was she had been injured when her car slid off the road. He rapped on the window and reached for the door handle. He saw her fingers flutter, and her head moved slightly. Her movements were uncoordinated, drunken. He wrenched the door open.

"Audrey?"

The inside of her car felt stuffy, and he smelled exhaust from her engine, which was still running.

"God, no." Raw fear, primitive as any he had ever known, churned through him.

Putting his hand beneath her chin, he tipped her face toward him. Unhealthy blue tinged her skin, and her eyes focused on him momentarily before rolling back into her head.

Carbon-monoxide poisoning was the one thing his imagination hadn't taunted him with.

Chapter 6

Gray reached inside and turned off the engine, then unsnapped her seat belt. In a rush, he pulled Audrey from the car and into his arms.

Her head lolled to the side, and her arms dangled limply. Hoisting her more firmly, Gray stood up.

Oblivious to the rain, he returned to the Blazer and jerked open the door. He set her on the seat and felt for a pulse in her neck. Beneath his fingers, he felt a steady beat.

His relief left him shaking. What the hell was basic first aid for carbon-monoxide poisoning? He couldn't remember. *Oxygen. It had to be oxygen.* He didn't have any. Just the cool fresh air. He hoped it was enough.

"Audrey!"

Her eyelids fluttered.

Gray wrapped one of her arms around his neck and put one of his around her waist. Pulling her from his car, he headed for the grassy bank at the edge of the road where there was less mud.

"C'mon, honey. Walk." Her feet dragged the ground. Gray took another few steps. "I know you can."

Her head drooped against her chest. Gray let go of her arm and lifted her face toward him. At the touch of the rain against her face, she gasped, and her whole body stiffened.

"That's it. Breathe!"

She shuddered, then gasped again. Her eyes opened. Though they were focused on his face, she didn't seem to see him. But they were open. That, at least, was something.

"Inhale again, honey."

She sucked in a huge breath. He pulled her arm more firmly around his neck and tightened his hold on her waist.

"We're going to walk, Audrey," he said, suiting action to his words. The first two steps, her legs dragged on the ground. On the third, she made her legs move. "That's it."

Most of her steps after that were uncoordinated, and she stumbled more than walked. The exercise was making her breathe harder, though, and at the moment that was all Gray wanted.

He glanced down at her. What he could see of her cheek wasn't as pale as it had been, and the blue tint to her skin was fading. With each step, her legs gained coordination. He kept talking to her, encouraging her, his response automatic. C'mon, love, he silently urged her. Fear curled through his gut, leaving behind a hole that burned.

Audrey coughed, and Gray stopped walking, holding her until the spasm passed. When it was over, she was trembling.

Suddenly, she stiffened and grasped his arms. "Gray?"

"Yeah," he answered.

She raised her eyes to his, this time thankfully focused and clear. The whites of her eyes still looked too blue to him. Sighing, she lifted her face into the rain, which was slowing to a stop. She closed her eyes, kneading her fingers into his arms.

"I stopped for a huge bull. If I hadn't, I would have

been on the bridge when a big crest of water washed it away.'' She shuddered. ''Oh, my God...''

Too easily, Gray followed her train of thought, and his grip around her tightened. If she had been on the bridge...if he hadn't been worried and come to check on her...

''You're okay,'' he whispered, pulling her more firmly against his side, pressing his lips against her hair. ''You're okay.''

''And I got so sleepy, and I never take naps.'' She started to shake. ''And I was sure I was dying, but I'd just fallen asleep....''

''You had carbon-monoxide poisoning.''

''No—''

''Yes.'' He cupped her cheek with his palm. ''When I got here, you were barely conscious, Audrey. Not asleep.''

''I could have...di— If you hadn't come...'' A hysterical bubble of laughter escaped. ''And I kept thinking I could have been on the bridge—''

The laughter ended on a sob.

Gray wrapped his arms around her. ''Shh. It's all right.'' He wished he had never said the words. Things weren't all right, and he was a fool for wanting her to believe they were. He wanted a look at the exhaust system on her car. If he hadn't come along, her death would have looked like a tragic accident. In his gut, he knew this was no accident.

The knowledge someone was willing to kill her made him shake. The deep anger was familiar, and so was his overwhelming need to protect. He hadn't felt this power- less, though, since he was a twelve-year-old, watching his father beat his mother. Then, Gray had known exactly who the enemy was. He wished he knew now. Richard? Hawk? Someone else?

Shocked that he had so much at stake in Audrey—view- ing her enemies as his own—he filed the realization away to think about later. The important thing was to figure why someone was after her.

"I have a headache that won't quit," she said.

"I have aspirin, but I don't know if it will help." He loosened his hold on her. "Are you ready to go?"

"Back to the ranch?"

He wished there were someplace else. His glance slid to the creek. Until the water receded, the choices were limited.

The ranch. Where Richard and Hawk were both glad to see her gone. Where one of them was evidently willing to murder.

The pueblo, he thought. Except Mary and Hawk both lived at La Huerta. Audrey wouldn't be welcome there, either.

His cabin. Which had a leaky roof, and since he had moved down to the lodge until it was fixed, he couldn't easily explain moving back.

Damn!

"Gray?"

He glanced toward the creek and Audrey's car. As soon as anyone saw her car, they would know she hadn't made it to the highway. Keeping her presence a secret would be impossible. Taking her back to his place was the only sensible answer.

He was on the verge of answering her when he heard the distinctive ping of a bullet striking metal.

He pushed Audrey down, dropping to the ground with her. His heart lodged in his throat, and he pressed his cheek against the sandy earth.

"What—?"

The heavy boom of a rifle's gunshot cut short her question.

Another bullet hit, this time striking a large rock a few feet away. A scant second later the gunfire resounded again.

"Damn," Gray muttered, dragging Audrey farther away from the road, seeking whatever meager protection the thick stands of rabbitbrush provided.

"I hear a gun," she said, disbelief coloring her voice.

"Damned straight."

Another bullet whizzed over their heads and struck the earth just beyond them.

"Oh, God, somebody's shooting at us." Amazement, more than fear, filled her voice.

"You got that right." Gray scanned the bluff above them. His eyes narrowed as he scanned the hillside. It was someone quite a distance from them, given the time between the bullet striking and the rifle's report. He wished he had the binoculars that were inside his truck. More than that, he wished he had the revolver hidden under the seat.

"Why?" she asked, lifting her head slightly.

Now, there was the sixty-four-thousand-dollar question. He pushed her head back down.

"C'mon, show yourself," he muttered. His revolver wasn't any good at distances. But he'd feel better if he had it anyway.

Gunfire sounded again. Without being told, Audrey curled completely against the muddy earth.

"Oh, God," she whispered. "Oh, God."

Another ping was followed by a brief hiss, accompanied by the thunderclap of an explosion.

Pieces of Audrey's car shot into the sky, driven by an orange and black fireball. The smell of burning gasoline permeated the air. The impact of the explosion thundered through Gray, and he covered Audrey's body with his. Pieces of her car crashed back to the ground. The odor of hot metal pinched his nostrils.

Above the sound of the fire, Gray heard more gunfire. He peered through the brush. A bullet struck the windshield of his car, shattering the glass. Another struck a tire, and another struck the radiator.

"Your car, Gray," he heard Audrey say from beneath him. "Oh, God, I'm sorry."

"What the hell are you sorry for?"

"If you hadn't come—"

"Don't even say it," he interrupted fiercely.

Feeling Audrey shiver, Gray opened his jacket and shifted slightly to his side, until he had it wrapped around her. Easing his weight off her, he put his arm under her head, then pulled her back more firmly against his chest.

He had no idea what he would say to her when she asked what they were going to do next. Thankfully, she didn't ask. They lay on the ground, listening to the fire burn, watching the black skeleton of her car gradually appear from within the diminishing flames.

Again and again, Gray's glance returned to the bluff. The more he thought about the shooter's location, the less he liked the possibilities. For one thing, the bluff was on the same side of the creek they were. Whoever was trying to kill them couldn't leave, either. Not unless he had wings. Equally important, getting back to the ranch was going to be a problem. Mud, little cover, rain and the cold were all concerns without the added threat of someone out there with a rifle.

The distinctive smell of rain filled the air, and Gray glanced up. On top of everything else, they were about to get soaked. His attention shifted to the bluff. Nothing. Wherever the gunman was, he was well hidden.

A veil of showers crept over the bluff.

"We're going to make a run for it in just a minute," Gray whispered in Audrey's ear, reasoning that if he couldn't see the bluff, the sniper wouldn't be able to see them. Gray figured if they were going to move, they would have as good a chance as they were likely to get in two or three more minutes.

"For your car?"

"I have a couple of things I want to get out of it, but we're going to be on foot. See that big boulder over there, the house-sized one that looks sort of like a pyramid with a balcony off the side?"

"Yeah."

"As soon as I say go, I want you to run for it. When you get there, hunker down behind it and stay put. Okay?"

She nodded.

A few sprinkles fell, and she glanced up the hillside to where the gunfire had been coming from. The bluff was hidden behind a curtain of rain.

Gray sat up suddenly and stripped off his jacket. He stuffed her into it as though she were a small child and zipped it to her neck. He looked so serious while performing the task, she couldn't help but reach up and smooth out the lines between his eyebrows. He paused, his gaze searching hers, then finished in a rush. He took her hand, and laced her fingers through his.

"Don't worry about a thing," he said. "I'm going to be right behind you."

She tried to smile. "Don't worry! Hah. Until last night, the biggest worry I had was not overdrawing my checking account."

"That's the spunk." Gray stood and pulled her to her feet. "Run, honey. And no matter what you hear, keep running until you get to the rock. Okay?"

"Okay."

He pointed her in the right direction and swatted her on the fanny.

All the fear that had been bottled up inside her let loose, and she ran as though the furies of hell were after her. When Gray pointed out the boulder, it hadn't looked so far away. Now it seemed miles.

Maybe not miles, she grudgingly admitted. She was a city kid. What did she know about distance? Before she was even halfway to the rock, her side ached. Fear and fear alone kept her running.

Within seconds, her legs felt weighted down, not just with the mud sticking to her shoes and sucking at her feet, but with fatigue. A stitch stabbed her side, and she pressed herself to run though her body demanded she stop.

Once, she glanced over her shoulder. She didn't see Gray
at all. Dear God, what would she do if something happened
to him?

An instant later, she saw him slip out of the vehicle, his
arms filled with a bundle. He crouched next to the door.

Run, she silently urged.

A pair of rapid rifle shots split the air.

Audrey tried to run faster, but she couldn't make her legs
move any quicker. Her lungs burned. And the damned rock
seemed no closer.

She glanced over her shoulder. Gray was running toward
her.

She returned her attention to the boulder and doubted
she would reach it before Gray caught up with her.

The huge stone was still a long way off when she heard
his pounding footsteps right behind her.

"You're doing fine," he said, sounding barely winded
at all.

She knew just how badly she was doing. Even under the
best of circumstances, she couldn't have run with his ease.
She vowed that just as soon as she made it back to Denver
she was going to get into shape.

The report of the rifle firing made her duck.

If she made it back to Denver, she thought. Reaching for
an additional spurt of energy, she thought, When. Not if.
When.

As he had when he walked with her earlier, Gray grabbed
her by the waist, half lifting her as they ran, making her
torturous progress more rapid. His support made her dig
deep for another spurt of energy. It was a mere dribble, but
he praised her anyway.

She looked ahead, and amazingly the outcrop was closer.
When they reached the huge boulder, Audrey wanted to
collapse at its base, but Gray pulled her around the back
side. Sheets of sandstone had broken off here and there,
some buried along the bottom, many piled on top of one

another. Gray pulled her beneath two huge perpendicular slabs carelessly leaned against the huge boulder's wall. The crude lean-to gave them nominal protection from the weather.

Audrey sank to the ground, sucking in huge gasps of air. Her chest felt tight, and her heart pounded. He put his arm around her shoulder.

"You okay?" he asked.

"Fine and dandy," she gasped. "I'm just getting warmed up. I'll be ready for a marathon in…oh…two or three minutes, max."

He squeezed her shoulder and brought her more fully next to him. The squall caught up with them. Thankfully, it was just a gentle drizzle. Audrey shivered and snuggled into Gray's abundant warmth. She noticed he had put on another jacket, which looked old and ratty compared to the one he had given her.

"I know this is gonna sound stupid," she said, "but I'm starved."

"That fine guest-ranch hospitality again," he said, his tone dry.

She chuckled. "I don't think I can blame Mary or Hawk for this. And Richard hadn't struck me as the outdoors type."

"He's not," Gray confirmed.

He leaned his head against the rock wall and closed his eyes a moment before shrugging out of a backpack. Unzipping the top compartment, he pulled out a pair of candy bars and handed one to Audrey. She studied the open pack and had the feeling she had just caught a glimpse of Mary Poppins's magic satchel.

"I don't believe it," she said with appreciation. Her stomach rumbled, a reminder she had been hungry before she left Puma's Lair. She unwrapped the paper around the Hershey bar, and the candy's sweet smell filled the air. "You're a saint."

She took a bite, savoring the taste and texture of the chocolate against her tongue.

His attention remained focused on the terrain they had just covered. "When I tell you we've got to get going, you'll think I'm a real bas—"

"I'll still think you're a saint," she interrupted, glancing at the gray clouds above them. "I've already figured out that if we can move under the cover of rain without being seen, the guy with the rifle can, too."

Gray nodded. "That's right."

"And since this outcrop is the only thing bigger than one of those bushes out there, it won't take a genius to figure out where we are."

"Smart girl."

She took another bite of her candy bar. "What next?"

"I'm going to climb up to the top of the rock and see if anyone is coming. If it's clear, we're going to take off for that set of foothills."

"The ranch is that way," she said pointing in the opposite direction.

"Yeah. And there's not enough cover between here and there to hide a jackrabbit." Gray stood up. "When I give you the high sign, take off at a good brisk walk. If you see anybody besides me, drop down and lay flat against the ground."

"What if they see me first?" She wished her question sounded flip instead of scared. Audrey had never felt so out of her element. This wouldn't have been fun even if somebody weren't shooting at them.

"They won't." He caught her glance. "It'll be okay. You don't have to run, but this isn't a Sunday stroll, either."

She rubbed her side where the stitch still ached. "Unfortunately, a Sunday stroll is about my best speed."

He patted her arm. "You're doing just fine."

Gray slid out from beneath the makeshift stone shelter

and climbed up the face of the boulder. Audrey's stomach clutched as she imagined what he might see. She still couldn't believe someone was actually shooting at them.

"It's clear, Audrey," Gray called. "I want to keep an eye on things for a while longer. Get going and I'll catch up with you in a bit."

"Define 'bit,'" she said.

"When you've got enough distance between here and the bluff by the creek that we can make it safely across the valley."

She slipped out from under the stones, immediately feeling the mist against her face. At least it wasn't raining hard the way it had been before, she thought. She tipped her head back and peered up at Gray. His weight was supported in one of the fissures of the big boulder, and he held a pair of binoculars to his eyes.

Flexing his shoulders, he pulled his arms back, and his jacket opened. Tucked in the waistband of his jeans was a black, lethal-looking gun. Audrey stared, and Richard's taunt echoed through her head. *He killed a man, you know.*

She swallowed, unable to look away from the gun. And someone was trying to kill her. *Don't trust anyone.* If she'd ever been around anyone besides a cop who carried a weapon, she hadn't known it. The whole business frightened her far more than she wanted to admit. Especially that this man might be willing to use his gun.

"Get going, Audrey."

She lifted her gaze to his. He looked the same.

Of course he looks the same, you ninny, she scolded herself. She understood why he wanted her to go ahead. The pistol didn't have a rifle's range, and staying here while she walked ahead gave her a better chance if the guy with the rifle showed up.

Dear God, what had she gotten herself into?

"Audrey?"

She rubbed her temple. One part of her wanted to argue

with him, say that if he stayed, so did she. Another part of her was completely baffled.

"You think it's best I go alone?"

"You won't be alone, hon—Audrey, I swear it. I just want to make sure we get a good head start."

"Toward those foothills, right?"

"Yep. Make a beeline toward those cottonwoods. And don't forget. If you hear anything or see anyone besides me, drop down and lay flat. Got it?"

She nodded.

"And Audrey?" He paused until she looked up at him. "Don't worry. You'll be okay. It may be a while before I catch up with you, but I will."

She believed him. If he had anything at all to say about it, they would be safe. Which led her thoughts straight back to the gun. She remembered her brother had once told her there was no point in carrying a gun unless you intended to use it.

She stuffed her hands in the pockets of her jacket and began walking toward the line of cottonwood trees.

The farther away from the road she got, the harder packed the ground became, which made walking easier and faster. She stopped and picked up a small flat stone to scrape the excess mud off the soles of her shoes. That, too, made walking easier, though she would kill for her Nikes and a pair of warm socks.

Kill. The word echoed through her brain, and she doubted she would ever again be so cavalier about the word. Had Gray really killed a man? Sensing he would kill to protect them if he had to, she was no longer so sure about her earlier conclusion that he couldn't have killed anyone.

The cottonwoods looked an impossibly long distance away, so she picked a landmark much closer to walk toward—a bush several hundred yards ahead. When she passed it, she found another small landmark and walked toward it. After the fifth or sixth time, she turned around and looked at the boulder. Gray was still braced in the narrow crack.

Audrey focused on the next marker and counted off the paces until she reached it.

Who would be shooting at them? she wondered. Despite Richard's comments last night, she couldn't imagine him wanting her dead. Of course, she couldn't imagine anyone she knew plotting murder, so what did she know? Even so, the image of Richard climbing a hillside in the rain to shoot at her just didn't compute. He'd get those expensive Tony Lama boots all muddy.

Her thoughts shifted to Hawk. She found it easier to believe Hawk capable of cold-blooded murder, but she suspected that was mostly because she had watched too many Westerns while she was growing up. And why would he shoot at her, anyway? Even though he had promised Richard he would take care of it if need be. *It.* There *it* was again, she thought. Figure out what *it* was and maybe she'd know who was shooting at her.

Cold realization washed over her. Someone had been shooting at her. Not her and Gray together, but her. For an instant, she thought she might throw up.

She tried to imagine what her brother's advice would be in this situation. As a Navy SEAL, she knew he courted danger, and she often suspected his world was so far removed from hers she would barely comprehend it. Until today, her personal experiences with danger had been no more risky than deciding whether to ride a roller coaster.

Trust your instincts, he'd probably say. That sounded good, but she had always found her mind to be far more reliable than her hunches.

After that, her brother would tell her to figure out who had the best resources she needed, then stick like glue. No doubt about it—Gray was far better equipped to get them out of this fix than she was.

Gradually, she realized the rain had stopped, and the clouds seemed to have lifted some. She glanced at her watch, wishing she had remembered to do that before she started walking. The time was just a few minutes past four. She had no idea how long she had been walking. She turned around and looked at the boulder where she had left Gray.

It was far behind her. Her attention became focused on walking as fast as she could. She glanced over her shoulder occasionally, trying to judge the point at which the trees were closer than the boulder. For a long time, she felt suspended between the two landmarks. Finally, when the trees seemed marginally closer, she saw Gray moving across the plain. He ran easily, covering the ground in a fraction of the time she had.

Knowing he was on his way lifted her spirits. She analyzed that, deciding no single thing accounted for the feeling. She was attracted to him. And she trusted him to do his best to keep them safe and get them out of this mess.

A little while later, she heard the sound of a car engine, and she stopped to look back in the direction she thought the road was. Worse, she didn't see Gray anywhere.

Then she heard him shout. ''Audrey, get down. Damn it, Audrey, lie down!''

Chapter 7

Obeying Gray's command, Audrey dropped instantly to the ground, lying flat. Against her cheek, the soil felt sandy, cool and damp. She could feel the rumble of a vehicle, as well as hear its engine. Peering through one of the spindly bushes that dotted the valley, she tried to see Gray. A hundred yards behind her, she saw him on the ground, belly-crawling toward her.

When he was fifteen yards away, he repeated, "Just stay put, honey. Our shooter has a Jeep and he's left the road looking for us."

"Do you think he saw us?" she asked.

"Nope. He would have fired by now if he had."

Again, she heard the engine. Gray didn't turn around to see where the vehicle was, so Audrey resisted the urge to look herself.

"I'll say one thing for this guy," Gray noted when he reached her. "He's persistent."

"Just before you yelled at me," she said, "I saw a gully

a little ways ahead. That's better than staying here, isn't it?''

"Sure is,'' Gray agreed. "Lay low, honey, and lead the way.''

On hands and knees, she crawled between the sparsely placed bushes toward the ravine. When Audrey reached it, she groaned. It wasn't better at all. Six or seven feet deep and about that many feet wide, the gulch zigzagged across the valley. Water stood in the bottom of the ditch, and the sides had crumbled away under the onslaught of all the recent rain.

"This is perfect,'' Gray said.

"Perfect is a room at the Marriott,'' she muttered.

"You'll get no argument from me. Room service and a hot shower are sounding better by the minute,'' he said. "But once we get to the other side, it's going to be real difficult for our friend back there to cross over. All we have to do is get there without leaving any obvious tracks.''

"If he hasn't already spotted our tracks.''

"He might not,'' Gray argued. "The rabbitbrush provides pretty good protection, and the soil was packed hard enough that your tracks weren't real obvious. If I hadn't known where you were headed and if I wasn't keeping a close eye out, I might not have seen them.''

Audrey smiled. "Thanks for trying to make me feel better, Gray, but the bad guys in the movies are always expert trackers.''

"Yep,'' he agreed. "And nine times out of ten, good prevails and justice is done. Only, life isn't the movies.''

They crawled along the bank of the gulch another hundred yards before Gray found a spot he liked. He took his backpack off.

"When was the last time you rode piggyback?'' he asked.

"Years,'' she said.

"C'mon. You can carry the pack for a minute, and I'll carry you."

"I don't think so," she murmured. "You walk. I walk."

He reached for her deck shoes, which he easily slipped off her feet. "You walk in the mud in these, and you'll lose them in ten yards."

"We're not going to walk in the mud for ten yards," she reasoned. "As soon as we get across—"

"We're not going across," he interrupted. "We're going to walk along the bottom of the gully for a while—it's our only hope of staying hidden until our guy gets tired and leaves." He put her shoes in the pocket of his jacket. "I'm walking, and you're riding."

"I can walk," she insisted.

He gazed at her, noting the bruised-looking smudges beneath her eyes. Without adequate protection for her feet, the chill from the mud would seep into her. If they had to make a run for it, she wouldn't have enough energy left to battle a feather.

"Gray—"

"No more discussion." He rose up, again checking the location of the Jeep. "He's headed back toward the road. Now's our chance."

He helped her put the pack over her shoulders.

"What do you have in here? Bricks?"

"Dinner," he answered. "And a few other odds and ends."

Audrey climbed on his back, and he grasped both of her legs, holding her thighs next to his sides. Layers of clothes separated them, but she was acutely aware of him. Against her legs, his body felt incredibly warm. His damp hair rubbed her cheek, smelling of rain, soap and the underlying scent that was uniquely him.

They descended over the edge of the gully in a rush. She looped one arm around his shoulders and grabbed on to his jacket with the other hand.

Gray's focus remained on the sound of the Jeep criss-crossing the valley as he trudged through the mud. The gully was barely deep enough to conceal them. As the sound of the vehicle ebbed and flowed, he could feel Audrey's tension. Did she realize she was the quarry?

Though he had been through his own life-and-death crises, never once had he been the hunted. If it scared and worried him, it must be terrifying for her. For the first time in his life, this was an insight to how his mother must have felt when she had fled his father's wrath.

The Jeep sounded much closer. Gray felt Audrey twist around on his back, looking behind them.

"See anything?" he asked.

"No," she said. "Nothing but the gully."

"Then he can't see us, either."

"Somehow that doesn't make me feel better."

It didn't make Gray feel better, either. Hidden as they were, they would be trapped if they were discovered.

The sound of the Jeep engine grew louder, worrying Gray more by the minute as he realized the gully was gradually becoming shallow, and they would soon be visible. He headed for a precarious-looking overhang that would shield them from view.

The water had worn away a wider course at the bottom of the gulch, leaving an overhang of four or five feet. From the top, the gulch would look no wider than it did anywhere else. He wouldn't give two cents for the ground above not collapsing, but it was better than being a sitting duck for the man chasing them.

Who the hell was he, anyway? And what had Audrey done, what did she know that would make her a target for murder?

The Jeep engine sounded directly above them, its tone changing as the vehicle slowed. There was a squeak of brakes, and a door slammed.

Gray eased Audrey off his back and edged deeper beneath the overhang. Pulling her to his side, he wrapped an arm around her and put his fingers to his lips. Her eyes wide, she nodded.

There was a whisk of footsteps directly above them. The edge of the overhang crumbled, and muddy clumps of earth splashed into the water in front of them. Directly above their heads, Gray saw a crack in the earthen roof, a crack that seemed to widen as he watched. He glanced at Audrey, her attention focused on the sounds above them, her head cocked slightly to the side.

Next to him, Gray felt Audrey tremble. He gave her shoulders a reassuring squeeze.

There was another brush of sound accompanied by footfalls, and a second later the car door closed. The engine revved and gears ground. The crunch of tires became more faint, and within a few seconds more, the sound of the engine had faded to a drone.

Easing out from beneath the overhang, Gray scrambled a couple of steps up the side of the gully. The vehicle was still close, and he ducked without taking his eyes off the driver. The man was bare headed, blond. Tall, judging by the way he sat behind the wheel. A red-and-silver lightning bolt was painted on the side of the vehicle, a design that was somehow familiar. From this distance, Gray couldn't read the plates, but they had the distinctive green and white of Colorado's. He had begun investigations with less to go on. He felt Audrey beside him, staring at the Jeep.

She shivered.

"I know who it is," she said, a quaver in her voice. "I've ridden in that vehicle."

She closed her eyes, and Gray noted the blue tinge beneath the surface of her skin, reminding him of all she had been through today.

"Howard Lambert." Her eyes blinked open, and she gripped his hands tightly. "My God, I should have figured this out sooner. All the signs were there, but I didn't want to—''

''You're sure?''

Audrey nodded.

''And I know why.'' She met Gray's eyes. ''Right before Howard sent me down here to do the audit, I was working on a deal for a resort he's buying in Tucson. And I discovered a bunch of irregularities with water and mineral rights on one of his other properties. He had sold the rights to raise cash for the new resort. Only trouble was, he sold one set of rights to two different buyers—we're talking millions of dollars here.''

''And you asked him about it.''

Audrey nodded. ''I was sure it had to be some kind of mistake. It had to be. That's deliberate, going-to-jail fraud.''

''And you told him that, too.''

''It came up, more jokingly than anything, but yeah. He told me he was sure there had been a mix-up and not to worry about it.''

''Then what happened?''

She frowned. ''He came back to talk to me before he left that night, and I told him my concerns. He said not to worry about it—he would take care of it. The next morning, he dumped a pile of files on my desk and told me to get down here. Which was strange.''

''Strange how?'' Gray asked, trying to recall anything he had ever heard Richard or Hawk say about the owner of Puma's Lair. Lambert hadn't come to the ranch often, but when he did, he loved to hunt.

''Puma's Lair was always his baby. I always reviewed the financials as part of the total package, but he didn't want any advice, didn't want any input, didn't want me to visit the place. Nothing. Until now.''

''What did you think?''

She shrugged. ''Howard is eccentric sometimes, and this

isn't the first time he's pulled me off one project to do something else." She gave Gray a faint smile. "I can't even believe I'm standing here talking about this. He's been a mentor, a friend. When my mother died, he was a rock."

Gray touched Audrey's hand. "But I hear an unspoken question in that."

"It's completely the kind of thing he does, and he knows just how to make you feel great. But he expects—almost demands—that same kind of loyalty in return."

"And asking him about the sale wasn't loyal?"

"It is if it was a legitimate error." Audrey's glance fell to her feet. "He sees himself as the last of the great individualists—the kind of men who settled the West. You never met him, did you?"

Gray shook his head.

"If you had, you'd understand what I mean. He dresses Western—blatantly so. Imagine a Buffalo Bill Cody fringed leather coat and a waxed mustache. He loves to hunt, and once he bragged to me there wasn't an animal he couldn't track."

An instant of silence followed, then she giggled, the sound verging on hysterical.

"Remember when I said the bad guys were always expert trackers?" Her eyes again locked with his. "Gray, if half of his bragging was true, he's an expert tracker."

"I see," was all Gray allowed, thinking that an old detective's adage had once again proved true—follow the money and you'll find the perp.

"How could he?" she whispered. She met Gray's glance. "He's ready to kill me, isn't he?"

Gray stared down at her, wanting to reassure her, unwilling to lie to her, hating the realization that clouded her beautiful eyes. Much as he wanted to promise her that he'd keep her safe, he couldn't even offer that. Bitter experience had taught him that would be a lie.

"Ready to go?" He rested one knee against a stone near the bottom of the gully.

She glanced from him to the bottom of the muddy gulch. "Why don't we just walk up there?" She nodded toward the flatter, drier terrain above them.

Gray lifted his head enough to see the Jeep continuing with a methodical search.

"We do, and it's only a matter of time before he spots us. Climb up."

"I should walk."

"We've had this conversation." Gray didn't add that the pallor of her skin worried him, that she needed to conserve her energy in case they needed to make another run for cover, that as soon as the adrenaline wore off she would crash.

She stood watching him, and Gray knew in that moment he admired her more than he had ever admired anyone else. She was obviously shocked about her boss, but she hadn't whined. Not about that, or a single other damned thing. Splotches of mud and a sheen of dust covered her jeans. Her hair was a mess, and her face was dirty. She looked beautiful to him anyway.

"I don't know how I was lucky enough to run across someone like you," she said. She suddenly brushed her lips against his cheek. "But I'm glad."

The statement surprised him, but not half as much as her soft kiss.

"Climb up," he ordered, his voice gruff. She couldn't know how alluring her trust was, couldn't know how much he wished he was worthy of it.

She settled her weight on his back, and he stood up, threading her legs between his arms and his sides. Desire, urgent and unexpected, lanced through him. Hell of a time to get turned on, he thought. He might want her, but she'd be crazy to want him back. He was filthy, and they would both be a lot dirtier before they got out of the ravine. That and the knowledge Lambert could return any time made him focus beyond the clamoring of his body to the problem at hand—finding someplace dry and safe to spend the night.

To keep her from thinking about her boss, Gray asked her about her life in Denver, her hobbies, her job. Her willingness to share surprised him; he hated talking about his past. The picture she painted was of a woman who worked too hard, took too little time for herself and who was good at her profession. In fact, he discovered they both used work as an escape from their personal lives. Unlike him, she admitted the cause—not wanting to come home to an empty apartment where she was reminded of her mother's death.

He liked listening to her, and he liked the moments of silence that fell between them, each comfortable, each giving him tantalizing glimpses of his life merging with hers when they got out of this mess. But that, he reminded himself, was impossible. He tried to imagine hitting her, tried to imagine being as mean and as mad as he'd seen his father and his brothers be with the women in their lives. The image simply wouldn't jell. Lifting a hand against Audrey? He couldn't imagine it. Even so, he didn't trust the feeling. Too many times he had watched his father apologize and beg for another chance with promises that were always broken.

Gray didn't know where they were headed, except into the foothills, but he was real sure of one thing. There was no place else he would rather be than with Audrey. His grip around her legs tightened marginally.

He wished they had a couple of the horses from Hawk's herd. Hell, one horse would be fine. Even riding double, they could make it back to the ranch or the pueblo long before it got dark. Of course, they wouldn't be able to hide as easily, and they sure wouldn't be able to outrun the Jeep.

Gradually the light began to fade, and the walls of the gully cast dark shadows across the bottom. Around another bend, they came to a sandstone wall, worn smooth by the water, that had enough handholds and footholds to climb out of the ravine without getting any muddier. Gray gave Audrey a boost, then climbed up after her.

He noticed she didn't have to be encouraged to lie flat when she came over the edge of the ravine. He followed, scanning the surrounding landscape. He was pleased with the progress they had made, and the line of cottonwoods were less than a half mile away. Taking the binoculars out of the case around his neck, Gray did a 360-degree search.

The heavy overcast of much of the past couple of days had lightened some. Behind the mountains to the west, there were a couple of patches of blue sky.

Gray didn't see any sign of Lambert. That was good. Or bad? The cottonwoods stood in water that hadn't been visible before.

"Well, so much for that," Gray said, adding that their destination was flooded. He scanned the terrain, then pointed. "See that steep ridge? It will be a hard climb, but once we're on the top, we can find cover in one of the mountain canyons." He glanced down at her, thinking of all that she had been through today. "Are you up to a climb?"

She grinned. "It beats some of the alternatives I've thought of in the last hour."

He pulled her to her feet, took the pack off her shoulders. Unzipping the top, he rummaged around inside and brought out a pair of socks. When he extended his arm, she smiled, delight lighting her face.

"Socks! You don't know how much—" She took them from him, and sat down. In the midst of brushing off her feet, her glance fell to his muddy boots. She stared a moment, then extended the socks back toward him. "I think you need these more than I do."

Hers was as unselfish an offer as he had been made in a long time. Gray sat down next to her and showed her the other pair of socks he had pulled from the pack. "I don't know why I had two pairs in here. Luckily, I also have another pair of shoes."

"Amazing," Audrey said, peering into the shadowed opening of the pack. "And there's still room for dinner in there, too?"

"I work on the theory that if you wait long enough to eat, you'll be hungry enough not to notice the food is terrible." He pulled off one of the boots and the muddy sock underneath.

Audrey pulled one of the tube socks over her foot. "In that case, I'm sure you're a gourmet cook because I'm starved."

"The one thing we need is water." He brushed off his other foot before putting on the clean sock and dry shoe.

"There's plenty in the bottom of the gully." She put on the other sock, then her shoes, which she pulled from the safety of his pocket.

"To drink." Gray put on the dry socks and a pair of walking shoes. "That's why we were heading for the cottonwoods—there are a couple of good fishing holes in the creek there." Tying the shoelaces of his boots together, he fastened them to one of the grommets at the bottom of his backpack and stood up.

She extended one of her feet and wiggled her toes, then looked up at him with a smile. "My feet are warm at last. I could just kiss you—"

He pulled her into his arms, and captured her mouth hungrily. A muffled whimper of surprise filled her throat, but she kissed him back, her mouth opening in invitation.

This wasn't the right time, this wasn't the right place and he sure as hell wasn't the right man. None of that kept him from accepting what she offered. Lifting her arms around his neck, he wrapped his around her back and edged his knee between her thighs.

Without warning, her arms slipped from his neck, and she shoved against him—hard.

His arms tightened around her as his emotions fought against the end of this one perfect moment. She tore her mouth from his, and shoved again, this time successful in breaking away from his embrace.

Gray opened his eyes. She wasn't looking at him, but at the gun tucked in the waistband of his jeans. Her breathing was as ragged as it had been when they sprinted away from her burning car. Realization, cold as rain, washed through him, reminding him no matter how much he wanted her, he was the wrong man.

With gentleness he had never once demonstrated to another adult, he lifted her chin with the merest touch of a finger. She met his gaze, her eyes wide. He expected to see fear. Instead, confusion puckered her brow.

"I'd forgotten about the gun," she confessed. "I felt it digging into my side, and all of a sudden I remembered Howard."

Gray smoothed away the knot between her brows with his thumb.

"And it scared me."

"I can understand that."

"You didn't pull the gun when we were hiding under the overhang." She looked up at him, her brows once again knit together.

He sensed the question within her statement, but didn't answer. He had killed a man—a hazard that came with being a police officer. Or so the police psychologist had encouraged him to believe. A righteous shoot. Gray knew better. And he knew he had lost the objectivity that had once made him a good cop.

Gray touched Audrey's cheek with a callused finger, his mother's warning echoing through his head. *A man who lives by the gun dies by the gun. And God help me, son, I don't want that for you.*

A promise. But, damn, he didn't see any other choice.

"I'll do everything I can to keep you safe," he promised.

Audrey raised her eyes to his, a sad smile curving her lips. "I know."

Picking up the pack, he slung it over his back and held a hand out to her. "Let's go."

Gray didn't point out to her how exposed they were in the half mile to the edge of the ridge, but knew she sensed it because she pushed herself to walk fast. Her panting worried him, but he figured there would be time to rest later, and he lengthened his own strides to keep up with her near trot.

Gray scanned the terrain in front of them, looking for cover, looking for an easy ascent up the first ridge. At the top, junipers and piñons grew, looking black against the fading light. The air had turned crisp, and Gray noted the clouds had pushed farther to the east, leaving an expanse of clear sky above them. This time of year, frost was a distinct possibility, which meant it could be a long, cold night.

Gray found another game trail that led toward the mesa. Determined to make the most out of the remaining light, Gray grasped Audrey's hand and led her on a zigzagging course up the side of the hill. Behind them, they left a clear trail, and he almost wished it would cloud over and rain again.

The sun set about the time they reached the top of the mesa, painting the clouds in brilliant shades of crimson. Ponderosa pines towered above them, the air pungent with their scent. Above the pines, another ridge loomed above them. Gray came to a stop in front of one of the piñon trees, where Audrey sank to the ground, her chest heaving.

"He could have been watching from somewhere," she said. "And even if he wasn't, even I could follow the trail we just left."

Gray gave her high marks for realizing exactly how exposed they had been on the slope, and he knew exactly who she meant by *he*. ''Yeah.''

Gray scanned the sky. ''We're fast running out of light.''

Audrey stood and brushed off the back of her jeans. Holding out her hand to him, she said, ''Then we'd better get going if we're going to find a place to spend the night.''

He took it, walking silently beside her as they headed away from the edge of the mesa. Gradually, the trees around them became thicker. Twice Gray saw deer gliding through the trees silent as shadows. He chose the hardest-packed ground to walk on, noticing that Audrey walked in his footsteps. If he stepped on a rock, so did she. The lady learned fast.

Suddenly, Gray didn't feel Audrey's presence behind him. He stopped walking and turned around. She was poised at the edge of a sandstone face they had just crossed fifteen or twenty feet behind him. Her attention was focused up a narrow canyon, its opening no more than fifteen feet wide.

''What is it?'' he asked.

She gave him a faint smile and nodded toward the canyon. ''Normally, I'm the last person to follow a hunch.''

''But?''

''What about up one of these small canyons?''

Gray looked toward the narrow opening. ''Most of these are going to be box canyons. We could be trapped.''

''But we don't know until we look, right?''

Maybe Audrey was on to something, he thought. Maybe this was the hiding place they had been looking for. ''Right.''

He led her through the notch, taking extra care to leave no tracks. Audrey followed suit. They came upon clear water running down a stream at the canyon mouth that was too narrow, too insignificant to be called a creek.

''It's safe to drink, isn't it?'' she asked.

"As safe as we're going to find without boiling it first," he answered.

She knelt and scooped the water into her hand, drinking thirstily. "I never knew water could taste so good."

Gray drank also. Fifty yards in from the canyon opening, it widened slightly. Huge boulders were spread over the bottom, a remnant from some ancient landslide. A single scraggly tree grew between a pair of the enormous rocks. Beyond, a faint path led up the windswept sandstone walls. Gray looked at the rocky bottom of the canyon and the high-water marks twenty feet above their heads.

"We can't stay down here," he said. "Do you want to go back out there onto the mesa, or follow that path?"

Twisting the silver bracelets as he noticed she did when she was thinking, she gazed at the faint trail that twisted up the canyon wall. "I think we should follow the path."

He glanced at the sky, and decided to play out her hunch, though the canyon was potentially a trap. "We'll give it fifteen minutes. If it turns out to be nothing, that still gives us time to get back here and get through the notch before it's too dark to see where we're going."

Gray led the way up the path, which became even more narrow as they climbed. They came to a sharp bend, and ahead of them the trail forked. One trail continued upward, where the light was steadily fading. Below the shelf, the narrow canyon was in deep shadow. Ponderosa pines grew at the base of the cliff, and the faintest hint of sulfur hung in the air.

"Wait here," Gray told her. Swiftly, he climbed the ascending path. At the crest, he stopped. To the northwest, the peaks of the San Juans rose, their summits covered with new snow. To the east, he could see the fold of land that nestled Puma's Lair and La Huerta. Closer, he could see the barn and fields where Hawk kept his horses. Miles beyond was the shadowed canyon where the Rio Grande flowed.

His attention returned to the field where the horses were, including his own. Sketches of a plan came together, a plan that just might work if they could get to the horses without being seen. He thought about leading Audrey off the ridge.

The trail was no more than a faint impression as it went down the crest before it was lost within the tumbled chaos of a talus slope that would be impassable in the dark. But tomorrow— It was a way to safety. He turned away from the crest. Hopefully, Lambert would look for them on the mesa, if he was still looking. The canyon below them was one of a dozen they had passed, which left Lambert with a lot of ground to cover if he began searching each one. The shelf below them was high enough to keep a campfire from being detected, and protected enough so it shouldn't be as cold as the valley.

So far, Audrey's hunch had been on target. Gray sniffed the air, again catching the faint scent of sulfur, and the corner of his mouth lifted. The lady had found herself a hot springs. He would bet money on it.

Gray returned to Audrey and gave her hand a reassuring squeeze. "There's a good lookout from up there. Let's see if we can find some shelter now."

Audrey let him hold her hand as they walked toward the plateau, hoping they would stop soon. Her occasional walk around the park at home and her couple nights a week on an exercise bike in front of the TV hadn't left her fit enough to meet the demands she had made on her body today.

Exhaustion crept over her, demanding she stop. An hour ago, she had been starved. At the moment, she was sure she wouldn't have energy enough to eat.

Beyond the trees, Audrey could see a cliff that rose a couple of hundred feet above them. Wind and water had hollowed out the stone at the base of the cliff, reminding her of the overhangs where the Anasazi had built their cliff dwellings in Mesa Verde. This one was much smaller, but it would provide them shelter for the night. Noticing the blackened stone at the back of the shallow cavity, she realized this had been a shelter for people before them. A shiver of awareness chased down her spine.

Gray whistled in surprise. "Yes," he said, as though answering an unspoken question.

Audrey lowered her gaze from the cliff's top to the ground in front of them. Gray wasn't looking at the recess. His attention was focused on a pool of water another thirty yards away. Beyond the pool, the water flowed into a narrow stream that wound its way across the shelf. On either side of the stream, the grass was lush and green, the first green she had seen since coming to New Mexico, she thought. Her gaze returned to the pool, and the steam rising from it.

Sliding his pack off his shoulders, Gray strode toward the pool, walked around it once, dipped his hand in a couple of different places, then looked back at her. "It's not a room at the Marriott," he said. "But I can offer you a hot bath."

That sounded heavenly, but what drew her toward him was the smile that lit his face.

Chapter 8

Audrey had wondered if a smile would make him look boyish. It didn't. His eyes were too haunted, his features too ruggedly masculine for that. Even so, the smile encompassed his whole face, revealing laugh lines around his eyes. Her breath caught, and her throat clogged with longing. She had been right. Smiling, he was irresistible.

She stretched her arms to him, and he took her hands.

"You did it," he said. "Your hunch paid off. This place has everything we need. Shelter. Water." He cocked his head toward the pool. "*Hot* water. I wasn't kidding about the bath, if that's what you want."

"It sounds great," she said, "though not half as good as dinner."

That alluring smile changed into a crooked grin, exposing a dimple in one cheek. "Hungry again?" He shook his head in mock concern. "The way to a woman's affection is through—"

"Her heart, you oaf." She slapped at his arm, loving his teasing. "But I've gotta tell you. Feeding her is a real good start. Besides, as you may recall I wasn't on the receiving end of good old-fashioned Western hospitality last night.''

"I remember.'' His smile faded, and Audrey could have kicked herself for saying anything that made his smile fade.

"I take that back,'' she said. When he cocked an eyebrow in question, she added, "Except for the dinner that you brought to my room, which was very nice.''

He shook his head and started to turn away, looking embarrassed. She caught him by the arm, touching his cheek to bring his gaze back to her.

"Being a nice guy is an okay thing, you know.''

He opened his mouth to speak, and she had a hunch it was to deny her assertion, so she pressed her fingers against his mouth.

"Don't you be saying anything negative about my friend Gray Murdoch. You hear me? I won't stand for it.''

That surprising smile reached his eyes again. "Yes, ma'am.''

"Now,'' she said, rubbing her hands together, "can we have a fire? Or will that give Howard a way of finding us?''

Gray glanced back toward the trail that had led them steadily up from the canyon floor.

"Nothin's a hundred percent,'' he finally said. "But we're high enough above the canyon bottom that we should be okay.''

"Good.'' She took off toward the towering ponderosa, sure the second she stopped moving, she would be too tired to be of any help at all. If Gray said it was safe to have a fire, she believed him.

She began picking up the first branches she came to, which seemed surprisingly dry in spite of all the rain that had fallen. Gray pulled evergreen boughs off a fallen tree, which he dragged back to the camp. Watching him, Audrey again uttered thanks he was with her. His self-assurance conveyed that he knew what he was doing, which was more than she could say for herself. In Denver, she could have navigated her way out of the worst traffic jam, taken him to any one of a half-dozen good restaurants and dialed 911 with the assurance that help would be on the way. Here, though, she was completely out of her element.

She didn't know why he had come looking for her after she left the ranch, but she was grateful he had. She kept thinking that if she just snapped her fingers, somehow her life would return to normal and the terror of having someone—Howard—shoot at her would fade away. And Gray had been there for her. Thank God. Why would he have willingly given up his safety to stay with her?

In the time she gathered one small armload of kindling, he had dragged a couple of good-size branches back to the camp, where he snapped them into shorter lengths, reinforcing how strong he was. He took off his jacket and tossed it onto the floor of the shallow cave that was to be their shelter. The green plaid shirt beneath the jacket followed, leaving him in a navy T-shirt that revealed to her for the first time the heavy rope of muscle in his arms and across his back.

She shivered, remembering the first instant after she climbed onto his back. He had lifted her as though she weighed nothing. Despite the danger, or maybe because of it, she had felt oddly vulnerable, her legs on either side of his waist. Now, as then, she wondered what it would be like to be in the same position—only face-to-face with him. Heat bloomed, and she studied him frankly, from the impressive proportions of his chest to the more subtle, equally fascinating curves and bulges behind his button-down fly.

"You doin' okay?"

Her glance flew to his face. If he had been aware of her staring, there was no clue of it in his expression.

"Yeah," she replied, her voice not sounding like her own. The man hadn't even made a pass at her, and she was hot and bothered. She glanced down at herself, noting the splotches of dried mud on the jacket and her jeans. Of course he hadn't made a pass. She looked about as appealing as the armload of kindling she dropped in a pile at the edge of the overhang.

He strode away from the camp toward another large branch lying under the copse of ponderosas. She followed him, noticing the twilight had deepened. Above them, the sky was still light, a narrow band of pale sky. A quarter mile away, the opposite wall of the gorge rose looking oddly like a fortress wall in the fading light. Fleetingly, she wondered which side of the wall they were on. The safe side, she hoped.

Her own mood more pensive, she rubbed her hands up and down her arms, glancing around the shelf. She had the feeling unseen threats lurked within the shadows.

"Howard won't find us here?" Realization that a man she considered a friend had tried to harm her rushed through her, making her feel exposed and anything but safe.

"He could," Gray answered, "but I doubt it. If he was watching us, he knows we came into the foothills from the valley. The first mesa is big, and I believe we hid our tracks well enough that he won't be able to pick up our trail. Not in the dark, anyway."

"What about tomorrow?" she asked, her throat still tight.

"We'll figure it out."

"And if he didn't see us come up to the mesa?"

"I'm hoping he'll think we're headed for either the ranch or the pueblo." Gray paused, his hazel eyes shadowed in the twilight. "And sooner or later, that's what we've got to do. We're okay, tonight, Audrey, but we don't have food or supplies to hide out indefinitely."

She dropped her head a moment, appreciating Gray's honesty. Another rush of emotion, this time gratitude, not fear, made tears burn at the backs of her eyes. The man had been a rock, and somehow he had been sucked into a problem that wasn't his. And he had done nothing but treat her with consideration and honesty. Not to mention saving her life.

Swallowing, she squared her shoulders and met his gaze. "A disclaimer, huh? I thought that was a magic pack you had. Candy bars, socks." She poked his stomach, hoping she would coax another smile out of him. "And you promised me dinner."

"So I did." He pulled her into his arms.

She sank against him, savoring the strength of his body and the ever present heat emanating from him. Silently, he held her a long moment before releasing her. She headed back to the tall pines for another armload of firewood, determined to keep her anxiety at bay by staying busy.

At the hollowed recess at the base of the cliff, Gray glanced at the ancient soot marks overhead, then he arranged a few loose stones into a ring. Within scant minutes, he had a small fire going. The ruddy glow provided a beacon of cheerfulness that lured Audrey closer. She hadn't been camping in years, and she had forgotten how absolutely dark night could be.

Forcing her attention away from the darkness settling into the canyon and creeping across the ledge, Audrey turned around and surveyed the hollow that was to be their haven. Aeons of wind had worn away the stone, leaving behind a smooth, rounded surface. Here and there, the sandstone slabs showed a darker stream of color where water had seeped into the surface, both from the recent storms and the hundreds before. She blinked and looked again. The random marks suggested the outline of a bird, a man, a deer. They weren't random at all, she realized. The patterns were definite...and man-made.

The back of her scalp prickled in response, and she stepped closer. The abstract symbols and figures were faded by time, barely more noticeable than a shadow.

"Gray, look at this," Audrey said.

He looked up from the fire, then came to examine the wall she was pointing to.

"I'll be damned," he said. "Petroglyphs." He traced one of the designs with a finger.

"Ancient graffiti?"

He almost smiled. "Maybe. At least a reminder that we're not the first to find refuge here."

"It's sort of spooky, isn't it?"

"Just think of it as a motel room where other guests have stayed." Gray let go of her hand and returned to the campfire, where he bent over his backpack. Opening the pack, he pulled out a battered aluminum pot and extended it to Audrey. "Would you like to get some water?"

"Sure," she said, taking the pot from him. At the lip of the shallow cave, she came to a stop. The water of the pool gleamed faintly, but what captured her attention was the absolute black nothingness at the edge of the shelf. Even the tall ponderosas were nearly invisible.

"Audrey?"

"Yeah."

"Everything okay?"

"Fine," she replied, tearing her attention from what she had feared most since childhood. The dark. Resolutely, she stepped off the sandstone and headed toward the water.

The steam above the pool shifted, undulating as though it had a life of its own. As she approached, she felt the air warm. A huge slab of sandstone bordered the pool on one side, almost looking man-made. She knelt at the edge, and dipped the pot in. It was surprisingly warm. Gray was right. Hot enough for a bath.

"Is this safe to drink?" she called to Gray.

"It won't be the best-tasting water you ever had, but it's safe."

She set the pot on the stone next to her and pushed up the sleeves of the jacket. Bending over, she washed her hands, then her face. The warm water felt good, and she

dipped her hands again. One of the bracelets suddenly loos
ened, and before she could grab it, fell to the bottom.

She peered into the black depths, unable to see the bo
tom, much less her bracelet. "Damn."

"What's wrong?" Gray asked from next to her.

She started. Once again, she hadn't heard his approach
"You've got to stop doing that."

"What?"

"Sneaking up on a person." She looked at his fee
"How in the heck do you walk so silently?"

"Habit," he said. Then he repeated, "So, what'
wrong?"

"I dropped my bracelet into the pool," she said, noticin,
she hadn't asked him to promise he would stop sneakin;
up on her. As if he was doing so intentionally, she reminde
herself.

Gray leaned over. "It probably sank to the bottom. We'
get it in the morning." He picked up the pot of water an
offered Audrey his other hand.

"What if it floats away?"

"The current isn't that strong. I got a pretty good loo
at the pool before it got dark, and I could see the bottom
There's a little sediment down there, but not much. We'
find it."

She gave the water a last dubious glance, feeling oddl
bereft. She had started wearing the bracelets all the time
few days after her mother died—a reminder of happie
times they had shared.

Gray took her hand, and she let him pull her to her feet
She followed him back to their shelter. A few red-hot coal
had begun to form at the bottom of the small fire. Gray se
the pot in the middle of the flames.

"I hope you like beef stew," he said, holding up
pouch. "Hermetically sealed and guaranteed. Beats the ol
freeze-dried stuff I used to bring camping."

"Gray, I'd eat broiled grasshoppers at this point," she said. She sank down cross-legged next to the fire.

The corner of his mouth lifted. "It's a little early in the season for grasshoppers."

"Lucky me."

"But if you're determined to eat off the land, I could try to find us a lizard or rattlesnake or—"

"Beef stew, freeze-dried, reconstituted or reconditioned, is just fine."

He opened the package and dumped the contents into the hot water. Almost immediately, a mouthwatering aroma filled the air, and Audrey's stomach grumbled in response.

Again, Gray smiled. "You weren't kidding, were you?" he asked, his eyes gleaming in the firelight. "It won't be long now."

Audrey felt like a little kid waiting for dinner. Gray left the stew to cook and went to the pile of boughs he had dragged beneath the overhang. With the same familiarity and efficiency that he did everything, he arranged the boughs into a pile, stripping away the larger branches. Gradually the pile came to resemble a mattress, and Audrey realized this was a bed. One bed.

She turned her attention back to the fire. She hadn't gotten as far as thinking about how they would sleep. Or where. Lifting her gaze beyond the fire, she admitted she was glad she was with him. Even so, this wasn't the way she had imagined spending the night with a man for the first time.

This afternoon—which felt like a lifetime ago, she thought—she had kissed him and felt as though she had found a missing part of herself. Once again, the memory of having her legs wrapped around him washed over her. Longing curled through her belly, and her awareness of him heightened another notch.

Whistling under his breath, he again checked on their

dinner. Using the sleeve of his jacket as a pot holder, he took the pan off the fire and came to sit next to her.

"This is a little informal for a first date," he said. "Community pot, and all."

She glanced at him. "Is that what this is, a date?"

"Sure." He pulled the pack toward him. "It's a pretty night, we've got a nice fire and—" he pulled his hand out of the pack as though brandishing a treasure "—a single spoon."

"Like sharing straws," she murmured, bemused at the thought.

"Something like that," he said, handing her the spoon and pushing the stew toward her. "Ladies first." He reached for his flannel shirt and put it back on.

The stew tasted almost as good as it smelled. She sighed and handed Gray the spoon. He took a couple of bites, then returned the spoon.

It was the most intimate meal she had ever shared, sitting shoulder to shoulder with him, eating from the same pot with the same spoon. Contentment, warmth and drowsiness stole over her.

Sometime later, she realized they were no longer sitting shoulder to shoulder. Instead, she was within the circle of his arms, and his body was supporting her. Though she was in his embrace again, she felt none of the sexually charged energy she had felt earlier in the day. With a yawn, she decided he was probably as tired as she was.

"The moon will be up soon," he said.

"How do you know?" she asked, resting her head against his shoulder and looking at the sky. With a faint sense of surprise, she noted a canopy of stars had replaced the gloom. More stars than she ever remembered seeing in her life.

"The sky is lighter to the east," he said, pointing. "See how the stars aren't as bright and the sky is more blue?"

"Yeah."

The Editor's "Thank You" Free Gifts Include:

- ⬤ Two BRAND-NEW romance novels!
- ⬤ An exciting mystery gift!

PLACE
FREE GIFT
SEAL
HERE

YES! I have placed my Editor's "Thank You" seal in the space provided above. Please send me 2 free books and a fabulous mystery gift. I understand I am under no obligation to purchase any books, as explained on the back and on the opposite page.

345 SDL CQUV

245 SDL CQUK
(S-IM-06/99)

Name:
_____
PLEASE PRINT

Address: _____ Apt.#: _____

City: _____

State/
Prov.: _____
Postal
Zip/Code: _____

Thank You!

"Moonrise."

Gradually the midnight color of the sky faded to a lighter hade, then the moon peeked over the edge of the horizon. ts silver glow seemed bright as a headlight, casting the helf of their camp in frosted light and shadows. It was eautiful.

"This is going to be okay," Audrey said.

She felt Gray glance down at her.

"What do you mean?"

"I'm afraid of the dark," she said simply. "I don't have personal memory of it, but my mother always said it was ecause I was trapped in a burning house when I was four r five." She held out her arm, revealing the mark the racelet normally covered. Gray gently traced a finger over he scar.

"You were burned in the fire?" His voice was very deep.

She nodded. "Silly, huh," she said. "When we first got ere it was so gloomy, and the canyon looked so black."

"Not silly at all," he returned. "Old events, whether emembered or not, can be the worst."

She twisted slightly so she could look up at him. "What bout you, Gray? Are you afraid of anything?"

He met her gaze, all expression gone from his face. Tracng the side of her face with a finger, he finally said, "My-elf."

"I don't understand," she whispered.

This time, he didn't answer, but instead kissed the tips f her fingers before returning his attention to the moonrise. he memory of Richard saying Gray had killed a man vashed over Audrey. She closed her eyes, comparing Rich-rd's statement with what she knew, with what she sensed bout Gray. He hadn't pulled his gun when they were hid-ng from Howard. And he might have been able to shoot Ioward as he was driving off. Everything she had seen bout him today was inconsistent with Richard's statement. f Gray had killed a man, and she couldn't imagine it, she

was positive it was in the line of duty. He had been a co
after all.

Relaxing more fully against him, she opened her ey
and stared into the flames. Safe, cherished, and... Sl
yawned. Don't trust anybody, he had told her. Especial
him. Nonsense. She had never met anyone more deservir
of her trust.

"Gray?"

"Hmm?"

She peered up at him, yawning once again. "I think I'
reached the end of my rope. If I don't go to bed soon, I'
going to fall asleep right here."

In answer, he pulled her across his lap, then stood
with her still in his arms. Being lifted was dizzying. Beir
carried so easily was wonderful, exciting. Another yaw
caught her, and she snuggled closer to him.

A few short strides carried him to the bed of boughs th
he had covered with a tarp. Kneeling, he set her in tl
middle of the bed, put his hands on either side of her hea
and brushed a brotherly kiss across her cheek.

"Kiss me, Gray," she whispered, her gaze locked wi
his.

He brushed his lips over hers in a chaste kiss.

"More," she whispered when he lifted his head.

"No," he answered. "Not now. Not tonight."

"Please."

He smiled, and it looked so sad it tore at her heart.

"I'm no saint," he said, brushing her hair off her chee
"And you're so, so tempting. And I won't be able to sto
with a kiss, Audrey."

She swallowed, her body tingling as she recognized tl
implications of what he was saying.

"Even if you want that, I don't have any way to prote
you. And..."

The silence stretched between them until she final
prompted, "And?"

"And if we make love tonight..." He paused, as if searching for the right thing to say to her. "I'm never going to know whether it was because you really wanted me or if it was just reaction to the danger we've been in today. It's the most powerful turn-on there is, Audrey. A way of proving to yourself that you're still alive."

Turned on, oh yes, she was. But it wasn't because of the danger they had shared today. "You could be right," she whispered, gazing into his eyes, remembering his confession that he was afraid of himself. "But I think you're just as scared as I am."

He glanced away and a moment later picked his jacket off the floor and laid it over her. "Go to sleep. I've got a couple of things to do."

"And then?"

"And then we'll sleep together." A hint of laughter filled his voice. "It's the only way we're going to stay warm."

Audrey watched him move around the camp. He hadn't denied being afraid, she thought. Her gaze returned to the small campfire, then drifted to the bright moon overhead, sleepiness once again overtaking her.

She heard a splash of water, and she looked from the moon to the pool. As if in a dream, she watched the steam above the pool undulate in streamers lit by the moonlight. Gray was nowhere in sight. Vague alarm dissipated the mirage. She sat up and called his name.

"I'm right here," he called.

The mist cleared slightly, and she made out the darker shape of his head in the middle of the pool, then noticed the pile of his clothes next to the edge. Fascinated, she watched. The faint aroma of soap drifted toward her. He remained motionless for what seemed a long time. She lay back down and divided her attention between the glowing coals of the fire and him. The streamers of steam alternately hid and revealed him. When he came out of the pool, the shifting mist closed around him like a shroud, then fell away, tantalizing her. His body gleamed in the moonlight.

He looked like a god. Muscles rippled as he sluiced water off his chest and legs. Broad shoulders and a deep chest tapered to narrow masculine hips.

Individual features were shadowed, which was a shame, she thought, because she had never seen a body that looked more beautiful to her. He pulled on a pair of briefs the same dark shade as his T-shirt, which he used to dry his hair before putting it back on. Jeans and the flannel shirt followed. Never once had she imagined watching a man dress could be sexy. But it was.

Sighing, she tore her gaze away from him and focused on the fire. Seconds later he appeared. He banked the fire and stowed their gear in the backpack.

She felt utterly exhausted, but at the moment sleep was the last thing on her mind. Even so, she let her eyes drift close. Sometime later, she felt Gray lie down beside her.

He gathered her spoon-style against him, his arm wrapped around her waist, and covered them both with his jacket.

Images of them locked together, skin to skin, poured through her. She longed to turn in his arms, press herself close and test the extent of his resolve not to make love to her tonight. Except that she wasn't sure what she would do if he caved in, and she was even less sure what she would do if he didn't. So she lay motionless, enjoying his arm wrapped around her, the heat of his body warming her and the masculine scent that was his alone.

"I could use a bath, too," she finally murmured. "I probably smell like something the cat dragged in."

"You smell fine," he assured here. "I'm afraid you'll get chilled. You've been cold all day."

"Yeah," she agreed. "I thought of that, too."

He adjusted his position slightly, making them both more comfortable. "Warm enough?"

"Mmm," she whispered. To her surprise, she yawned. "I like this," she murmured.

"Me, too," he said. "Go to sleep, Audrey."

Sometime between staring at the full moon and the fire, she did.

The wind softly moaned through the pines, and Audrey stirred. Opening her eyes, her gaze focused first on the fire. The flames were gone, but coals burned brightly. The light from the moon didn't seem as radiant, and she lifted her eyes to it.

It gleamed brightly at one edge only, and she frowned. It had been a full moon. Hadn't it?

Another whisper of wind moaned in the trees, and Audrey snuggled more deeply beneath the covers. Gray's arm was still curled around her waist, and against her back his body felt warm as a furnace.

Her attention returned to the moon. The band of light seemed smaller. A huge orange-hued ball hid the moon's brilliance. The stars in the sky twinkled more brightly, a planet—Venus or Jupiter, she couldn't remember which—gleamed like a beacon. The moon became even more mysterious.

She should understand, she knew she should, but some important piece eluded her.

The shelf where their camp was lost all definition, and Audrey felt as though she was at the edge of an abyss. The only real things in her existence were Gray at her back and the glowing embers of the fire at her front.

"Gray?" she whispered.

"What?" he asked, sounding instantly awake.

"Look at the moon."

Moment by moment, the curve of light disappeared as a shadow over the face of the moon increased.

"I've never seen a full lunar eclipse before," he said.

Relief flowed through Audrey at his matter-of-fact state-

ment. At one level, she had known what it was, but at
another it seemed so surreal, so mysterious.

He grasped the top of his jacket, tucking it around Audrey. Her breathing slowed, and he realized she had fallen
asleep. Then, he, too, drifted off.

Sometime later, he awoke. Lying quietly, he listened to
the sounds of water from the pool, the moan of the wind
through the pines, the occasional snap from the fire. But
something didn't feel right. The hair on the back of his
neck rose, and he scanned the shelf.

The eclipse was complete, the moon looking like an amber ball hung high in the sky. A coyote broke the silence,
its eerie song echoing through the canyon. Others joined in
the chorus in a song old as time.

"I've never heard the coyotes sing before," Audrey
whispered. "It's beautiful."

"Yeah." Something besides the eclipse and the coyotes
still didn't feel right. Gray scanned the dark shelf, visually
searching for anything out of place.

Steam covered the pool like a blanket, spilling over the
edges. Movement beyond the campfire caught his attention,
and he reached for the revolver that he had set on the
ground next to their makeshift bed. With his other hand,
he pressed a finger against Audrey's lips, hoping she would
understand. Beneath his hand, he felt her nod.

The breeze picked up, stirring through the pines in a
ghostly whisper of sound. Out of the mist next to the pool,
a woman wearing buckskins emerged.

Chapter 9

She wasn't real. Gray knew she wasn't. And yet...

Almost transparent, she appeared as though projected onto the black screen of night. As she came closer to the camp, her image became more opaque, more full bodied...more real. Gray's scalp prickled, and his arm around Audrey tightened.

The Indian woman glanced over her shoulder toward the narrow trail that led to the canyon floor below, her body taut, her head cocked to the side as though listening for an intruder. Her wariness increased Gray's apprehension, and he listened intently, as well. She sighed, then she resumed walking toward the camp, carrying a clay pot filled with water.

"Who are you?" he asked, admitting to himself that he didn't expect an answer.

She gave no indication she had heard him.

Reaching the campfire, she gracefully knelt next to the fire, added more wood to it and settled the pot in the middle of the flames. Opening a pouch tied to her waist, she sprinkled dried leaves of some kind into the water, going about her business as though she was alone. Her posture, however, remained wary.

Gray strained to hear anything that would indicate someone approached from the canyon below them. Ordinary sounds—the crackle of the fire, the faint trickle of water over stone, the whisper of pine needles touching one another—came to him.

As the woman had, he concluded they were alone. Safe…at least for the moment.

She glanced up, her dark eyes fixed directly on him. Gray returned the stare, his throat becoming more dry. Maybe she did see them.

She looked enough like Audrey to be her sister. The same fine, nearly translucent skin. Expressive dark eyes. Her hair was black to Audrey's rich brown. He wondered where the horsemen were. Had they chased her here? Or would that moment somehow come after this one?

"Who are you?" he repeated.

She picked up one of the sticks of kindling that Audrey had laid near the fire, stirred the coals, then let it fall into the flames.

"Miss?" He raised his voice slightly.

She sighed, then pressed her hand into her side as though easing a cramp.

"Where did you come from?" She might be deaf, but she would have to be blind not to see them. How was it possible they saw her, but she didn't see them?

Her expression became pensive, and she spoke, the words in a language he didn't recognize. He couldn't decide if she had really heard him or was simply talking to herself.

Beneath his hand, he felt Audrey stir, and she tugged his hand away from her mouth. He squeezed her shoulder reassuringly.

Gray sat up and got out of their bed of pine boughs,

tempted to pick up his revolver, resisting the urge, uncertain how this apparently unarmed woman could pose any threat. "Where did you come from?" he repeated. "Who are you?"

Figment of his imagination...or...ghost, she looked real. He stepped toward her. "What are you doing here?"

The Indian woman turned slightly away and began speaking softly again, the words rapid, and her arm lifted in a gesture that encompassed the camp and all of the sky above them. Gray came to a stop directly in front of her, and if she saw him, she gave no indication.

"Are you all right?" he asked, waving a hand in front of her face.

She rose, stumbling slightly, again pressing her hand to her side. Gray reached out to steady her.

His hand encountered nothing but air.

A chill crawled down his spine. The woman frowned, touching her shoulder where his hand should have brushed her. Then she turned away from him as though he were invisible.

Just as she had the day he had seen her running from the horsemen.

She peered into the clay pot, made a sound of vague satisfaction and walked toward the stone pool.

At the edge of the pool, she undid the lacings of her gown, which slid off her body, the steam shrouding her. Moccasins and leggings followed. As she stepped into the pool, the veil of steam shifted, revealing her profile—a too slim body ripe with advanced pregnancy. As she settled into the pool, the steam sank toward the water, as well, shielding her from view. Her murmured sound of satisfaction rose above the mist.

Gray returned to the bed and sat down next to Audrey.

"I saw her," she whispered, shivering badly and wrapping her arms around herself. "Oh, God. I've got to be dreaming."

"If you are," he returned hoarsely, "I'm having the same dream."

"I saw your hand…" Another huge shiver made Audrey's voice break. "Last night, I saw her. I just didn't know…I thought it was a trick of the light."

Gray wrapped an arm around Audrey and pulled her to his side. She burrowed closer. He had a sense of awful danger, but he couldn't pinpoint its source. His usual instincts were of no help. The woman herself was of no danger. But the horsemen he had seen chasing her, what of them? He wanted to scoop Audrey up and run with her to safety—wherever the hell that was.

He stared at the shifting steam above the pond, seized by uncharacteristic indecision. There was no way at all they could prudently traverse the trail back to the canyon bottom. After the eclipse was over, the top of the trail would be lit well enough, but the lower part would be blacker than a witch's dream. But to stay here with a ghost…

"We've got to get out of here." He stood up, pulling at Audrey's hand. She didn't move. Finally, he looked away from the pond to her.

"Why?"

"Why?" What kind of foolish question was that? He waved a hand in the direction of the pool. "She…"

"I don't think she means us any harm."

"How do you know that?" Again, he pulled at her hand, urging her to stand. She pulled back, urging him to sit back down.

When he did, she said, "Look at her. She can't see us, can't hear us. I don't know why we can see her, but…" She looked up at the moon, the eclipse nearly complete. The moon looked huge, mysterious, awe inspiring. "It has something to do with the eclipse. Don't you think?"

"I don't know," he admitted. "Maybe."

The woman began to sing, her voice deep, carrying the rhythmic cadence of a native chant. In all her life, Audrey had never heard anything so beautiful or so mournful. An answering sensation rose within her. She felt as though she had merged with the woman somehow. Keenly, powerfully, the woman's emotions surged through her. Loss. Fear. Heartache. Mourning for a man who had died. Audrey knew, as certainly as she knew Gray held her, this woman was mourning for her man.

On the other side of the canyon came an echoing sorrowful cry in chorus. The hair on the back of Audrey's neck stood on end. Even though she had watched Gray's hand pass through the woman, she had seemed so…real. And now the coyotes heard her song, too. As the mist above the water shifted, she looked just as solid as Gray had when he was in the pool.

"I'm not dreaming," Audrey said, talking more to herself than to Gray. "I've lost my mind. I don't believe in ghosts." Her voice caught on another shiver.

"You're not losing your mind," Gray assured her.

She wanted to accept that, but couldn't. Until now, her life had been measured by ordinary standards. Ghosts and omens had no part in her life. Ever since she had arrived at Puma's Lair, her world was tilted. This was simply the latest in a series of inexplicable, senseless events. She clung to Gray, feeling as though he was her only anchor in an unfamiliar world. Solid. Real. Trustworthy.

Lifting her gaze to the sky, she stared at the moon. It looked huge, ethereal. The coyotes' chorus and the woman's mournful song fit perfectly.

She risked a glance toward the pool. Steam hid the woman as her haunting voice soared into the night. When the last of the song faded away, she silently appeared once again, carrying the bundle of her clothes. As she approached the fire, her body gleamed, her belly round and full, making her look too fragile for the burden of her pregnancy.

Dropping the clothes next to a buckskin bag, she re-

moved a square of cloth that looked to Audrey like a piece
of chamois. She dipped it into the pot over the fire,
squeezed the excess liquid from it, and wiped her body, her
actions those of a woman who believed she was alone.

"What is your name?" Audrey asked, not at all sure
what she would do if the woman really heard her or saw
her.

The woman didn't respond.

"Are you from the pueblo?"

Again, no response. Suddenly, the woman tensed, her
face taking on an expression of intense concentration. The
muscles across her abdomen rippled, then clinched in a
spasm that lasted long, long seconds. When it ended, the
woman patted her belly, murmuring words, conveying a
feeling Audrey understood despite the barrier of language.
Encouragement for the child coming into the world. Reassurance of love. Promise that all would be well.

Another contraction seized the woman, and she sank to
her knees. She was a woman alone, about to deliver a child
with no one to help her. She might feel as though all would
be well. It was a feeling Audrey didn't share.

"I can't just sit here and do nothing."

"You can't help her," Gray said. "She can't see us."

Audrey stood and stepped close to the campfire, holding
her arms slightly out as though approaching a child she
didn't want to frighten.

"Maybe you can't see me or hear me or touch me," she
said, her voice trembling. "But I'm here to help you…if I
can."

Abruptly, the woman's gaze shifted, and her eyes widened, first in astonishment, then in fright.

"So you do see me," Audrey murmured softly, hoping
her tone was reassuring. "I won't hurt you. See?" She held
her hands up, trying to convey her intentions.

A volley of words followed, incomprehensible but for
the tone. It was filled with fear. The woman glanced wildly

about, as if torn between picking up a weapon with which to defend herself and fleeing into the night.

"I know," Audrey said. The consuming fear coursing through her belonged to them both, she thought. "This must be very scary for you. It is for me, too. The idea of you being alone and delivering this baby is terrifying. Not to mention you may be a ghost. That's pretty scary, too." She glanced toward the bed where Gray sat watching her. "I wonder why she can see me, but not you?"

"I don't know," he answered.

She knelt next to the woman. "My name is Audrey." She patted her chest. "Audrey."

"Odd Ree?" The woman gave the consonants a hard inflection as though the sounds were unfamiliar.

"That's right. Audrey. What's your name?" she asked, pointing at the woman.

The question appeared to confuse her.

"You were a cop, Gray," she said. "Did you ever deliver any babies?"

He shook his head. "And, I'm no first-aid expert, either."

She took off her jacket and put it over the woman's shoulders, who seemed only then aware of her nakedness. Another contraction gripped her. Audrey held out her hand in reassurance, and the woman took it.

Gray left the bedroll and added another log to the fire. A cascade of sparks shot into the sky, which caught the Indian woman's attention. He came around the campfire and knelt next to her. "If she can see you, you'd think she could see me, right?"

"You'd think." She patted the woman's shoulder and pointed at Gray. "This is my friend."

Her gaze followed Audrey's finger, but she seemed to see nothing at all. Audrey turned to look at Gray, needing to make sure he was still there, suddenly terrified she might have been consumed by whatever it was that connected this woman's world with hers.

He gave her shoulder a reassuring squeeze, and she swallowed, grateful for his touch.

Shrugging, the Indian woman turned away and gathered the jacket more closely around her shoulders. Seconds later, another contraction seized her.

When the contraction passed, Audrey smiled reassuringly at the woman. "You're doing fine," she said, aware she was probably telling a blatant lie. She had no idea whether the woman was fine or not. Almost before the contraction ended, another one began, this was intense enough to draw a long, anguished groan from the woman.

Pulling a buckskin bag toward her, she reached inside. She removed a knife, which she set in the coals of the fire next to the pot.

Audrey's gaze went from the knife to Gray. "What—?"

"To cut the umbilical cord," he said. "Maybe to cauterize the baby's so it won't bleed after it is born."

"Oh, God," she murmured. She had wondered how women had given birth without benefit of hospitals or doctors, but she had never thought through the details. Face-to-face with the prospect of birth, she was reminded just how out of her element she really was.

Another spasm gripped the woman, and Audrey once again offered her hand.

Noticing that the light above them had changed, she glanced at the moon. The eclipse was beginning to pass, and a brilliant white halo appeared on one side.

The contractions came one after another over the next few minutes. Sweat beaded on the woman's forehead, and she wiped it with the soft chamois cloth, dipping it in the astringent-smelling liquid in the pot.

Minutes flowed one into another. The woman's pain transcended the moment, bringing into sharp focus another woman's pain—in death, though, not in the process of giving life. Now, as then, Audrey felt helpless. A woman suffering, and nothing she could do to help except offer her hand in support that was pitifully too little.

This was a feeling she had never wanted to experience again, and for an instant, she wished she had agreed with Gray—they should have left. The instant the thought surfaced, she felt ashamed. Whatever her discomfort, it was insignificant compared to what this woman endured. It wasn't enough to be a presence, offering her hand and her support, while someone else faced unbearable fear and pain. She wanted to shout her frustration at her own impotence to really make a difference. Instead, she blinked away the tears burning at her eyes and squeezed the woman's hand, murmuring words of encouragement and reassurance.

Audrey felt the woman's emotions as if they were her own. Fear at being alone when a woman was at her most vulnerable. Worry for the unborn child. Loss of her man. Isolation and loneliness so huge she didn't know how it could be borne. The woman straightened suddenly, squatting over a much stained square of buckskin. Audrey knelt behind the woman, supporting her, holding her hands. The woman groaned, gripping Audrey's hands as though they were a lifeline. Then she screamed, the sound splintering down the canyon walls and drowning out the mournful wails of the coyotes.

Audrey felt Gray behind her, holding her body as she supported the woman. She glanced over her shoulder, tears in her eyes blurring him. So strong. So solid. As long as he was here, she could do this.

New images filled her mind—just as real as the moment now, just as powerful as the woman's grip on her hand. Images of Gray holding her, supporting her…cherishing her…when the labor to deliver a child into the world was her own.

The woman cried out again, perhaps calling the name of

her warrior husband who could not come to her. So powerful was the connection, Audrey felt a cry tear up her own throat, felt the overwhelming grief of continuing this life without love and companionship. She leaned her back into Gray's solid form, seeking the reassurance of his presence. His warm hands slid down her arms, bracing her trembling muscles as she supported the woman.

Overhead, the moon grew steadily brighter, the shadow of the eclipse gradually fading. The light reassured her, and she talked to the woman, soothing incessant sounds, encouraging her, goading her, sure that life—not death—was the reward at the end of this struggle. Surely the child would ease the woman's isolation and loss and loneliness.

"Just a little more," Audrey urged.

The woman's hard labor intensified. How much more could she bear? Audrey wondered. She felt the woman's energy change, as though she had nothing else to give the labor. A thousand anxieties for the woman's safe delivery chased through her.

Suddenly, the woman slumped within Audrey's arms as though she had no more energy left.

"You can't quit now, you can't." Audrey lifted her eyes to the bright moon, the eclipse nearly gone. The bright light felt cold, empty, flat. A shiver of apprehension chased through her.

In one instant, her body supported the woman. In the next, she didn't feel her at all. No heat. No touch…no pressure from the grip of the woman's hands. Only the chilly evening air and the faint heat from the campfire.

The woman shifted, looking over her shoulder, meeting Audrey's gaze. She murmured something, squeezed Audrey's hand and simply, instantly disappeared.

Vanished.

Numbly, Audrey looked down. Everything—the chamois cloth she had held, the pot in the fire, the stained buckskin—was gone. Only her jacket lay in a heap at her feet.

Unbearable loss welled within her.

"No," she wailed, holding out her arms.

Gray's arms came around her, and she turned toward him.

"She was here," she cried. "She was *here*. I saw her. I held her. I *touched* her!"

"I know," he answered. "Look at your hands."

Bruises were beginning to form where they had been squeezed. Gray examined first one hand, then the other, gently smoothing his thumb over the marks. She wasn't crazy, and she hadn't been dreaming.

"Oh, God," she moaned, turning into Gray's arms. "What happened to her? Did sh-she have th-the baby? Did she…live or…die?"

"I don't know, love."

"Hold me." She clasped Gray around the neck. "I felt her, Gray. She…was fl-flesh and…blood. And here."

"I know she was," he murmured.

His arms came around her, and she held him more tightly. He was real. Solid. Warm. As warm as the woman had been. She gripped him tightly, half expecting him to vanish. Without him, her world would be utterly bleak. Just as the woman's had been without her man.

"She was so alone." Tears welled from beneath her eyelids. "No one should be so alone. Oh, Gray…"

"It's all right. I'm here."

Primal emotions erupted from the depths of her soul. More tears squeezed beneath her lids. Turning Gray's face toward her, his cheek feeling like sandpaper beneath her hand, she brought her mouth to his. Surprise held him rigid beneath her touch.

Instinct and raw need guided her. Boldly, she brushed her lips over his, savoring the texture. Briefly, she touched the seam of his mouth with her tongue, then withdrew. Once, twice, she repeated the action, needing his deep, hungry kisses more than she needed her next breath. A third time. Solid. Real. Warm. Resilient beneath her touch. Feeling as though she needed to absorb him within herself, she pressed herself closer.

Greedy need built as she explored all the textures and tastes he had to offer. Someone groaned, and she didn't know if it was him or her. She didn't care. She wanted more.

Her hands slid into his hair, her nails running over his scalp. He shivered in response, and her kiss, if anything, became bolder as an ache of longing spread from her center. His heat, his response, reassured her, made her feel as though she had arrived at home after a long, trying journey. He felt right.

The world shifted suddenly, and she realized Gray had picked her up. A few steps later, he laid her on the pine-bough bed and stretched out beside her, returning her hungry kisses. Turning, she put her arms around his shoulders, urging him closer.

He slipped a leg between hers, and she wrapped one of hers around him, shifting to her side. The pressure of his knee against her pelvis eased the emptiness, but not enough. She leaned into him. Urgent need flared again, leaving her feeling even more hollow. She held him tightly, but it was not enough.

His hand traced the line of her collarbone, his touch generating a trail of awareness. She ran a finger down the strong column of his throat, touching the fringe of hair that extended above his shirt. And through it all, she continued to kiss him deeply, drinking from him as though his taste were the sustenance of life itself.

Her hand feathered across the expanse of his chest, then to his back, trying to find the tail of his shirt. Warm skin, not cloth, was what she needed. She found a way through his clothes to the warm, smooth skin of his back. Touching him this way was exciting, frustrating and satisfying all at once. She loved the feel of him, but she wanted more.

His skin felt so good. From back to side to front. Beneath her fingers, she found his chest covered with surprisingly soft hair. In stark contrast to the silky hair was the tight nub of his nipple. He shuddered when she lightly ran a finger over it, and so she returned to it again…and again.

Rolling her onto her back, he broke the kiss, and grabbed her hands, holding them above her head. He gazed down at her, breathing hard. She lifted her head to kiss him, settled for sampling the texture of his neck when she couldn't reach his lips. He shuddered as she tasted him.

"Tell me what you want, Audrey."

The words he had uttered earlier echoed through her mind. *And you're so, so tempting. And I won't be able to stop with a kiss.…* Tempting. He absolutely was. That she might be equally tempting was new. More than anything, she wanted to be just as alluring as she found him to be.

Slipping one of her hands from his grip, she touched his cheek. "You."

Wrapping her other leg around his, she returned his intense stare. She tried to pull his head down for another kiss, but he was immovable, so she lifted her head and kissed him, teasing his lips, encouraging him to open his mouth and give her what she wanted.

Never in his life had anyone wanted him like this. She was a siren in his blood, belying the feeling that she was an innocent. She couldn't be—not kissing like this.

He was at once reassured and disappointed. He'd gotten used to thinking of her as an innocent, and he liked that. How much simpler, though, that she knew satisfying mutual desire wasn't the same as a commitment to anything beyond the moment. He had been crazy to think they could sleep together without giving in to this.

He returned her kiss, allowing his own hunger free rein. Desire clawed through him, testing his determination to go slow. Except she didn't want slow. She pushed his shirt off his shoulders as though she must touch him or die.

He knew exactly how she felt.

He somehow removed her calico shirt and the sleeveless sweater under it. Her skin felt satiny smooth and soft, but only for an instant before goose bumps rose on her arms.

She inhaled deeply, absorbing his scent. Nothing had ever felt as sensuous as the texture of his hair against her cheek. His hands roamed over her, cupping her bottom, sliding down the outside of her thigh, up the inside, across her bare midriff. Touching everywhere, lingering nowhere, feeding the inferno of longing that consumed her.

She needed to touch him in the same way, needed to show him with her own hands how much she enjoyed his caresses. She worked free the tight buttons of his jeans, warm from the heat of his body. Finally, one popped free. Then a second. After an eternity, a third. She reached inside, found more cotton, softer than the denim, but not the resilient skin she needed to touch. She found the waistband of his shorts and slipped her hand inside.

His breath hissed out.

She kissed his neck, feeling powerful and feminine, then tested his skin with her teeth. He tasted good, felt good. She smoothed her hand over his hip bone, then followed a ridge of muscle across his lower back to the base of his spine.

Once again, his breath caught, then rushed out on a sigh that sounded like "Good. So...damned...good."

His pleasure excited her, making her tremble, intensifying the ache within her.

She flexed her fingers into the muscles of his buttocks and abruptly stilled her exploration when she felt his hand on her breast. He fingered the silky fabric of her bra, then found the fastening between her breasts. Her breath caught, held as he slid his palm over her skin. Heat was her first impression, closely followed by another intense rush of desire at the feel of his thumb drawing tight circles around her nipple.

He trailed a line of openmouthed kisses down her neck and the swell of her breasts. For an instant, he held her in suspense as he paused at the valley between her breasts, his breath hot. Then his mouth was over her nipple, tracing it lightly with his tongue. Deep inside, her muscles quivered, and a rush of heat poured from her.

Every caress made her need more, but calling it simple need was too tame. Slowly, he increased the intimacy of his mouth against her breasts, a pace that was sure to make her lose her mind.

A single thought surfaced. More. It beat to the galloping cadence of her heart. More. Swamped in the sensations of his touch and the powerful emotions gripping her, she knew only one thing. She needed more.

She shoved his jeans down his legs.

She wanted more.

His mouth against her breast was more beautiful than anything she had ever imagined.

She wanted more.

His kisses drugged her and excited her.

She wanted more.

Sensations blurred one into another. The touch of his palms beneath her panties warm against her bottom. The rasp of his hair-covered leg against her smooth ones. The feverish heat of the bunched muscles of his shoulder. All focused into a sole nucleus when he pulled the panties from her, then cupped her intimately. Her breath caught, then expelled in a rush when his fingers slid between to touch her where no one else ever had.

She opened her eyes and found him watching her, his eyes very bright. His caress, if possible, became even more intimate, and she spread her legs wider, looping one of them over the top of his leg, inviting him to touch her more deeply.

He did.

She shivered as a tiny piece of the pressure splintered and washed through her.

Gray had never seen any woman more beautiful to him, her eyes dark and mysterious. She seemed surprised at each response of her body, which told him something of the pleasure he was giving her. Just now, nothing seemed more important, not even satisfying his own hunger.

She reached for him, her fingers curling around him, cool in comparison to the heat of his skin. And he knew he had been lying to himself. Nothing was more important than burying himself in her until they were closer than a heartbeat.

He closed his eyes and pressed himself into her palm. She explored all the textures of him as though nothing were more important to her. Beneath his fingers, he felt the flooding warmth of her arousal, knew she was ready to accept him, wanting her to climax again and again before he took her. Carefully, he teased her sensitive flesh, adjusting his pace and his touch in response to the tiny surprised catches in her breath.

Suddenly she stiffened, and he bent to kiss her. She curled against him at the first pulses of her release. He had intended to wait, had intended to bring her repeatedly to the brink. Urgent, undeniable need clawed through him.

He loomed over her, parting her legs with his knees, needing the completion he would find within her.

At the touch of his blunt flesh against her softness, her eyes flew open. He bent and kissed her, taking her mouth deeply, and pressed into her.

And found she was a virgin.

Chapter 10

He was the first. The realization pierced him to his soul. He had never been the first. Ever.

Thinking was impossible.

Stopping was impossible.

Still, Gray poised at the brink, barely comprehending what he was feeling.

"Please," Audrey whimpered.

Please what? he wondered, alarm settling in his gut, Stop? Continue?

Her hands curled around his waist, then slid to his buttocks, and she pressed against them, urging him forward.

"Please," she whispered again.

She wanted him. He was the first. And she wanted...him. He would make this right for her. Better than right. Perfect.

Lifting his head far enough to see her, he followed the insistent demands of her hands and pressed into her. Her eyes widened when he again reached the barrier. He withdrew slightly, then pressed forward...gently...with more control than he knew he had. Nothing had ever felt this good to him, but not hurting her was more important, so he patiently inched forward, then withdrew, then forward, feeling her body gradually accommodate his.

"Oh, please..."

"Soon," he promised, recognizing that renewed desire, not fear, was the source of her breathy request.

His slow taking of her was the sweetest torture he had ever indulged in. Her ragged breathing and the heat of her body told him all he needed to know about her pleasure. With slow, careful strokes, he eased into her a bit farther, hoping to find a way past the barrier without hurting her.

Beneath him, she felt soft, totally feminine. Woman. The aroma that rose from her heated, aroused body was uniquely hers. Nothing had ever smelled better to him. Until the day he died, he'd remember this.

She put her arms around his neck and pulled his head down to her. In the moonlight, her eyes were fierce, but no more so than the grip of her legs as she suddenly shifted and wrapped them around his waist. He stilled, her movement opening her wider and bringing them even closer.

"Please," she repeated against his mouth. "More. I...want, need...more."

Kissing her deeply, he withdrew slightly, then pressed into her. There was a fractional hesitation, then he slid fully in until his pelvis rested against hers. She groaned, her eyes wide. He held perfectly motionless, absorbing the pressure and warmth and softness squeezed around him. Nothing in his life had ever felt this good. Nothing.

He brushed his lips across hers, then kissed her more deeply. She returned the kiss, and tried to move her hips toward him.

"Shh," he murmured, stilling her movements. "Are you okay?"

"I feel as though I'm going to split open."

"I'm hurting you." He tried to withdraw, regretting he hadn't taken her more carefully.

She clasped him more tightly with her legs. "Don't you dare leave me. And you're not hurting me." She brushed his cheek with her palm. "I think I was made for you."

That simple declaration shattered the last remnants of his control, and he began to move. He crested to a higher plateau of sensation, expecting any moment to explode into release. Except release didn't come.

In the moonlight, he watched her. Her features held intense concentration, and she panted as though she had been running a long, long time. Bracing his body on his elbows, he smoothed the hair away from her face. Her eyes opened once again, and she tried to smile.

"You're beautiful," he whispered, bending to kiss her, possessing her mouth as thoroughly as he had possessed her body.

Audrey felt as though she were riding a surging wave, thrusting her into sensations she hadn't dreamed existed. Her awareness narrowed to Gray and the pleasure his body gave hers. He felt like a missing part of her. She clasped him more tightly, and in response he gathered her even closer, body to body...soul to soul.

She wanted to tell him how much she loved what he was doing, but she had no words. She wanted to show him how she felt, but could not. The feelings he evoked swirled to a single vortex that became tighter...brighter...stronger.

Without warning, the pleasure spiraled to a peak, then shattered. Pure feeling enveloped her, more brilliant than the full moon. Piercing...sweet...fulfillment.

Audrey held on to her only reality. Gray. He murmured words of reassurance and praise against her ear, holding her fully within his powerful embrace as though he sensed how much she needed him.

The spasms slowed, and breathless, she pressed her cheek against his. His movements slowed, too, giving her sensitive flesh a moment's rest. He withdrew almost completely, then slowly entered again, repeating the languid thrusts that soothed and excited her at once. The beautiful, unbearable tension began to coil through her again, and as though he anticipated her need, his rhythm increased.

Knowing what to expect this time, she held on to him tighter, seeking his mouth, wanting that mating as much as she wanted the other. His alluring heat accompanied the soar toward completion. Her senses heightened, and she became aware of everything. His scent...bunched biceps on either side of her shoulders...his hands cupping her face...his taste...the soft hair on his chest against her nipples...the pressure of his pelvis against hers...the feel of his thighs against the soles of her feet...his heat...the ragged rasp of his breath.

Opening her eyes, she watched him. He looked like a man in great pain, and as pressure built inside her, she understood he rode a wave of consuming ecstasy as great as her own. The awareness she had the ability to bring that kind of gratification carried her own desire toward the pinnacle.

Groaning her name, he buried himself within her again and again. His excitement, his pleasure in her body, carried her to a shimmering peak where she hung suspended within feelings too intense to bear, too beautiful to let go of.

As before, her climax washed over her. She wrapped her arms and legs around Gray—the only solid, real thing in her universe. His release poured into her, his convulsive throbs igniting another spasm of purest pleasure within her.

Gradually, the moon slid across the night sky. Audrey must have fallen asleep, though all she remembered was holding on to Gray as though he were a lifeline after he collapsed on top of her. Then he cradled her in his arms as though she were precious, a feeling that she savored.

Gray's breathing changed, and she realized that if he had been asleep, he had awakened. She felt him kiss her cheek, and she shifted her gaze from the bright moon to him. His eyes, as he looked down at her, were equally brilliant.

"Hi," he said, his voice husky.

"Hi."

He raised himself on his elbows, and his gaze traveled from her face down to the shadowed cleft where their bodies touched, lingering at her breasts. She felt her nipples tighten in response.

He groaned an instant before he bent and kissed first one, then the other. Sitting up, he pulled her across his lap. He put his arms beneath her back and her legs, then stood as though his arms were empty instead of holding 127 pounds.

Being carried this way made her feel cherished as she never had before. Looping her arms around his neck, she pressed a kiss against his collarbone.

Seemingly oblivious to their nakedness and the chilly air, he walked toward the edge of the overhang, then into the night toward the steamy pool.

"What are we doing?" she whispered, intensely aware of his hands on her thighs and under her arms.

"Taking a bath," he whispered back, a trace of laughter in his voice.

"Why?"

"Because...I want to hold you in the water, and...because maybe you won't be so sore if you have a long soak."

New awareness throbbed at her core, tingling in an intimate, tactile memory of his possession. Anticipation coiled through her, once more waking the ache only he could assuage.

As they approached the pool, the air became thicker, the steam inviting. Carefully, Gray stepped into the water, gradually lowering her into its depths. The water felt welcoming, its warmth perfect. He found a stone seat at one edge, and sat down, still cradling her in his arms. Above

them, the moonlight sifted through the steam, which wa
vered like gauzy streamers of white chiffon.

Audrey felt as though they were sheltered inside a warm
protected cocoon. Gray smoothed his hands up and down
her arms, then her back before sweeping down the length
of her legs. When his palm slid back up the inside of her
thigh, she sighed and opened her legs for him.

He laughed softly. "So you like that."

"You know I do."

He cupped her with the palm of his hand, then eased one
of his fingers between the folds. "Hurt?"

She shook her head.

"Tender?"

She shook her head again.

"Ah, sweet, sweet Audrey. You don't know what you
do to me."

As she felt his arousal pressing against her bottom, it
was Audrey's turn to laugh softly. "You think not?"

She shifted in his arms and straddled his lap. Leaning
forward, she kissed him, then whispered, "Love me
again."

In answer, he put his hands beneath her bottom and
brought her toward him. She sank down on him, his flesh
even hotter than the water, and infinitely more pleasurable.
She sighed.

"I...like this," she said, testing the length of him.

"I can tell," he said, his voice gritty.

She moved slowly, intending to torment him as he had
done to her earlier. Except the relentless tension curled
through her once again, making her abandon all thought
except to relieve the pressure building inside her. He
brought her head down, and kissed her. Without warning,
the climax consumed her. An instant later, he groaned, and
she felt the pulses of his release. He wrapped his arms
around her and pressed her head against his shoulder. One

of her palms slid to his chest, and she felt the race of his heart.

Gray shifted them to a more comfortable position, still holding her on his lap, so only their heads were out of the water. They sat quietly for a long time. Audrey tipped her head back, the moon again brilliant, the eclipse completely gone. She stared at the spangle of stars flung across the sky, the night huge and timeless. What was real? she wondered, touching the tender marks on the back of her hand. The Indian woman? Gray?

She turned her head toward him, seeing that he, too, was staring at the sky. Beneath the water, she sought his hand, twining her fingers with his.

He brushed his thumb across her palm. Beneath the back side of her hand, she felt something smooth, round. Letting go of his hand, she searched the stone surface of their seat with her fingertips. She closed her fingers around the object and lifted it out of the water.

Her bracelet.

"Amazing," she breathed. "Look at that."

"Told you we'd find it," he said, taking it from her and putting it around her wrist with the other bracelet.

She touched the surface of the bracelet, relieved it had been so easily found. "That you did."

He clasped her hand within his once again, and they leaned against the edge of the pool. Audrey closed her eyes and let the moment engulf her, simply enjoying the heat of the water, the crisp night air and the feel of Gray's body next to hers. If this was complete contentment, she wanted it forever.

"Why?" he asked, the question so soft it might have been a lap of water against the edge of the pool.

"Hmm?" she responded.

"Why were you a..."

"Virgin?" she finally finished for him.

"Yes."

"It...just sort of happened...or rather, didn't happen."

He turned his head until she met his gaze. "It's a little unusual. What are you, twenty—?"

"Eight," she finished. "My mom had a stroke eight years ago—not long after she was diagnosed with leukemia."

"And you lived with her."

Audrey nodded. "When I was nineteen or twenty, it didn't seem like such a big deal. Over the years, I had a couple of casual boyfriends, but...my situation kept things from getting serious, you know?"

"It's a gift you should have given to someone special."

Audrey turned to face him more fully. "I did."

"You can't be sure of that." He traced the side of her face with his finger. "We hardly know each other."

"We've shared more in the last twenty-four hours than most people do in months or even years. I know my own mind, Gray."

"There are things you don't know—"

"Gray." She touched his cheek. "You're right. I don't know your history, beyond being a cop-turned-sculptor. But I do know you're honorable, kind—"

"I'm a killer," he said, his voice harsh, his judgment of himself breaking her heart a little.

"I know. Richard told me." Hopefully, Gray would never guess how difficult it was to keep her voice even, though his admission tore at her. Whatever Gray called himself, she had no doubt it had been his only choice at the time and in the line of duty.

"You know? And you gave yourself to me anyway?"

"That's right," she returned. Whatever he had done, the man in her arms was all the things she had secretly dreamed for. Smoothing his hair away from his forehead, she added, "Maybe you killed someone, once. But I watched you this afternoon, and you had the opportunity to shoot Howard when he was driving away. And you didn't do it."

"That doesn't prove anything."

"To me, it was a lot. Richard taunted me not to trust you, which was sort of funny, since you had told me the same thing. But I knew, even then I could."

"And look at what it got you—"

"Life," she interrupted. "Life, when I surely would have died without your help." Her voice softened. "And greater pleasure than I ever imagined possible."

He stared at her, his gaze intense. "I don't deserve that kind of trust."

"Tough," she said, putting her hands around his neck, then easing her fingers into his hair. "If you want to fight with me, you're going to have to do better than this."

"I don't want to fight with you," he whispered, touching her lips with his own.

"Good," she said.

Gray wrapped his arms around her, wondering how he was ever going to let her go. To the depths of his soul, he wanted to claim her as his woman. Was this how the cycle began? Needing one special woman so much you'd kill to keep her? The questions tore through him as his arms gently cradled her. He couldn't imagine hurting her. Had it started this way for his father, his brothers?

He had been the first, and damned if he wanted anyone else touching her so intimately. And someone else would. His woman…a dream to forever be denied. He had watched the cycle too many times with his father and his brothers, and he knew what came after this fierce sense of possession. Jealousy. Violence. Remorse. It was a pattern he had vowed never to repeat. The sooner he let her go, the better.

She lifted her face, kissed his cheek, then traced the line of his jaw with her lips. This kind of gentleness, this kind of trust, he had no defenses against. When her mouth reached his, he kissed her deeply, possessively.

And damned fate for tempting him.

* * *

Much later, Gray carried her back to the campfire, drying her with his T-shirt, a favor she returned, taking as much time as he did. His big body fascinated her, and she doubted she would ever get tired of touching him. He made no move to escalate their gentle caring of one another into passion.

It was another facet of the man she admired.

So many things about the night tempted her to believe she was having a dream.

The pleasure Gray had given her.

The Indian woman.

Audrey's gaze fell to the area around the campfire. Nothing was left of her. Nothing. Audrey touched her fingers to her hand, felt the tenderness where the woman had gripped her so tightly. But it wasn't proof she had really been here.

Audrey sat down on their makeshift bed, the tarp rough against her skin, the scent of pine heavy in the air.

"We're gonna freeze if we don't get dressed." He handed her a shirt.

Her glance fell to his groin. He was aroused. Warmth flooded through her, and she reached for him.

"Sure you want to get dressed?"

He shuddered as her fingers closed around him, his skin hot beneath her hands. His eyes were tormented when they met hers.

Lying down, she held out her arms. "It's okay."

"We're not going to make love again tonight," he stated.

"I want to." She traced a line down the center of his body. "You want to."

"What I want…" He swallowed. "I don't want to hurt you."

"You won't," she assured him. "Besides, I'm willing to risk it."

"I'm not." He thrust her clothes into her hands, then put his own on. She watched an instant before reluctantly deciding he was right. The night was cold.

After they were dressed, he lay down on the tarp beside

her and arranged his jacket over them, gathering her closer into his arms. "I want to sleep with you in my arms."

"I'd like that, too," she returned, laying her cheek against his chest. Beneath her ear, she heard the steady beat of his heart. The campfire was once again reduced to a few flames and red coals. Her arms tightened around Gray, and her eyes drifted closed. No home anywhere could feel better than this man and this place.

For years, she had associated home with a cheery hearth and comfortable furniture. Gray's warmth was even more alluring, and she couldn't imagine being any more comfortable than she was in his arms right now.

Gradually, the arousal faded into a feeling just as potent—belonging. The steady beat of his heart reassured her that she wasn't alone and lulled her toward sleep.

One last time, her gaze lit on the small campfire. What had happened to the Indian woman and her child?

Hours later, she felt Gray gently shake her awake. Where her body nestled against his, she was warm.

"Time to go," he said, sitting up.

"Already?" Pale sky had replaced the canopy of stars, but sunrise was a mere promise. She sat up, then shivered. "Why so early?"

He nodded toward the trail. "Hear that?"

She cocked her head to the side, listening. The faint rumble of a vehicle. Alarm, too familiar now, settled in her belly.

"If that's Howard, aren't we better off staying here? Hidden?"

"We'd be trapped." Urging her off the bed, he gathered up the tarp and shook it out before folding it. "And we need help."

"We've done okay so far."

"We've been lucky."

"Where are we going?"

He stuffed the tarp into his backpack. "Hawk's place.
He keeps a herd of horses between here and the ranch. That
also gives us transportation so I can get you to safety."

"If transportation, as you put it, was so easy, why didn'
we go there yesterday?"

"Yesterday we would have been caught out in the
open." He pointed toward the trail. "Listen."

They fell silent, and once again heard the rumble of a
vehicle.

"I think he found the trail we left when we climbed the
mesa. It's only a matter of time before he backtracks and
starts checking the side canyons. If we can get to Hawk's
place while Lambert is looking up here, we'll be safe."

Everything Gray said made sense. Sensible or not, she
felt as though he was pushing her away.

She stepped close to him, looped her arms around his
waist and kissed his cheek, which felt sandpapery beneath
her lips. "Did I dream last night?" she whispered.

He put his arms around her and rested his cheek against
her hair. "Which part?"

"The eclipse? The Indian woman?"

He took her hands from around his neck and examined
them. Even in the predawn light, several dime-size bruises
showed clearly against her pale skin. Gently, he smoothed
his fingers over each one. "That could have been a dream."

"And making love with you?"

He met her gaze. "That could have been a dream, too."

She smiled and lifted a hand to his face. "I'd like to
have that particular dream again, then."

He turned his face far enough to kiss her palm. "Me,
too."

Within minutes, they took apart the camp, returning the
pine boughs to the base of the towering ponderosas, dous-
ing the campfire, then covering it with a layer of soil. As
they left the camp, Audrey looked back one last time.
Again, the transparent mist shrouded the stone pond. To

her, it looked as though no one had been there in a long, long time.

Instead of heading back down the way they had come up, Gray led her up the trail he had investigated yesterday when they first arrived. They reached a notch at the top where the view was breathtaking. Snow-covered mountains in one direction, and the expanse of the valley in another. He didn't give her any time to enjoy it, though, as they picked their way down a steep talus slope. Gray remained only a couple of steps ahead, offering his hand when the going was particularly rough.

When they were halfway down the hillside, the sun came up, brilliant and warm. Off to the south, low clouds hugged the ground, threatening rain.

When they reached the bottom, she looked back. Above them, a cliff towered, and from here it was obvious that at some point, part of it had given way. She shuddered, imagining the rockslide that had created the nearly vertical ridge they had just descended. Gray offered her water from the canteen before taking a sip himself.

Her stomach rumbled, but she didn't ask if he had anything left to eat. If he had, he would have offered it already. She sat down on one of the boulders, took off her shoes one at a time, emptying the bits of rock from the insides before putting them back on.

They began walking again, their pace brisk. They didn't talk much, and she found herself listening for the vehicle they had earlier heard. There was no cover, no way for them to hide, and she knew Gray was right. If they had taken this route yesterday, Howard would have found them.

What seemed like hours later to her, they ducked through a barbed-wire fence. In the distance, horses grazed.

"If we have any kind of luck at all," Gray said, "now is the time." Then he whistled, a shrill, piercing sound. In the distance, the horses lifted their heads.

"See that big sorrel," he said, pointing, "the one coming toward us? That's D.J."

"Our transportation?"

Gray nodded. "If he'll be a gentleman and let me catch him."

"I would have thought this guy's name would have been Cat," she murmured. "Since you have a cat named Horace."

He grinned, the first smile he'd given her all day. Knowing how rare they were, she cherished each one.

"So what does 'D.J.' stand for?"

The grin widened. "Don Juan."

"Ah," she teased. "A family name."

"Not even."

Within moments, they were surrounded by a half-dozen horses, including D.J. He seemed happy enough to see Gray, but shied away each time Gray reached for him.

"How come the hero's always able to leap on the back of his horse in the movies?" she asked.

"Because they forget a horse's basic nature. He's a herd animal. And much as he likes me, his instinct to stay with the herd is stronger."

Movement at the edge of the field caught her eye—a horse, this one saddled. "Someone is coming," she announced.

Gray turned to watch the approach, his posture becoming even more alert.

As the rider came closer, Audrey recognized Hawk. When he was a couple of hundred yards away, the horse's trot became a lope, which scattered the horses that had been walking with them.

Hawk brought his horse to a skidding halt. He looked from Gray to Audrey and then back again.

"It's really you," Hawk said.

"Who else would I be?" Gray retorted.

"I thought you were dead."

"Dead?" Gray repeated.

He dismounted and slapped Gray on the back. "As a doornail. Man, am I glad to see you."

Possibilities raced through Gray's mind. Why would Hawk think he was dead? There were no bodies. Even with the fire in Audrey's car, there would have been a skeleton. So...

"Aw, damn," Hawk muttered, rubbing the back of his neck. "You shouldn't find out this way...."

"Find out what?"

"Your cousin...Richard shot himself last night."

Cold disbelief slithered down his spine even as he asked, "What happened?"

"He committed suicide."

"That doesn't make any sense."

"I hear you," Hawk answered. "But there's not much doubt about it. He left a note. Which is why we thought you were dead."

"A note?" In his experience, suicide notes were damned convenient and didn't necessarily prove anything. He felt Audrey move closer to him, her small hand sliding within his, squeezing in reassurance. "What did it say?"

Hawk shrugged. "That he had shot you and Audrey."

"My God, why?" Audrey asked.

Hawk shrugged. "He didn't say why, only that he had made a huge mistake and that he couldn't go on living."

"That makes no sense," Gray said. "Where'd this happen?"

"In his quarters."

Gray wanted to see the room. He didn't believe for a minute that his cousin had killed himself.

"Were you able to reach the Denver office?" Audrey asked.

Hawk shook his head. "Nope. The telephones are still out."

"Has the sheriff been notified?" Gray asked.

Hawk tipped his Stetson back. "Well, as it happens, I'm headed over to John Toosla's place to use his phone. Since the bridge is out, need to rely on good old-fashioned horse power." He patted the horse on the neck.

"Did you find Richard's weapon?" Gray asked.

"Sure," Hawk responded. "It was in his hand."

"What about a rifle?"

Hawk shrugged. "All we found was a .38 revolver."

Gray turned away and stared into space. To the best of his knowledge, Richard had never been much of a hunter. Somewhere, hiding out, was a man who was. There was no way the person who had been shooting at them could have been Richard. None. He wouldn't have thought so even if they had not seen Howard Lambert. Gray frowned, the pieces forming a new puzzle he didn't like at all.

He and Audrey weren't dead. And his cousin hadn't committed suicide.

Richard had been murdered.

Chapter 11

"You can't be serious about ruling Richard's death a suicide," Gray told the county coroner some seven hours later.

He had bullied his way into Richard's quarters, ignoring the doctor's protest and dismissing the deputy for the kid he was.

Gray was in no mood to be reasonable, and he had questions he didn't trust anyone else to provide answers to. It had been a long horseback ride back to the pueblo where Gray had stashed Audrey with Francie. He hadn't wanted to leave Audrey, but he didn't want her anywhere near a murder scene, either. And Francie was the one person he trusted to keep Audrey company until he had seen for himself where Richard died.

Then he had gone back to the ranch while Hawk rode across the river to find a working phone. A helicopter carrying the coroner and a young deputy arrived a couple of hours after they were called.

"That's the way I see it." The doctor made a couple of

other notes, then looked at Gray. "I can understand how difficult this must be for you—the deceased being family and all—but he did take his own life."

"I've seen my share of suicides, and I'll tell you, no one shoots themselves in the chest—"

"Perhaps…the gun discharged prematurely."

Gray knew the good doctor was a family practitioner, not a pathologist. If the coroner had investigated a murder at all during the past year or five, Gray would have been surprised. He sure as hell didn't know how to read a crime scene.

The deputy, who looked as if he should still be in junior high school, was no help, either. The closest the kid had probably ever come to a murder was textbook pictures when he attended the law-enforcement academy. Assuming he had even that much training.

The doctor's gaze fell to where Richard's hand was wrapped around the pistol. "And then there is the matter of the note."

"Yeah, he left a note, all right. Which is pretty damned vague." Gray stalked across the room to the dresser, where the note had been found. "'I've made a terrible mistake,'" he read without touching the paper. "'After I killed Gray Murdoch and Audrey Sussman, I realized I could no longer go on living.'"

"People contemplating suicide are often not rational," the doctor said in tones meant to be placating.

"He wasn't suicidal," Gray stated flatly, pinning the doctor with a hard glance. "He had no motive for murdering me. And as you can see, I'm not dead!"

"And Miss Sussman?"

"She's not dead, either," he snapped.

"Mr. Murdoch—"

"He was murdered," Gray insisted. "Check for powder residue on his hands. I'm willing to bet he didn't fire this gun."

"Of course, that will be checked as part of the autopsy. But, I'm telling you, there's nothing here to indicate anything other than a suicide."

"I'd like the sheriff to take a look at the scene," Gray said.

"He's on vacation for the next two weeks," the deputy responded.

"And you two are the experts—"

"As close as you're going to get," the coroner countered, his voice rising to match Gray's. "This isn't a big city, but that doesn't mean we don't know what we're doing."

"When was the last time you investigated a murder?" Gray asked.

"That's irrelevant in this case—"

"It's exactly the point."

"And how the hell would you know?" the doctor returned. "I know you're upset—"

"I was a detective on a homicide unit for six years," Gray said, his voice clipped and a thousand times more calm than he felt. "I've investigated more murders than I can count, and I'm telling you. This is no suicide."

"You see what you want to see," the coroner said with a shrug. "Because you're related, and we never want to think a loved one is capable of this. Because of your training, you think along certain lines automatically."

"That's a crock."

Within minutes, the coroner had finished up his job. They loaded Richard's body into the helicopter. The deputy and coroner climbed aboard, and the chopper took off in a cloud of dust.

Gray went back inside and found himself at the doorway of Richard's quarters. The stench of death hung heavily in the air, and a dark red stain marred the Navajo rug in the middle of the floor. Gray opened a window. A billow of fresh air flowed into the room, reminding him of the ancient custom of leaving a window open so the departing soul could escape.

From ghastly to surreal, Gray thought, wondering if Richard's spirit had made it on to the next world or if it would hang around and haunt this one, becoming another ghost of Puma's Lair.

"Not much else to be done here," Hawk said from the doorway.

"Not much," Gray agreed, continuing his study of the room. Surely Howard Lambert had left a clue somewhere that would nail him.

"I can see why you thought your cousin was murdered," Hawk said, stopping just inside the doorway. "Richard didn't know much about guns. In fact, he used to hate the hunting trips Lambert insisted on when he came down. But maybe the coroner's got it right."

"Let's hope so," Gray finally said.

Hawk lifted an eyebrow.

"If he's not," Gray stated, as though he were explaining a hypothetical case, "there's someone out there who wants Audrey or me or both of us dead."

He rolled his shoulders, realizing the adrenaline that had kept him going the past day was beginning to wear off. He glanced down at his jeans and shirt, both of which were filthy. "I want to shower and put on some clean clothes before I go get Audrey."

"I'm going to head back," Hawk said.

"See you in a while," Gray responded, watching the other man stride down the hallway. Relieved to no longer be suspicious of Hawk, he nearly called out. Instead, he quietly closed the door to his cousin's quarters. He headed for his room, uncomfortably aware that he was alone in the sprawling hacienda. Gray stopped just inside the doorway of the room he had been using. Nothing was obviously out of place, but he would bet his last dime the room had been methodically searched. Pulling his weapon from the back waistband of his jeans, he silently moved toward the closet and, standing to one side, opened the door. No one was inside the closet, but that didn't keep his heart from pounding. Gray snagged a pair of chinos and a shirt off a hanger, then pulled underwear out of a drawer.

Even though he wasn't ready to confide in Hawk, Gray wondered if he should have asked the man to wait. If he were Howard, he would be looking for just this kind of opportunity. There would be no witnesses, just as there hadn't been for Richard.

Almost as an afterthought, he picked up a straight-back chair, which he took to the bathroom. After locking the door, he wedged the chair back under the door handle. It wouldn't hold if someone was really determined to get in, but it would give him warning.

He figured Lambert's plan hadn't been all that bad. Kill them, then blame it on Richard. It was an easy way to explain two dead bodies plus removing any opposition to his plans. Only Lambert should have made sure he and Audrey were dead before he killed Richard. Things were messier now. Unpredictable. Men desperate enough to plan and carry out a murder weren't the most predictable sorts of people. And Gray didn't like that a bit.

Setting the weapon within easy reach, Gray stripped and stepped into the shower. He finished showering and dressing without hearing anything out of the ordinary. Gray stole quietly through the vacant hacienda, listening to each nuance of sound, but heard only the usual creaks and groans of the old building.

Outside, he headed for the corral, where he saddled D.J., then he headed across the open valley between the ranch's hacienda and the few dwellings of the pueblo where Hawk lived.

The ride to the pueblo was only a couple of miles, which to Gray was a couple of miles too many. The longer he was separated from Audrey, the more he worried that Lambert had somehow found her.

The sun was scant minutes from setting by the time Gray reached the pueblo. The ruins cast long shadows across the plaza. A number of people in native costume stood in small groups, talking. Men with blackened faces, wearing buffalo skins and horns, indicated to Gray the buffalo dance had been performed during the afternoon. Gray dismounted and led the animal into a corral near Hawk and Francie's house. After he unsaddled the animal, he went looking for Audrey.

The tense, edgy feeling that had ridden him all day intensified. He scanned the small clusters of people talking here and there without finding her, then methodically searched the group again.

He found Francie first, with a young woman dressed in off-white and a couple of young men who seemed intent on explaining the significance of their costumes. Gray's gaze returned to the young woman.

Audrey.

Her hair was loose around her face, and he imagined easing his hands around her head, feeling the silky strands against his fingers. He wasn't the only one who had showered and had a change of clothes. She was wearing a full tiered off-white skirt and a tunic similar to Francie's.

She smiled at something one of the men said, and Gray heard her chuckle ripple across the plaza toward him. Though he loved her laughter, he hated the thought that she was laughing with someone else. Stopping short, Gray cursed at himself. Someone else, hell. Admit it. A man.

The feeling that rushed through him was new, but he knew it. Jealousy. The monster twisted through his gut, making his breath grow short and his temper even shorter.

Gray slowed his stride, then finally stopped. If he followed the primitive impulses surging through him, he would sweep her away from the two men, knock them both flat for even looking at her and make sure she knew she was his. An impulse he had hoped he would never feel, had vowed he would never act upon.

His gaze slid over her face as he remembered how soft her skin felt, how her eyes became very black as her climax approached, how she had wrapped her arms around him and held him as though he meant everything to her. She was the sum of all he had ever dreamed of having...and she was not for him. No matter how jealous he was. Especially because he was so damned jealous.

She didn't need this. No woman did.

And so help him, Audrey deserved better. Long years of solitude flashed before him, stark counterpoint to one vivid day of being surrounded by her laughter, her honesty, her newly awakened passion, her trust. The last hit him like a blow. Trust.

And he rewarded that with searing jealousy that she'd done nothing to invite.

He was on the verge of walking away when she looked up and saw him. Her smile became even brighter, punching him in the gut with need and wanting he could not deny. He clenched his jaw when she patted one of the men on the arm before murmuring a goodbye.

She made her way toward him, the skirt swirling around her bare legs.

"You look beat," she said, giving him a hug, smelling clean and fresh.

Her open arms, her easy hug—both were a woman's gesture of welcome to her man. Convulsively, Gray's arms tightened around her until he lifted her off her feet. She felt...so damned good. He forced himself to loosen his hold on her, letting her slide down his body.

"I am," he admitted, letting go of her, mostly to prove to himself that he could.

"I saw the helicopter come."

"The coroner— As soon as the autopsy is finished, Richard's death will be ruled as a suicide." Telling Audrey the coroner was an idiot wouldn't do any good, so Gray kept his mouth shut. Besides, he didn't want to talk about Richard, didn't want her thinking about his death.

She seemed to sense how bothered he was because she ran a hand down his arm in an unspoken gesture of sympathy.

"Hawk called Lambert Enterprises and let them know about Richard," Gray added, pausing until she looked at him. "And I had him call a friend of mine who runs a charter helicopter service in Albuquerque. He'll come get you and take you to Albuquerque. From there, you can catch a flight to Denver."

"Trying to get rid of me, huh?" she said lightly, laying her doubled fist against his arm.

"That's right," he returned, his voice gruff, knowing he had never told a bigger lie in his life. If he had wanted her gone, really wanted her gone, he would have insisted she leave with the coroner and the deputy. But he didn't, so he rationalized she would be safer with him until they figured out where the hell Howard Lambert was.

"When?" she asked, her eyes dark, luminous.

"When what?" For the life of him, he couldn't remember what they had been talking about.

"Your friend—the one with the helicopter," she explained, a trace of impatience filling her voice. "When is he coming?"

"Tomorrow afternoon." Gray half hoped she would tell him she didn't want to leave. Conversely, the sooner she went, the better.

Instead, she surprised him with a total change of subject. "Did the office know where Howard is?"

Gray shook his head, wishing he could reassure her. "He's supposed to be in Arizona, but no one has seen him."

"Except us." Her brow was puckered with worry when

she looked up at him. He longed to ease the furrows away with his thumb. Even more, to ease the cause of her worry.

She stared into space a moment, then glanced back at him. "I wouldn't have made a mistake like that."

"I know."

"So, what's next?" she asked.

"We get some dinner and figure out where we're going to sleep tonight."

She grinned, then poked him in the stomach. "Here I ask a serious question and you—"

"Food is serious." He grabbed her finger.

"And beds?" Her eyes sparkled, and he damned himself for being tempted by her.

"Extremely serious." Especially knowing tonight would be his last night ever with her. If he allowed himself that.

Who the hell was he kidding? He wanted the night with her—wanted a whole bunch of them, in fact. He'd take this night, though, and pay the devil his due later.

"Food is taken care of," she informed him. "Francie invited us for dinner." She looked away, worrying her lower lip between her teeth. "And, Gray?"

"Hmm?"

"I know this probably sounds stupid." She turned to face him, all teasing and all playfulness gone from her expression. "But I'm not real crazy about going back to Puma's Lair."

"Then we won't," he said.

"And I don't want to be away from you," she added. "This afternoon was bad enough."

He took her hand and brought her palm firmly next to his. "Then you won't be."

A slow smile lit her face. "Good."

She'd had the same smile on her face last night in the pool when she had come to him, whispering, "Love me again." He had never glimpsed a dream he wanted more. Never had a dream felt more impossible. For the moment, though, he was tempted to believe. So he took her hand, commanded his conscience to leave him alone for a while and led her across the plaza.

The few homes that surrounded the plaza were mostly traditional adobe structures, as much from economic necessity Gray knew, as from aesthetics. Adobe may be the picturesque building material for Taos or Santa Fe—here it was made by the Indians themselves because material for the adobe bricks was cheap and plentiful. Hawk's house was typical, set a quarter mile away from the pueblo. A huge cottonwood tree grew near the house, its naked limbs stretching into the pale evening sky.

Francie met them at the doorway and ushered them inside with the same warm hospitality she had shown earlier in the day. Audrey was still surprised that not only had Hawk's wife fed her, provided a shower and clean clothes, washed her dirty ones, but had also made her feel welcome.

Hawk was inside, as well. Audrey found the transformation in him so complete she could not imagine he was the same remote man who had greeted her so coldly when she'd arrived at Puma's Lair. Though still taciturn, he demonstrated unexpected gentleness toward Francie. Within minutes after their arrival, they would sit down to a meal of red and green chili, *posóle,* bread and peaches.

"A traditional feast," Gray commented. "What's the occasion?"

"Why, the eclipse, of course," Francie answered, motioning them to sit down. "Can't let those celestial events pass without proper notice, you know."

"Peaches are a traditional food," Audrey said, though she recalled what Mary Maktima had told her about the orchards.

Francie smiled. "At La Huerta, yes. According to my mother, it's a remembrance of a time when the pueblo was known for its orchards."

"It's a heritage we have a chance of reclaiming if Howard Lambert doesn't sell off all the water belonging to the land.'' Hawk met Audrey's gaze across the table.

"I don't…I didn't know anything about that before I got here,'' she said.

"Without water, land is worthless,'' Hawk stated flatly.

"I know.''

"It's theft. Pure and simple.''

"She knows that, too, Hawk,'' Francie said, touching Audrey's shoulder and sitting down next to her.

After they were finished eating, Hawk and Gray went outside and stood talking quietly while Audrey helped Francie clean up the dishes. As they worked, Audrey wondered where she and Gray would sleep tonight. So long as they were together, she didn't care where.

The day had seemed endless after he and Hawk had gone back to the ranch. When she had watched the helicopter arrive, her focus stretched beyond the confines of Puma's Lair. For the first time since Gray had rescued her from her car, she had thought about returning to Denver.

In some ways, she wanted desperately the familiarity of her own home. In others, she didn't want to contemplate leaving here. The thought had left her aching, and now, hours later, things were no better. Gray had made the preliminary arrangements for her to leave. Relief and denial surfaced simultaneously, leaving in their wake a dull ache knotting the pit of her stomach.

She would go home a very different person than she had been when she came here. It seemed more had happened to her during the past two days than in her entire life. Threats, then attempts that had almost been successful. Being connected with a ghost. Finding a man who felt like the other half of her soul.

Audrey stared through the window where Hawk and Gray stood talking. More shadows than substance in the darkness, she imagined Gray…as he had been when she first arrived, his eyes intense, then the softening of those eyes before he had kissed her…his heat and his gentleness when he transformed her from virgin to woman…a man who had become her protector. How could she leave him? She loved him.

The realization left her shaking, even as logic denied love's possibility. She had just met him not even two days ago. How could she love him? She didn't know anything about him.

Except that he had risked his life for her.

Except that he had loved her, giving her more joy than she had dreamed of in any fantasy.

More to the point, the man hadn't promised her love or commitment or anything else. But he had given her something as valuable—he had put his life on the line for her when he could have just as easily left her to fend for herself.

"Hawk has a place where we can spend the night," Gray told Audrey a few minutes later.

"At the ranch?" she questioned.

He shook his head. "No. Here at the pueblo. He built a guest house, which Mary used until recently." Gray smoothed his hand over her hair. "I wouldn't take you there if I didn't think you'd—we'd be safe."

"I trust you," she said.

"I wish I deserved it."

Chapter 12

Gray stopped just inside the doorway to the guest house, blocking Audrey's entrance. For the life of him, he didn't know how he was going to suppress his need for the one thing he wanted most—to make love to her again. Now that they had arrived, he had a choice—do what he wanted or do what was right.

The guest house, separated from Hawk and Francie's home by a line of piñon trees, consisted of one large room and a bathroom. A double bed and a couch were the two primary pieces of furniture.

The bed, large and comfortable looking, was covered with a patchwork quilt and crisp white sheets. Just looking at the damned bed made him hard. Sighing, he turned his gaze on the couch, which was too short for his six-foot frame, and too short, in fact, for Audrey.

She tapped him on the shoulder. "Is there a problem?"

As he stepped aside, she moved past him, setting her bundle of clothes on a table. She slipped out of her shoes, her bare feet drawing his attention to the slender curve of her calves beneath the swirling fabric of her skirt.

He shut the door, then locked it. Just the two of them. Alone.

They had been alone for most of the past two days, but this was different. Intimate. No fear riding them, at least for the moment. Private. Secluded. A haven where he could show her just how special he thought she was. He glanced toward the bed again. He shouldn't touch her. If she gave him even half an invitation, he'd be all over her like warm sunlight. If the lady had a lick of sense, she'd kick him out. Now. But she had said she didn't want to be alone. And he didn't want her to be alone. Ever.

"This is nice," she said, turning around to face him. Her smile widened, and she nodded toward the bed, stretching her arms to him. "In fact, very nice."

He swallowed and caught her hands against his chest when she would have put them about his neck. If he had an ounce of honor, he wouldn't take what she offered.

The smile slowly faded from her face. "Gray?"

He brought her hands to his mouth, kissed one, then the other. "I don't believe in happily ever after, you know."

"I kind of figured that out already."

"I want you."

"I figured that out, too." She took a step forward, closing the gap that separated them, her soft body making contact with his. "And I'm glad. I want you, too." She stood on tiptoe and kissed his jaw, her lips feeling incredibly soft against his skin. "So, what's the problem?"

"I don't want you to get the wrong idea."

"That we might have something going after the sun comes up in the morning, after I go back to Denver?" She tipped her head back. "That kind of wrong idea?"

He gazed into her eyes, noting the fringe of nearly black lashes, the dark brown irises. Beautiful eyes that looked at him with such trust. He had always wanted to be a man worthy of that kind of trust. He wasn't. Not where he kept his darkest secrets hidden.

''Yeah,'' he finally said. Except that he had never wanted anything more than to…court—what an old-fashioned word, but he couldn't think of anything that better fit how he felt about her—wanted to court her until she agreed to spend the rest of her life with him.

He wouldn't, though. She deserved so much. Tying herself to him would surely condemn her to the brand of misery his mother had endured for most her life.

She kissed his cheek. ''Then we'll have to make sure tonight is one to remember, won't we?'' A hint of sadness filled her voice, but just as she had given her trust before without asking questions, she gave it now without any recriminations attached.

He stared down at her a moment longer, his breath catching in his throat when she moistened her lips with the tip of her tongue. Still holding her hands within his, he bent, brushing her nose. He kissed her cheek, inhaling the aroma of her skin, then kissed her other cheek. If tonight was all they had, she was right. It had to last a lifetime.

Letting go of her hands, he cupped his around her face and explored it with gentle, roving kisses. Eyelids, softer even than her cheek. The gentle sweep of her brows. The delicate line of her jaw. The erratic pulse beneath her chin. Her breath became shallow, and he smiled. He was giving her pleasure, and so help him, that was all she would ever know from him. Mind-consuming…endless…pleasure.

''Let me love you,'' he whispered against her ear.

Her hands curled into loose fists and rested against his chest as though she had forgotten to put them around his neck. He lifted her arms over his shoulders, then slid his around her back until they were heartbeat to heartbeat. Still, he didn't kiss her mouth, though he wanted to, though he knew she wanted him to. Tonight was a night to heighten the wanting until there was nothing else. They had time to do this right.

He wasn't much of a dancer, but he began moving to a slow beat, swaying with her. Having her in his arms like this was heaven, and he intended to savor and prolong each moment.

Her arms tightened around him, and she stood on tiptoe, bringing her pelvis into closer contact with his. He shuddered.

"I hear your music," she whispered against his ear. As they danced slowly to a rhythm only they heard, she explored his face the same way he had hers. The brush of her soft lips sensitized his skin. It seemed impossible to be so achingly hard over these innocent kisses, but he was.

Removing the belt to her tunic, he grasped its hem and pulled it over her head. In the dim light of the room, her skin glowed, pale in comparison to his hands. She surprised him by snaking his belt out of his waistband and letting it drop to the floor. Pulling his shirt free, she unbuttoned it and pushed it off his shoulders.

Still rocking to the slow beat they had established, she kneaded the firm muscles of his shoulders through the fabric of his T-shirt while he traced the delicate network of veins between her neck and the top of her lacy bra.

"This isn't fair," she said. "You have more skin to touch than I do."

He grinned. "You can fix that, love."

She smiled back, slid her hands beneath the cotton and pulled the T-shirt over his head. She smoothed her hands over his collarbone, down the length of his arms and up again, then the backs of her hands down his chest.

"I like being petted by you," he said huskily.

"I like petting you," she responded simply, her gaze not leaving his chest.

Her frank admiration of his body and her gentle touches made him feel ten feet tall. Dropping his hands between her breasts, he unfastened the catch, pulled the bra open and slid the straps down her arms. Last night, he hadn't taken the time to look. He did now, using his cupped hands to support the soft weight of her breasts. Beautiful. Her nipples beaded into tight points that he knew would be sensitive and aching for his touch.

With his thumbs, he lightly circled the nipples, watching them grow even tighter.

She imitated his caress, making him realize his own nipples were just as sensitive as hers.

Her breathing grew ragged. "Gray, you're torturing me."

"That's the whole idea," he murmured.

She suddenly pressed herself against him, then sighed as their skin touched. "Yes," she whispered. "This is what I've been remembering all day. How—" she brushed her breasts across his chest "—this feels."

Gray gathered her closer, loving the feel of her breasts pillowed into his chest. Against his neck, her breath felt hot. He pressed her head closer, until it rested on his shoulder.

"You're so beautiful," he whispered against her hair. "So special. I've waited my whole life for someone like you."

In answer, her arms tightened around him.

The need she had been teasing to life curled through him. He wanted her naked. Now. Discovering the waistband was elastic, he simply pushed the skirt off her hips, taking her panties down at the same time. Gracefully, she stepped out of the skirt, her long bare legs brushing against him. He gathered her close again, cherishing the feel of her slender body against him.

Long moments later, she breathed, "This feels so naughty, you being dressed, me bare…"

"More so than me being naked with you?" he asked softly.

She nodded.

"Do you mind?"

Catching the lobe of his ear between her teeth, she said, "I like it. A lot."

His hands roamed down her back to the cleft of her bottom, then down farther, until his fingers curved inward at the top of her thighs. The skin beneath his fingers felt smooth, softer even than her breast. He flexed his hands, and she shuddered.

"Are you okay?" He pulled his head back far enough to look at her.

She opened her eyes, her pupils fully dilated, her lips pink. "I can barely stand," she said. "Am I okay?"

He smiled. "Perfect. That's just the way it's supposed to be."

"You affect me so much. Yet you don't seem…bothered much at all."

"Want to bet?" Boldly, he took her hand and pressed it against him. Hard enough he thought he might burst. At the touch of her palm flattened against him, separated by layers of cloth, he became even harder.

"You're a little overdressed for the occasion," she said, meeting his eyes, a smile lighting her face.

"Then undress me," he commanded.

She unzipped the fly and, as he had, pushed the pants and his shorts over his hips. But he couldn't step out of them because his shoes were still on.

"What's the problem here?" she asked, looking down. The corners of her mouth twitched.

He looked down, too. His pants and shorts were tangled around his legs.

"Oh, Gray." She brought her hand to her face to hide a grin. Then she laughed, a delighted giggle. "We seem to have forgotten something important."

"I'll say," he responded. He was aroused to the point

of pain and she was laughing. Even so, he found himself smiling.

Her giggles were contagious, and in spite of himself, he laughed. A look of surprise chased across her features.

"One of us is supposed to know what we're doing," she teased, poking him in the stomach.

"It had better be you, then," he murmured with a chuckle, "because I can't even think."

"I like your laugh," she said, poking him again, making him step backward toward the bed. "I've never heard you laugh before." She poked him again, and he stumbled.

"Watch it," he said, grabbing her finger.

"I'd love to," she murmured, her gaze dropping inches below his waist.

He stepped back, feeling the bed on the back of his legs. She pushed him, and he sprawled backward. He grabbed at her, and she fell across him, giggling and tickling his ribs. Making love with a woman was serious business, a test of his performance. Which she didn't seem to know, because she blew on his stomach. He laughed harder. Sheer, carefree fun. He hadn't done this while making love...ever. He loved knowing Audrey was secure enough with him to laugh, secure enough to play.

Sliding off the bed, she dropped to her knees, pulled off one shoe, then the other, then each pant leg. He sat up. The sight of her kneeling in front of him, his arousal inches from her face, was totally erotic to him. His laughter slowly died away as new awareness filled him.

She glanced back up at him, deliberately teasing him by ignoring that part of him that most wanted her attention.

"Better?"

"Take the damned socks off," he said, lifting a foot, his smile a contrast to his gruff tone.

"I thought you might have cold feet," she teased.

"I want to make love to you more than I've ever wanted

anything,'' he answered, ignoring her obvious double meaning.

"Then you want what I want." She threw the socks aside, pressing firmly against the bottom of his foot. She ran her palms up the inside of his thighs, cupping him intimately.

Fierce, possessive need swept through him as she explored the contours of his body as no woman ever had. He endured her incendiary caress as long as he could, then lifted her onto the bed and pulled her into his arms. No part of her went untouched, unkissed, from her ankles to the top of her head. He hadn't thought he had anything new to learn about making love. He was wrong. She touched him as though she had found a treasure, exploring his body as thoroughly as he explored hers.

She kneaded the muscles of his shoulders as he caressed the flat plane of her stomach. She tested the pebbly nubs of his nipples as he stroked the inside of her thighs. She arched against him as he took one breast, then the other, into his mouth.

Locked in her arms, he gazed down at her, loving the way she looked. The time for teasing was long past, and he took her mouth in a hungry, carnal kiss. He knew the pressure was too hard, but he couldn't make himself let her go, even a little. She didn't seem to mind, and as she had done last night, became fire in his arms.

Kissing her deeply, he positioned himself between her legs and entered her. Raw sensations of heat, pressure and searing softness exploded the last vestiges of thought from his mind. He needed to slow down, to make it right for her, but he could not. Within his arms, she trembled, soft mewling sounds coming from her throat. His kisses roamed over her face, and he tasted…tears.

That stopped him cold. He lifted his torso away from her body, breathing heavily.

Her eyes flew open, her breasts rising and falling and

shiny with a sheen of perspiration. Tears trickled down the side of her face. "Don't—"

"I'm hurting you," he said. "Oh, Audrey—I'm sorry."

"You're not," she said, pulling his head down so she could kiss him. "Please don't stop."

"Why tears?"

"Because this is…almost too much to bear."

Cautiously, he moved within her, and she smiled.

"Oh, yes."

Wrapping her close, he increased the tempo. Within seconds, her sweet cries began again, her response to passion, he realized, not pain. Scalding possession poured through him, denying any other reality.

She was his.

"Mine," he groaned as his climax pulsed through him.

They made love twice more before crawling under the covers, and Audrey suspected she should be exhausted. She wasn't. She had too much to think about.

Gray lay on his back, his arm curled possessively around her. She rested her head on his shoulder, one of her arms resting on his chest, one of her legs tucked between his. She knew he wasn't sleeping, either, because she had caught him staring at the ceiling.

"You gave me a first tonight," he said.

She twisted slightly so she could look at him.

He glanced down at her and kissed the tip of her nose. "I never laughed while making love."

"I was happy."

"Me, too."

"You don't laugh—or smile—enough." She combed her fingers through the hair on his chest. "I'd give you laughter if I could."

"You already have, love."

Love. There was that endearment again. If she asked him, she would bet he didn't realize he had called her that.

"Why don't you believe in happily ever after?" she whispered, almost afraid to ask the question.

She sensed his withdrawal, though not so much as a muscle moved. Time seemed to stand still; even his breath seemed suspended. Finally, he sighed and turned toward her.

"That's a fair question, I guess." He tucked a strand of her hair behind her ear, tracing the shell with the tip of his finger. "I'm the youngest child in my family."

"That's important?"

He nodded.

A dozen rejoinders came to mind that would lighten the mood slightly, but the tension beneath her hand on his chest kept her silent.

"My two older brothers—"

"No sisters?"

"No. No sisters."

A beat of silence followed.

"Your brothers?" she prompted softly.

"They take after my dad. And I guess I probably do, too."

The tautness in his voice warned her that taking after his dad, though normal for boys, wasn't necessarily something Gray liked. She smoothed her hand across his chest and down his side in long, soothing strokes.

"My mom spent years tiptoeing around him, never knowing when she might set him off. Things would be fine for a while, and then something would happen. An unexpected bill. Her being friendly with a neighbor."

Another long pause followed, and Audrey asked, "And then?"

"He'd beat her senseless."

The stark words painted vivid images in Audrey's mind far more effectively than any detailed description would have. She would bet her life's savings that Gray, as a boy, had hated what his father had done.

"Is your mother—?"

"She died about eighteen months ago."

"I know what that's like—losing your mom," Audrey whispered. "I'm sorry."

Gray raised her hand to his mouth and kissed her fingertips. "Me, too. She was finally happy, and she didn't have much time to enjoy it."

"Your dad?"

"She finally divorced him. He came back one more time. She ended up in the hospital with two broken legs, a concussion and more cuts and abrasions than you could count. She filed charges, and he went to prison." Gray sighed, a huge shudder that racked his body. "He died there."

"And your brothers?" she asked though she had a good idea where this was going.

"One of them is serving time for assaulting his ex-wife. The other one has a restraining order to stay away from his wife."

"And you?"

He glanced suddenly at her, the question seeming to catch him off guard. "What do you mean?"

"You said you take after your father," she said. She understood Gray wanted her to believe he was an abuser like his father, like his brothers. "So, there's an ex-wife or a girlfriend somewhere that you've beaten up."

"No, there isn't."

"Who have you beaten, then?" Audrey asked.

He shook his head. "No one."

"But..." Deliberately, she let her voice trail away.

"My dad would have sworn on a stack of Bibles that he loved my mother. That didn't keep him from hitting her. He hated what he did. And he'd bring her flowers and candy and jewelry, and he'd beat her the next time he got mad."

"What does that have to do with you?" she insisted.

"I vowed I would never be that kind of man—"

"And you aren't."

He shook his head. "I won't risk a woman's safety by allowing myself to get that close."

"No wife?"

He shook his head.

"No long-term lover?"

"I can't risk it," he whispered.

Another long silence passed, and Audrey wondered what it would take to convince him that he wasn't like his brothers or his father. She knew next to nothing about men, but she was sure it was a rare one who would stop in the middle of making love with her because he thought he was hurting her. That didn't strike her as a man likely to beat a woman.

"There's more," he said, looking at her. "Remember me telling you I killed a man?"

"It's not something I would forget."

"I was assigned to a domestic-violence unit in Dallas."

Given his family history, she understood why he was drawn to that area of law enforcement.

"There was one case, a young mom with three little kids, not one of them in school yet. She had filed for divorce, and she'd gotten an injunction against her husband. He didn't just beat her...." His eyes closed, as though shutting out some painful memory. "The oldest little girl was fair game, too."

"And he didn't stay away," Audrey concluded.

"That's right."

"And you shot him."

Gray nodded.

"In the line of duty?"

"Yeah."

Audrey placed her palm against his cheek and gently turned his face toward her. "I knew it had to be something like that."

"Don't be making me into a hero, because I'm not. I wanted that bastard dead."

Audrey nodded. "I can see why you would."

"You don't understand," he said fiercely.

Gently, she said, "Then make me understand."

"I lost my temper. I became judge, jury and executioner."

"Then why aren't you in jail?" she asked.

He rolled onto his back, and she followed, propping her head on her elbow.

"Did the D.A. file charges? Whatever review boards you answer to, did they find you had overstepped your bounds?"

"No. The D.A. thought it was a righteous shoot." Gray looked at her. "And his widow thanked me for saving her life."

"Well," Audrey said. "There you have it. With all that, I can see why you don't believe in happily ever after." She searched his face, realizing how much he had revealed of himself, how deeply he believed he was flawed. She would find a way to show him that he wasn't. For now, it was time to turn his attention away from this. "Thank you for telling me."

"You're welcome," he answered gravely.

She rolled on top of him, straddling his hips with her legs. Bending, she kissed his lips, then rose and smiled at him. Placing the backs of her arms against his chest, she rested her chin in the palms of her hands. "I want to make love again."

He ran his hands down her sides, lingering next to the fullness of her breasts. "I'm an old man. I'm not sure if I can just yet."

"Old? Not you."

"In comparison to you, I'm ancient."

She wriggled closer to him, then smiled as she felt him stir against her thigh.

"Not that ancient," she whispered against his mouth. Then she kissed him, deeply, as he had taught her to do.

Seconds later, she felt his rigid length pushing against her. "Not that ancient at all." And she took him inside her body, showing him as best she could the kind of man she thought he was. Protective. Gentle. Honorable.

At least she now knew what demons haunted him. She would find a way, she vowed, to make him see that anything was possible between the two of them. Even love. Even happily ever after.

Chapter 13

The following morning, Audrey awakened to the sound of the shower running. She stretched, absently smoothing her hand over the sheets, still warm from the imprint of Gray's body, still holding the indefinable scent that was uniquely his. Aware as she was that a future with him was unlikely, she couldn't help but imagine this was the first of many mornings she would awaken, sated from his loving.

Turning on her side, Audrey wrapped an arm around Gray's pillow and listened to the shower. Last night, he had caressed her and explored her body in ways she had heard about but never imagined for herself. And he had encouraged her to explore him in the same way. She had never imagined doing those things, either. But she had, and she loved it.

The idea of his sharing such intimacies with any other woman sent searing jealousy through her. Skilled or not, experienced or not, he shared with her as though their experiences were a first for him. That she might have shown him something new was both a thrill and a puzzle to her.

How could she have given him anything he hadn't ha
before? she wondered.

She had not gotten her fill of him; it would take year
for that. She was determined that even if she returned t
Denver today, this would not be her last day with Gray
During the night, she had rested in his arms, frightened tha
if she didn't fight for this chance at love, she might neve
have another. Sure, she had led a sheltered life, both b
choice and necessity. But she had dated, and not a singl
man had ever attracted her the way Gray did.

She wanted to believe he was just as drawn to her. Sh
had paid attention to the way his body responded to he
and he had shown her in uncountable ways that he wa
Even the things he said were revealing, despite his assertic
he didn't believe in happy endings. His husky declaratio
would stay with her the rest of her life. *I've waited m
whole life for someone like you.*

His concern and care for her while they made love–
those weren't the actions of a cruel or careless man. Wit
her, he smiled, and she had noticed he didn't smile wit
anyone else. He was protective of her from the very begin
ning. For a man determined to keep his distance, he hadn
kept any from her. Not from the moment he had put h
hand over her mouth and hidden her from Richard's dis
covery.

Gray would never harm her.

She believed it, knew it as certainly as she knew her ow
name.

The trick was to make him believe that. She had see
his iron control over his emotions, and she wondered wha
it would take to overwhelm that control, to make him angr
enough to be violent. She would bet all she had that goad
ing him into a rage so violent he would hit a woman wa
simply not possible.

Audrey couldn't imagine what his life must be like car
rying around a fear so huge, so consuming. She understoo

she believed he was capable of being an abusive man like his father and his brothers. Somehow she would find a way to prove to Gray that he was not.

The shower shut off, and she sat up in bed, gathering the sheet over her breasts. He was whistling between his teeth, and she wondered if that was his usual habit.

A scant minute later, the bathroom door opened, permeating the air with the fresh scent of soap. He stepped through the doorway, dressed in the pants he had been wearing last night, his chest bare, his hair towel-dried and looking shades darker than it did when the sun shone on it.

"Hi," he said, the corner of his mouth lifting. The smile went no further. No crinkling of his eyes. No revealing of the dimple in his cheek.

Even though she had anticipated his withdrawal, the face of it disappointed her.

"Hi, yourself," she said, holding out her arms.

He watched her an instant, almost as though he was reluctant to touch her. Then he came to the bed, allowed a quick hug and kissed her cheek.

"Did you sleep well?" he asked, stepping away, avoiding her eyes.

"What sleep was that?" she returned with a smile. They hadn't slept more than a few hours, but she felt good. Better, in fact, than she could ever remember. For the first time in months, she realized, she had woken up the past two mornings with something—*someone*—other than her mother on her mind.

The platitude was true, Audrey thought. Time did heal. The grief that had been so overwhelming even a month ago was much less pronounced today. Memories of better times surfaced first instead of the months of illness. Snippets of her mother's values seeped through the loss, values this morning that related to marriage and love.

Though Audrey's father had died when she was young,

her mother had made it clear that marriage and living a fu
life with a man were the normal state of things. If a woma
was lucky, she would have a grand love that would last h
a lifetime. And if she wasn't that lucky, she had to cheris
the time she had without bitterness. Audrey knew she ha
found the grand love her mother had talked about, and sh
wanted a lifetime with Gray.

Instead of returning her teasing remark in kind, he busie
himself with putting change in his pant pocket. Though sh
had anticipated his withdrawal, she didn't like it, and sh
didn't intend to make it easy for him. She climbed out
bed and moved toward him.

"Hungry?" He put on his shirt, his back still to her.

"Famished," she answered. Coming up behind him, sh
put her arms around him. "Starved, in fact." She rubbe
her cheek against the crisp fabric of his shirt, wishing
were his skin.

Fragments of sensation came back to her. The hard rop
of muscle in his arms and shoulders. The pressure of h
palm flattened against her spine. The surprising softness
the hair covering his chest and belly. The heat of his brea
between her breasts. The heat and strength of his erectio
covered with the smoothest, softest skin she had ev
touched. The feel of his cheek against the inside of h
thigh.

Her arms tightened around him. She had never thoug
of herself as so intensely physical. She was, though, an
she wanted to repeat everything they had done during th
night.

He stiffened and clamped a hand over one of hers, pu
ting pressure against the bruises the Indian woman had le
on her hand. When Audrey flinched, his grip instantl
eased. In tune with her, he realized the source of her di
comfort. Lightly, he ran a finger over the back of her han

It was a small gesture, but another that confirmed h

could never hurt her. To do so, she suspected, would be hurting himself.

"Audrey." Gently, he manacled one of her wrists and loosened her hold on his waist, then turned around to face her. Whatever he had been intending to say was lost when his gaze fastened on her breasts. Her nipples tightened as though caressed by his hands or tongue instead of merely subjected to his gaze.

His scrutiny of her nude body fell to her feet and swept upward...slowly...as though he intended to memorize each feature. She gloried in the way he looked at her, as though her body was something to worship. The ache in her intensified, an ache he was a master at teasing to unbearable proportions before easing.

His eyes, when they met hers, belonged to a man being tortured.

In that instant, she knew she could not—would not—turn her back on him, no matter how flawed he felt himself to be. Counting up the hours she had spent with him, she decided they made up weeks of dating under ordinary circumstances. And those ordinary circumstances would have never shown her the true mettle of the man.

She smiled sadly. "Is what you're feeling so very bad?"

"You've no idea."

"I can ease what's ailing you," she whispered, tracing her index finger down the center of his chest where the shirt hung open. His breath sucked in when she reached the waistband of his pants.

"No doubt," he answered in a hoarse whisper.

"Maybe you should give in to it." She flattened her palm against his zipper, reassured to find him aroused.

He shook his head, taking her errant hand in his and kissing the backs of her fingers. Pulling her into his arms, he held her tight. The unbuttoned shirt allowed her access to his bare skin, and she returned his fierce hug, loving the way his hair-dusted chest felt against her. This was, she remembered with a thrill that chased through her stomach, how their lovemaking had begun last night. She nuzzled his neck, encouraging him to lower his head and kiss her deeply. He did not.

He let go of her, except for her hands, which he held in both of his as though he was afraid to let her touch him. His eyes searched hers once more. "Go take your shower, and I'll rustle up some breakfast."

He walked out of the guest house without a backward glance. She stared at the closed door, feeling empty, bereft, her skin cold after caressing his heat.

The surprising urge to throw things at him swept through her. Never had she met a more stubborn man. Unless she did something drastic, he'd finish shoring up the wall he had put between them. He was on the verge of shoving her out of his life. She knew it without a single doubt.

He had warned her not to get any wrong ideas, she thought, her frustration tinged with anger. And she had lots of them, wrong or right. Ideas and hopes and plans and dreams that would be nothing more than dust if she believed what he wanted her to believe—he was a man who could not be trusted.

Maybe she gave her trust too easily, but he was too stingy with his own. She trusted him not to hit her, and she could think of only one way to prove that. Fight with him. Show him that even when he was mad at her, he wouldn't hit her.

If she was going to pick an argument with him, it couldn't be something benign, something inconsequential. To prove to him he would not hurt her, she would have to attack the heart of his belief about himself—that he was flawed, that he was violent. Whatever she decided to do, she had to do it soon. This morning.

She showered, dressed in her jeans, red sleeveless sweater and calico shirt, and pulled her hair into a French braid that fell down her back. Gray still hadn't returned, so she went to the door and opened it.

The morning outside was glorious, the kind she had been expecting for a springtime in New Mexico, the kind that had been absent her first morning here. Birds chirped in a nearby tree. The sky was dotted with a couple of fluffy clouds, and the sun felt warm. Audrey stepped into the sunshine, wishing her mood matched the day.

She prided herself on being direct, but she hated conflict. She hadn't deliberately picked a fight with anyone in years. And she had no idea how to start an argument with Gray. He was the last person she wanted to fight with. But she had to. How? Over what?

Praying for inspiration, Audrey's gaze focused on the pueblo. Before she saw it yesterday, she had been expecting it to be like the one outside Taos. It was not. The multistory adobe structures were smaller, and even from a distance, it was clear no one lived in the pueblo itself. The buildings had been condemned several years ago, Mary had informed her yesterday. Its abandonment seemed all the more forlorn this morning as Audrey remembered how alive the plaza had been the day before.

Men, women and children, wearing off-white tunics with the brilliant patchwork accents, had filled the plaza. At the time, the pueblo had seemed to Audrey like a majestic monarch, pleased with the dances and songs and children learning their heritage. This morning the crumbling adobe and the broken roof supports were all too apparent.

A moment later, Gray came around the line of piñon trees, carrying a basket and a blanket. Watching him stride toward her, Audrey was sure she had never seen a finer-looking man anywhere, nor had she ever known a better man. The lonely life he had condemned himself to hardened her resolve. He deserved more than he gave himself credit for.

"You look all lost in thought," he said as he approached

her. A mouthwatering aroma of fresh bread rose from the basket swinging from his hand.

"I was just thinking it's going to be hard to leave here. What's in the basket? It smells wonderful."

"Fry bread and honey. Fresh fruit. Coffee." Sliding the blanket under his arm, he offered her his free hand. "There's a real pretty place over on the other side of the pueblo where we can eat."

Surprised and pleased, Audrey took his hand, which closed warmly around hers. She had expected him to be as aloof as he had when he left the guest house. Maybe the darned man would come to his senses and realize they shared something rare and special. Hope filled her with buoyancy, and she raised her eyes to the sky. It was a glorious morning.

The place he took her to was a low stone wall that surrounded one edge of the pueblo. Gray told her there once had been a tower at the corner, a place for a sentinel to keep a lookout.

He spread the blanket on a knoll just beyond the wall, and Audrey looked out over the land knowing what she saw wasn't so very different than what a sentinel might have seen. No buildings marred the landscape. The rumpled contours of the valley gave way to a mesa, the one where she and Gray had hidden, she realized. Above the mesa were taller ridges with deep canyons, and finally the rugged peaks of the mountains.

They dug into breakfast, talking of inconsequential things. Within minutes, Audrey realized her hope had been premature. His silences became longer, and when he spoke to her, it was about some anecdote about the pueblo or some facet of the surrounding geography. Interesting, sure. And she appreciated his knowledge, even as she hated seeing him withdraw from her. Instead of looking at her, he focused his attention more on the landscape.

"Seeing all this makes me wonder why anyone lives in

the city,'' she murmured, wondering how she would ever find an opening to argue with him if they stayed with bland topics like the weather, like the scenery.

"You'd give up living in Denver?'' he asked. "Away from the hustle and bustle?'' The corner of his mouth quirked up. "The shopping?''

She chuckled. "I don't like shopping all that much. And yeah, to have a slower pace of life. I'd like that.''

"I would have thought you loved living in the city, going to concerts, eating at fine restaurants.''

"Coping with rush-hour traffic and eating microwave dinners at home is more like it.'' Her smile faded as she realized he had given her an opening. Not a very good one, admittedly, but life-style was a personal choice with the potential for conflict. "Did you like living in Dallas?'' she asked, knowing this wasn't the question she had wanted to ask, knowing she had sidestepped the opportunity.

"I came to hate it,'' he said, his gaze on the distant mountains. "That's why I came here. For the solitude.''

Another opening. A better opening.

Carefully, Audrey wiped her hands on the napkin. "Then maybe you came for all the wrong reasons,'' she said, forcing a harsh note into her voice that contradicted what she really felt. She understood his need for solitude; she wished for the same during the last, painful months of her mother's life.

"After the circus my hearing had been, solitude was exactly what I needed,'' he said as though he hadn't noticed the argumentative tone in her voice.

"Or maybe you were running from yourself.'' Deliberately, she made her voice sharper.

He arched an eyebrow and slowly dragged his gaze from the scenery to look at her. His eyes were intense, completely focused on her. She resisted the urge to squirm or look away.

"Maybe,'' he acknowledged. "Funny thing how that

works, though. Hell of a thing—trying to run away from yourself.''

His even tone fueled her frustration.

''Maybe you're running from commitments. A full life.''

''I like my life.''

''Do you?'' Genuine curiosity prompted her question, overriding her intentions, erasing her belligerent tone. She covered his hand. ''You seem so lonely to me.''

''I'm not.''

''Will you be after I leave?''

He swallowed, pulled his hand away, and looked away from her. ''I already told you—''

''Gray, let's get married.'' She hadn't intended to say that, but those incautious words were the truth. She couldn't—wouldn't—take them back.

His jaw clenched, but he didn't look at her. The minute that followed was the longest in her life.

''You know that's not possible,'' he finally said, his attention still directed at the horizon.

''I don't know any such thing.'' She touched his cheek. ''I know that I love you. I know that you're the finest man I've—''

''Stop!'' He surged to his feet and towered over her, his hands resting on his hips. ''You don't know what you're saying.''

''Yes, I do.'' She stood, tilting her chin and meeting his gaze straight on. She had surprised herself by asking him to get married. Surprise or not, marriage was exactly what she wanted. ''I'm in love with you.''

He shook his head, raising his gaze to the sky. ''That's the stupidest thing I've ever heard. Do you know what kind of man I am?''

''Yes!''

''Do you know how long we've known each other?''

''Three days. So what?''

''So, I'm not going to let you throw your life away like

that.'' He raked a hand through his hair, held his hand halfway out to her, then curled it into a fist that he rested against his hip, the gesture revealing his frustration more clearly than words.

''It's my life to throw away if I want.'' She took a step toward him. ''You seem to think I don't know my own mind.'' She stabbed the middle of his chest with her finger. ''Well, I do.''

''You can't be in love with me.''

''I am.''

''It's just the situation. You're grateful, that's all. I happened to be in the right place at the right time to save your life.''

''You're right. I am thankful you saved my life. But I know the difference between love and gratitude. What's going on with me is not the issue here.''

His Adam's apple bobbed. ''At least you got that right. You can't trust me.''

''Hah! I trusted you with my virginity. I trusted you with my life. And I would again in a heartbeat.'' Remembering why she had started all this in the first place, she stabbed at his chest again. ''What you're really saying is that you can't trust yourself not to hit me.''

A look of sheer anguish crossed over his features. ''You don't want to risk that, love—Audrey.''

Love. There it was again. Did he even realize what he'd called her?

''Want to bet?'' She took another step toward him, and he backed up. At any other time, she might have found his retreat funny. Instead, she wanted to hit him for not standing his ground.

He lifted his hands, palms toward her, and backed up another step.

''If you're such an abusive man, we might as well find out right now.'' She doubled her own hand into a fist and punched him in the stomach—a hard wall of unyielding muscle. He sidestepped away from her. She followed.

"Don't you think?"

She hit him again, this time clipping his chin.

He backed up again. "Audrey, don't do this."

"And don't you run from me," she commanded, her own anger suddenly at the surface, her control eroding. "Show me what a tough guy you are." She lifted her own chin and pointed at it. "Go ahead. Hit me."

"I can't." His hands fell loosely to his sides.

"Sure, you can," she taunted, her voice shaking. "You're the man who takes after his daddy. Remember? You told me you're just like him. Just like your brothers." She swung at him again, accompanied by a cry of frustration.

Gray caught her fist, kissed it, then drew it close to his chest. "I know what you're trying to do." Wrapping an arm around her and pressing a kiss against her temple, he added, "And it's admirable. But it's not going to work."

"See," she sniffed, trembling as she leaned against him, tears burning at her eyes. "I knew you couldn't hit me."

"But I don't know that. I may never know that."

"I have enough trust for both of us," she said.

He tipped her chin toward him, and she gazed into his eyes. Beautiful, dark hazel eyes, flecked with all the colors of the desert. "What you're feeling is just a reaction from making love for the first time."

She shook her head, and opened her mouth to speak. He pressed his fingers against her lips.

"I'm flattered you asked me to marry you. Someday you'll be glad I turned you down."

She wrenched from his grasp, her anger back at the surface. "You keep talking like I just fell off the turnip truck. Being a virgin didn't make me stupid. I know the difference between hormones and my own mind. I'm not some charity case so hard up I asked the first guy who took me to bed to marry me. And you're not hard up, either. You're a good man, Gray.''

He snorted.

"You are," she insisted. "The best man I've ever known. Look me in the eye and tell me that we don't have something pretty special."

Folding his arms over his chest, he said, "We do. There's no future in what we have, but you're right. It's damned good."

"I knew it," she responded, a niggle of hope worming through her fear. "The things you said to me while we were making love—"

"Should be ignored in the cold light of day," he said, his gaze on the ground in front of his feet. "A man says...things...in the heat of the moment."

"Do you know what you call me?" she asked, then added without waiting for his answer, "Love."

His lips compressed, and a muscle at the corner of his mouth twitched, but he didn't look at her.

"Not honey or darling or babe. Love. So tell me, is that the usual endearment for the women you take to bed?"

He turned his hands toward her in a gesture of supplication. For a moment, Audrey thought he would look at her, then stretch his arms toward her. An endless moment passed while she watched his struggle chase through the expressions on his face.

His jaw hardened, and he jammed his hands in the pockets of his chinos. "Sometimes."

"You've told other women you've waited your whole life for them?" When he didn't answer, she added, "You said I was yours, Gray."

"For that moment, you were." His gaze touched her briefly.

"And you've said the same thing to other women?"

The call of a meadowlark seemed no less loud than the pounding of her own heart while she waited for his answer.

"I've said a lot of things to women to get what I wanted," he finally said, a derisive smile curving his lips.

She remembered all the times she had wanted him to smile, and never had she imagined he possessed one so cold, so mocking.

"I'm exactly the kind of guy your mother should have warned you about."

"Did you tell other women they were yours?" she demanded, positive he was saying what he thought would drive her away, hoping he'd slip and confess he loved her.

"Probably."

Since he again answered without looking at her, she stepped in front of him so he had no choice but to meet her gaze.

"And I think you're lying." Throwing the last of her pride to the wind, she said, "Look me in the eye, Gray, and tell me you don't love me."

"I don't love you," he said immediately, his voice gravelly, his gaze intent on her. His body language, his expression, his voice conveyed the truth of his statement.

She felt herself shatter into a million tiny shards.

Chapter 14

He didn't love her. She had been so sure he did. No hesitations, no looking away as he had when she thought he was deceiving her.

Hot tears filled her eyes, and when he took a step toward her, she put her hand up, backing away from him. "My tears, my choices," she said, putting a hand flat against her breast.

He didn't love her. She had gambled...and lost.

She turned away from him and bent her head, admitting in her heart of hearts that she hadn't expected this outcome. He wouldn't hit her—that much she had proved, even if she hadn't convinced him.

Maybe in time, he would trust himself enough to leave his solitude. Maybe in time, he would love...someone else.

Silent sobs shook her shoulders, and she wrapped her arms around herself. She wanted to be that someone. Oh, God, how she had wanted it.

"I never meant to hurt you," he whispered.

His big hands cupped her shoulders, and she wrenched away from his grasp.

He sucked in a breath and stepped away from her.

She squeezed her eyes shut, tears seeping from beneath the lids. There was no law that said when you loved someone they had to love you back. She recalled reading that somewhere, sometime. A stupid thing to remember just now.

"I think…" Her voice choked, and she cleared her throat. "I'm ready to go home."

"Rafe promised me he'd be here this afternoon."

This afternoon, she thought, seemed an eternity from now. "The sooner the better."

They stood there for a long time. Numbness stole over her, but not enough to block out the consuming pain that constricted her heart. Her head pounded, and her feet and hands felt cold, discomforts that she noticed from within a fog. Her only goals were to make it through the day without making any more of a fool of herself than she already had; to hold on until she was safe in her own house; to keep the broken pieces of herself together until she got home.

Gray repacked the picnic basket and folded the blanket.

"I'll call Rafe from the ranch if the phone is working again," Gray said. "See if he can't be here sooner."

"Fine."

"Audrey?" He paused until she met his gaze. "If he's delayed, we can go on horseback to get to town. I'll make sure you're on your way home today. Just like you want."

She nodded, not trusting her voice or her composure.

"Do you want to go with me back to the ranch?" he asked. "The closest phone is there."

She caught his glance, then looked away. She supposed there was something she ought to be doing there, but she had no idea what. More to the point, she was very afraid that she might beg him to love her…if only in body. Eventually, she shook her head.

"Well, then." He thrust his hands into his pockets. "Nobody's seen Lambert."

His statement gave her a jolt; she had forgotten that her boss had been trying to kill her. "Then I'm safe, at least for the moment."

Gray sighed.

"Go on with you," she said. "I'll be just fine." The command was sheer bravado. She was a long way from fine. Light years, in fact.

He gave her another of his long, thorough gazes. She straightened beneath his scrutiny, determined that he wouldn't see how much she was hurting. Finally, he walked away without a backward glance, his long strides carrying him swiftly away from her. She watched until he was out of sight, stricken with the conviction that she might never again see him.

For as long as he lived, Audrey would haunt him, Gray thought as he walked away from Francie's house. So much had happened over the past couple of days. Things that should be more vivid than one woman's grieving expression. Seeing Audrey's car blown up. Having a close encounter with a hundred-year-old ghost. Being confronted with his cousin's murder. None of those compared with Audrey's eyes the moment he told her he didn't love her.

Gray saddled his horse and rode it out of the corral at a canter. D.J. seemed anxious for a run, and a hard one suited his mood just fine. He galloped across the valley as though demons chased him.

In his mind, they did.

The last thing he had ever wanted to do was hurt her.

Then you should have stayed away from her, his conscience taunted. You knew exactly what would happen if you got involved. She's not for you.

However true, no one had ever felt more right to him. Her openness drew him as nothing else ever had until she gave him her trust. She believed in him, dared him to confront the demons that now chased him across the empty plain.

She had seemed unaware that he could have injured her with a well-placed blow, seemed oblivious that he outweighed her by close to a hundred pounds and that her strength was no match for his.

But she got to you.

And she had. With nothing more than her courage and her honesty and her trust.

His eyes burned—surely because of the air rushing past, surely nothing more—as he relived the moment he told her he didn't love her. He couldn't have hurt her any more cruelly if he had taken a strap to her.

She believed in him, and her faith tempted him more strongly than anything ever had. But, dear God, if he could hurt her this much simply by trying to push her from his life, what would he be capable of if he did what she wanted—marry her.

They would have moments like last night when they laughed together. But it couldn't last. He had seen the cycle too many times to delude himself. He'd do anything to be close to her, to make her love him. And then he'd do anything to make sure she was his woman, including treating her the way his father had treated his mother.

Gray shook his head, tortured at the idea of Audrey bloodied and bruised at his hand. His eyes focused on his fist. For the life of him, he couldn't imagine hitting her. Yet he had seen the monster in his father, had seen it in his two brothers. He was his father's son. And Gray knew. The monster was there inside him, waiting for its release.

He shook with the knowledge. Pictures exploded in his mind, ancient, old and new all mixed together in his head. A terrified young boy who hid in a closet to avoid his father's unpredictable rages, a boy who later ran away instead of staying to protect his mother. The shame of it blossomed through his chest, choking him. A man who took another man's life and was glad for the death. A man stabbed with jealousy when Audrey laughed with another man. A man who would surely die if he harmed her in any way at all.

The sooner he sent her on her way, the better. End of story.

When he arrived at the hacienda, it seemed to have more creaks, groans and wispy drafts than he'd ever noticed before. Every sound made him jump. Fortunately, the phone was working again. His friend Rafe was on his way, but according to their original plan. He wouldn't be here for hours.

When Gray finished his call, he went back to the front of the lodge, restless and edgy, and half tempted to go back to see Audrey. A better use of his time, far better, would be to ride back into the valley and track down Howard Lambert.

He had just mounted his horse when movement behind him caught his eyes. Hawk's battered pickup racing toward him. The driver honked the horn.

The pickup came alongside him. Inside was José Romero, one of the teenagers from the pueblo who helped Hawk with his herd of horses.

"There's been a stampede," José said through the open window. "Hawk asked me to come get you. He needs all the help he can get."

"What happened?" Gray asked.

José waved in the direction of the corral across the valley. "I don't know, but they're plenty spooked."

"I'm on my way."

A relieved smile flashed across José's face, and he gave a thumbs-up before whirling the pickup around and speeding back in the direction he came from.

Gray reined his horse away from the road, and headed

directly across the valley. He'd help Hawk round up his herd, and then he'd go find Lambert.

Both would keep him away from Audrey…and temptation…until she was gone.

Audrey hoped against hope that Gray would come back. But he'd gone to the corral, saddled his horse and ridden away without a backward glance. She watched until he disappeared from view.

Finally, she turned back toward the guest house. Inside, the tumble of sheets on the unmade bed reminded her of what she had shared with Gray. Firming her chin, she stripped the sheets from the bed. Just when she thought she might get through it, she inhaled his aroma. Burying her face in the bedcovers, she let the cries come, sobs so huge they brought her to her knees.

She rocked back and forth, the pain as huge as any she had ever borne.

"Audrey?"

At the sound of Francie's voice, she snapped her head up.

Francie stood in the doorway. "What's happened? Are you hurt?"

Audrey wiped at her tears with the backs of her hands, struggling to find a modicum of composure.

The other woman came the rest of the way into the room. "When I saw Gray heading toward the ranch alone, I was afraid something had happened." Francie lifted a brow. "Did you two argue?"

"Not exactly."

"And not anything you're going to confess to a brandnew friend, either." Francie touched her shoulder. "C'mon. I bet you could use a cup of coffee or tea." She smiled when Audrey met her gaze. "Or a Bloody Mary." She clapped a hand over her heart. "And I promise not to pry…too much."

"A woman of her word." Audrey's tone was dry.

"Exactly. If I can make my patients distracted enough to keep them from knowing I'm drawing blood, then I ought to be able to get your mind away from Gray Murdoch for three or four seconds. Unless you'd like to see a couple of his carvings."

"I'd like that," she responded. "These patients of yours, where are they?"

"There's a clinic back in town where I work part-time." She smiled. "A welcome change from an ER, I can tell you."

Audrey nodded, remembering that Gray had told her Francie worked at the clinic.

She followed Francie out of the guest house, noticing the sunny day wouldn't be with them much longer. Already, clouds had moved far across the sky, and in the distance, it looked as though it was already raining.

"Mud season," Francie said, following the line of Audrey's gaze. "Can't wait for it to end."

"Why are you being so nice to me?" Audrey found herself asking. "I'm not on your husband's list of favorite people."

"Sometimes I agree with my husband. Sometimes I don't," she said cheerfully. "After twenty-seven years of marriage, he's kinda used to it."

"What about your mother?"

"Let's just say that I trust Gray's judgment. He thinks you're okay." Francie opened the door to her house and waited for Audrey to precede her inside. "Besides, if my mother is to be believed, the eclipse the other night was an omen and all our troubles are going to be over."

She seemed to realize that Audrey wouldn't have anything to add, so she continued, pulling a couple of mugs out of the cupboard as she talked. "Of course, after everything else that's happened in the last couple of days, ghosts and broken curses might be a little tame."

Because asking was a way to numb her pain, Audrey asked, "The Indian woman who's chased—that ghost?"

Francie nodded. "My mother is convinced that she—the ghost—is her grandmother."

"That's possible?"

Francie shrugged. "Who knows?"

Audrey shook her head, again thinking she had somehow stumbled into an alternate universe. The sooner she returned to her ordinary, albeit boring, life, the better. She took a sip of coffee from the mug Francie handed her, absently playing with the familiar weight of the bracelets on her arm.

"Be right back." Francie left the kitchen, talking over her shoulder. She came back a couple of moments later holding several wood carvings. One was of a bird of prey, a hawk or eagle, the carving smooth without a hint of feathers, only the powerful outline of the bird. The second was a woman, sitting with her knees against her chest, her head bowed. Both were stunning pieces.

"These are amazing," Audrey whispered, caressing the bird, then picking up the woman. From any direction, her expression was impossible to discern, but the figure seemed to convey a deep sadness. Or maybe it was her own state of mind, she decided.

"How did you know about the ghost?" Francie asked, sitting down across from her.

Unwilling to admit she had seen her—touched her—Audrey glanced down at the bruises on her hand. "Gray told me," she said, carefully setting the figure on the table. Him again. She sighed and glanced at Francie, deciding Mary's fixation on a ghost was a much easier topic than Gray. "Why does your mother think she's the ghost's...granddaughter?"

"My grandmother was found out there in the middle of the valley when she was only a few weeks old. Around her neck was a necklace with a medallion—the symbol of Kokopelli, like your bracelet. The necklace was supposedly a wedding gift from a man of the people when he married a Comanche woman—the one who became the ghost. The legend says she was captured on her way to Santa Fe, where she was supposed to have delivered a deed that would have returned all this property to the people.

"And when my mother was a young girl, she had a spirit dream that led her to a sheltered box canyon up on the mesa. There's a protected overhang there that has petroglyphs. One of them is in the symbol of Kokopelli."

Audrey glanced down at the bracelets. On one, the abstract symbol of the buffalo looked as it always had. The other bracelet, she didn't recognize. Instead of the familiar stylized tree rising from a lake, a hunchbacked man playing a flute was etched into the silver.

A chill crawled down her spine. Except for the unfamiliar engraving, the bracelet looked as it always had.

"What is it?" Francie asked. "You look as though you've seen a ghost." Then, laughing at her own joke, she chuckled.

"My bracelet," Audrey whispered. She stared at the engraving, then shook her head. She'd worn this jewelry every day since her mother's death. She knew what it looked like...and it *wasn't* this. She knew what it felt like...and it *was* this.

"What?" Francie asked, her voice growing serious.

Audrey swallowed, knowing she would sound crazy. "My bracelet isn't supposed to have this figure on it...Kokopelli." She met Francie's eyes. "I swear to you, until yesterday, it had another symbol on it. Are you familiar with Sipofene?"

Francie nodded. "It's the name of the underworld where the people lived before this one was made."

Audrey nodded. "My bracelet used to have an etching of a lake with a tree, a symbol of the journey from Sipofene—not this hunchbacked figure."

"Used to have?"

She nodded, then whispered. "We saw the ghost. Up there on the mesa in one of the hidden canyons."

"What happened?"

Audrey closed her eyes, remembering the moment the Indian woman had appeared out of the mist at the height of the eclipse. And she told Francie almost all of it. The woman's long, intense labor. How she'd simply vanished as the eclipse ended. How she'd lost the bracelet in the pool and how they had later found it.

"You've got to tell this to my mother," Francie said.

Audrey shook her head.

"Don't you see? I know she'll believe this is the sign she's been looking for all her life."

"Why is it so important?"

"It's her heritage—mine, too. But she's also convinced my great-grandmother's disappearance—and the ghost's haunting—is the reason our pueblo doesn't really belong to us, not legally, not in the government's eyes. It's one more step to help her solve that mystery."

"You don't think I'm crazy?" Audrey asked.

Francie grinned. "I definitely don't think you're crazy. Stranger things have happened."

Audrey didn't want to imagine what those things might be.

"Where did you get the bracelets?" Francie asked.

"My mother bought them for me," she answered, remembering vividly the day in Santa Fe they had bought them from an old woman with a booth in the plaza. Audrey touched the bracelets. "It was the last trip we took before she became too ill to travel."

"Good memories, then."

"The best.

"Anything special about Kokopelli?" Audrey asked.

Francie laughed. "The hunchback of the pueblos, and to all accounts, a Don Juan. He was a peddler or storyteller, depending on which legends you believe. But always associated with fertility.''

''Kokopelli. Don Juan,'' Audrey muttered. The connections in the story to all that had happened the past few days were too close to be believed, including the name of Gray's horse.

''We've got to go see my mother.'' Francie stood. ''C'mon. It's a nice day—or at least it is until it rains, which it surely will.''

Audrey followed Francie out of the house. Outside, she paused, again glancing at the bracelet, hoping she'd see the old symbols etched in the silver instead of Kokopelli. She didn't.

The rumble of an approaching vehicle made her look up. A Jeep came around the corner at the front of the house. In the driver's seat sat Howard Lambert.

''No,'' Audrey murmured. She whirled around. The piñon trees were too sparse to hide within, even if he hadn't seen them. And the broad valley didn't provide any place to hide at all.

''Small world,'' Francie said. ''Hawk has been going nuts the last two days trying to get hold of him.''

Audrey glanced around. There was no place to hide.

He waved, shut off the engine. ''Francie,'' he called. ''How the hell are you?''

He vaulted out of the vehicle instead of using a door and strode toward them, his rapid footsteps echoing exactly the sudden frantic beating of Audrey's heart.

''I've been looking all over the place for that reprobate husband of yours.''

''Hawk wants to see you, too,'' she said.

Unwillingly, Audrey turned around to face her boss. He looked as he always did—waxed mustache, fringed jacket and an air of total self-confidence. A demanding employer. A man she had considered a friend. A man who tried to kill her. She knew the last as surely as she breathed.

He caught her glance. In a fleeting instant, surprise and horror flickered across his face. He smiled hugely and came toward her. "Audrey. My God, I didn't expect to see you."

"I can imagine."

"Are you all right?" He took both of her hands within his, then hugged her. Unable to bear his touch or the duplicity of his smile, she stepped away from him.

"My Lord, girl, you look like death warmed over," he said. "But of course you do. You've been through hell the last couple of days. I bet you're anxious to blow this place."

He didn't seem to notice her lack of response at all, because he turned to Francie. "You wouldn't happen to have some more coffee?"

"Of course," she said, turning back toward the house.

"Actually, we were just on our way to Mary's house," Audrey said, tugging Francie's sleeve, urging her back down the walk.

"I wouldn't want to detain you," he said in a tone that indicated otherwise.

"It's no problem."

Francie gave Audrey a puzzled glance and headed back into the house. Howard made a sweeping gesture, removing his hat in the process.

"After you," he said.

Inside, Audrey followed Francie into the kitchen, determined to warn her. Before she could utter a single word, Howard followed her into the room and sat down on one of the chairs, setting his hat on the table.

"I saw your friend riding toward the ranch," he said. "He wants you to meet him there."

Audrey shook her head. "I'm positive he doesn't want to see me at all."

"Really?" Howard shrugged. "He said he did." He said *did* with such an exaggerated drawl that the word almost sounded like *dead*. Audrey shivered.

"How do you take your coffee?" Francie asked.

"You're taking off to see your mother," Howard began. "Anything special going on?"

"Audrey—"

"No," Audrey interrupted. "Just morning coffee. We promised." She made a point of glancing at her watch. "And we really should be going."

"Even though your friend wants you to meet him at the ranch?"

"He knows where to find me," she answered.

Howard took a long swallow of his coffee, then stood up. "I think you've imposed on Francie long enough, Audrey. It's time to go. The sooner we go to the ranch, the sooner we can go back to Denver."

"It's okay," Francie interjected. "We don't have to go visit Mother."

Howard beamed. "See? Even Francie agrees."

Audrey met Howard's gaze, positive she'd be signing her own death warrant if she left with him.

He leaned closer, looking solicitous and concerned, and he whispered in her ear, "If you don't come right now, Francie's going to get hurt. Understand?"

Shaking, Audrey nodded and stepped away from him. Gray hadn't said so specifically, but she was sure he thought Howard had killed Richard. And he certainly had tried to kill her. She swallowed hard, the realization flooding through her that he might yet succeed. And she didn't want to be responsible for any harm coming to anyone else.

Clearing her throat, she said to Francie, "Howard's right. I've imposed long enough. If you see Gray, please tell him—" Emotion clogged her throat, and she had to stop. "Tell him that I won't be needing his friend's help to get home."

"Are you sure?" Francie asked.

"She's positive," Howard said, urging her toward the door. "Aren't you?"

"Yes." She glanced back at Francie, wishing she could convey her desperate plea—*I need help!*

The essence of a gentleman, Howard opened the Jeep door for her and handed her the seat belt, waiting until she buckled herself in. He got in the vehicle and started the engine, waving at Francie as they drove away.

"So poor old Richard shot himself," Howard said after they were in the Jeep. "Damn, but that's a shame. Did you know that his great-grandfather once owned the place?"

"No."

"Hell of a thing, wanting what you can't have."

"Like double water rights for a property?"

He looked at her briefly. "Yeah. Like that." Then he smiled. "A little car trouble should have left you stranded. And it would have been such a tragedy, you know. A young woman shot by a sniper while she was waiting for help to come."

"A lot of effort," she said, managing to keep her voice even. He made his plans for murdering her sound so ordinary. Like ordering takeout. "The thing is, why?"

"A business problem." He shook his head. "You drew entirely the wrong conclusions from the facts."

"Conclusions that are worth millions of dollars to you," she countered. Outside, she didn't see a soul. It was far too soon to expect Gray back. And based on what Francie and Hawk had told her last night, fewer than a dozen people lived on the pueblo. Who knew where they all might be?

"Yes, there is the money," Howard said.

"I have to know. Was Richard helping you?"

Howard laughed. "Good God, no."

"He wasn't responsible for the carbon-monoxide poisoning?"

"No. I wish I had thought of that sooner. It almost worked. Who would have guessed you'd find a champion in Richard's cousin?"

Awful visions filled her head since Howard had been

aware that Gray was on his way to the ranch. What if…? "You didn't hurt Gray?" She couldn't say out loud what she most feared. What if Howard had killed him?

"Who's Gray?"

"Richard's cousin," she snapped.

"Oh, him." Howard directed his attention across the valley. "I'm afraid I lied about his wanting to see you. He's busy with Hawk." He clucked his tongue, and shook his head. "Horses. They're so unpredictable."

Relief made her eyes burn. Gray was busy with Hawk. Safe.

"And Richard?" She hated asking, hated thinking this man she had once considered a good friend was capable of murder. "You saw him yesterday?"

"I'm afraid so, yes." He twisted his mustache between his fingers. "If you hadn't so completely vanished, it would have been so much cleaner." He snapped his fingers. "Two business problems. Gone. Richard was merely greedy. But you. Disloyal after all that I've done for you. You should have known better, Audrey."

She swallowed. "He didn't commit suicide, did he?"

Howard pinned her with a glance. "That's a suspicion you'll never be able to tell anyone."

"You can't—"

"Simply kill you?" he questioned. "It should have looked as though Richard killed you, then was so stricken with remorse that he took his own life. You should have been in your car when it blew up." Howard shrugged. "You're right. After all the misfortunes of the last day or two, you're about to have another."

Audrey reached for the door handle. She didn't know how fast they were going, but anything had to be better than this. "Just in case you have decided to be uncooperative…again." A snub-nosed revolver appeared in his hand, pointed directly at her. "I don't want to have to shoot you, Audrey, but I will if you force me."

Audrey shook her head.

"This is a nice act of defiance," he murmured. "But you will go. Life always chooses life." He aimed the gun toward her head. "Are you so sure you want to die right now?"

Audrey's gaze focused on the small black hole at the end of the gun's muzzle as she pushed away a seething bubble of fear. She wanted to speak, but she couldn't make her mouth open. She wanted to move, but fear held her in the seat of the vehicle.

How could it have come to this? Howard had been a friend. A good friend. This kind of thing didn't happen to her. Her life was dull. Ordinary. And about to end.

He drove the remaining mile to the ranch, one hand on the wheel, one holding the gun aimed at her. When he came to a stop in front of the low wall surrounding the entry to the lodge, he got out of the truck and pulled her after him. Then he grabbed her by the arm and twisted it behind her.

"Let's go," he ordered, his voice harsh.

Audrey stumbled up the walkway and through the door into the main room of the lodge. She wondered where Gray was. Had he made it to the ranch? Had he called his friend? Dear God, somehow help had to be on the way.

Howard pushed her down the maze of hallways, then stopped in front of one of the doors—the linen closet, Audrey realized. He opened the door and shoved her inside. Immediately, she focused on the carved doors at the end of the closet. They were open. Beyond the doors, the black interior of the hidden room yawned—evil, beckoning.

Chapter 15

Audrey struggled to wrench free of Howard's grasp. With a last heave of force, she freed herself. Before she had taken a single step, he pushed her, and she fell forward. With no effort at all, he thrust her into the musty hidden room, the odor of dust thick around her.

"No. Please, Howard. Not in here."

Before she could stand, he closed the carved doors. She rushed forward and pushed against them, but the crossbar held the doors firm. She beat against the wood.

"Howard, not this. Please, don't do this."

"Begging, Audrey?" He clucked his tongue. "I am surprised."

Begging she had been, and she hated it. She stepped back from the door, angrily wiping the tears from her eyes. Beg a man who was intent on killing her? The absurdity brought a bitter smile to her lips. She might die, but damned if she was going to beg.

"It's a good place to escape from the smoke, don't you think?" he said. "Goodbye, Audrey."

Those simple words filled her mind with awful images as she realized he intended to set fire to the hacienda. Her resolve not to beg vanished. "Howard, wait!"

Howard walked out of the linen closet, turning off the light, and shut the door behind him. Its slam resounded through her like the gate to an inescapable prison. She cried out again, near panic surfacing.

The room was left in absolute darkness except for a sliver of light that shone underneath the door. Stronger than her fear of the moment were her phobias rooted in the distant past. Abruptly, she remembered searching the linen closet with Gray, thinking this hidden room would be a terrible place to be trapped. Little had she known.

She was a child no longer, but the fear was just as huge, just as powerful as it had been so many years ago. Pressing a fist against her mouth, she took a deep breath. Then another. Panic made her weak. Control gave her power. She took another breath, and with more resolve than she had suspected she possessed, she forced herself to think.

Thinking seemed impossible, and old, old memories surfaced.

Her mother had related the events, but until this moment, the memories had not been her own. Memories of being five, memories of running from a fire.

She had hidden, seeking an escape from the heat and the smoke. She had waited and waited, and a long time had passed before her daddy came for her. Caring for the burn left behind from a poker, he had hugged her and cried that she was safe.

Audrey touched the burn scars beneath the bracelets. Her daddy, who had died less than a year later, had come for her that day long, long ago. Today, no one would. Not Gray. Certainly not Howard.

Her gaze glued to the tiny sliver of light, Audrey pushed against the door. The crossbar held it fast. Leaning her head against the panels, she took a deep breath.

"Think," she whispered to herself. "Calm down, and just think. You can do this. He's so confident, he didn't tie you up."

And she knew why. He'd said this was to be a tragic accident. So it wouldn't do to have any marks left on her that would cast any suspicion. She looked out to the linen closet and shook the barred doors again.

The way out was not through the linen closet.

Turning, she faced the black cavern of the room—ominous as her worst nightmares. The space was so dark she couldn't tell if the room was a few feet wide or much more. Howard wouldn't have stashed her somewhere with an escape route, but hope made her think maybe he hadn't checked. Remembering that Gray had told her the passages were used to connect rooms and spy on unsuspecting houseguests, she took a step forward. Maybe this was one of those passages. Extending her arms until she touched the wall, she took another step, half expecting the floor to become a bottomless pit. Or at the next step. Or the next.

Abruptly, the wall she followed with searching fingertips turned a corner. She glanced over her shoulder, knowing she had to keep each turn she made clear in her mind or she might never find her way out.

"Left," she whispered, noting the direction she turned. A few feet later the wall turned again, right this time. "Left, right," she said, repeating the first turn and adding the next one.

When the wall angled off in another direction, she repeated the turn she took, reciting it with the others. When the maze turned again, the tunnel seemed less dark, and ahead she saw the ornately carved silhouette of a door, daylight seeping into the hallway, if only for a few inches.

Sure she was on the verge of finding a way out, she moved forward, her attention fixed on the light beyond the silhouette. Reaching the carved panel, she touched the wood and peered into the room beyond. Though she had never been in the room, from the furnishings and personal items, she knew this must be Richard's quarters.

The rustle of papers made her cock her head to the side. An instant later, Howard passed in front of the door less than a foot away from her; only the panel kept her safe from discovery. Audrey's breath caught, and she didn't let it out for fear of being heard. There was another flutter of papers, and she realized he was looking for something.

He stood so close she could smell his aftershave lotion and hoped no equally telltale signs gave her away.

Finally, he moved away from the door, and she slowly let her breath out, taking a silent step back away from the panel. The way she had come looked absolutely black, and the tunnel leading in the other direction wasn't any lighter. She hated leaving the source of light, but feared Howard's discovery more. So she pressed into the darkness, wishing she knew how to move as silently as Gray did.

Twice more the tunnel turned, then became so narrow Audrey could feel the walls on either side of her shoulders. Tempted to turn back, she stopped walking, her fingers lightly touching the cool walls. What if it was the way out? What if it was a dead end? Either way, she wouldn't know until she got to the end or until the tunnel narrowed so much she couldn't go farther.

Far ahead of her, she thought she saw light. Faint gray against the utter black of the tunnel. She moved toward it, and the light became more pronounced, a disk so small she couldn't judge how close or far away it might be.

The temperature and smell of the air changed, and she began to think the tunnel no longer wound its way through the interior of the hacienda. Gradually the light became larger and the smell of fresh air more pronounced. She increased her pace, hopeful she had found a way out of Howard's death trap.

Beneath her feet, the texture of the floor changed, and she looked down. In the dim gloom, she saw that the stone floor she had been walking on gave way to packed dirt. Items piled next to the wall caught her eye, and she paused. A couple of old pots, their designs faded, but distinctly pueblo. Another item she didn't recognize lay next to the pottery.

She almost passed the artifacts without stopping. Some awareness made her stop, however. She turned around and studied the items. Audrey knelt, her fingers tracing the pots. One of the pots seemed so much like the one that had held herbs and warm water the night of the Indian woman's labor that Audrey picked up the pot and sniffed at the opening. The only aroma was dust. Disappointed, she gently set the pot back down. She turned over the object next to the pots and discovered it was a cradle board.

Carefully, Audrey lifted it and held it in her arms. The leather lacings were stiff, the suede brittle. Moving toward the light, Audrey studied the cradle board, wondering how long it had been here.

Caught up in her examination, she ignored the faint tremor beneath her feet. Within seconds, the tremor became a more pronounced rumble. A moment later, a boom from an explosion echoed down the tunnel.

She ran toward the light. A couple of big junipers grew in front of the opening, their branches reaching into the tunnel. Held fast by the branches was a wrought-iron gate.

The acrid smell of smoke caught up with her, accompanied by roiling dust.

Audrey pulled on the gate. It didn't budge. She pushed. Still it didn't move.

Setting down the cradle board, she pulled harder, this time with both hands. On a screech of protesting hinges, the gate opened, and she slipped out, surrounded by the pungent aroma of the junipers. Her glance fell on the abandoned cradle board. Obeying an instinct she didn't question, she reached back inside and grabbed it.

Behind her, dust poured from the tunnel.

Audrey crouched beneath the junipers to get her bearings, none too anxious to leave her hiding place. To her surprise, she was a hundred feet away from the hacienda. A plume of dust hung above the roof, but there was no black smoke that would indicate a fire. Either the adobe building had not caught fire or the thick walls hid it. Audrey hoped the building was intact. Too much history had passed within its walls to so casually destroy it.

She glanced back into the tunnel. And thankfully, she had escaped. She wasn't going to become one more ghost haunting Puma's Lair.

Absently fingering the cradle board's laces, Audrey gazed out onto the landscape. She must have lost track of time, she decided, because the storm clouds that had been over the mountains when she rode to the ranch with Howard were now directly overhead. They looked as ominous as they had the first day she was here.

The billow of dust above the roof gradually settled, and she wondered if anyone else had heard the explosion.

Seeing something flutter to the ground, Audrey looked down. A couple of yellowed sheets of paper lay on the earth, apparently fallen out of the cradle board. Sitting down, Audrey picked them up, noting the paper was as fragile as the old leather on the cradle board.

Carefully, she unfolded the first sheet, covered in an ornate script and written in Spanish. Unable to read the words, she folded it and picked up the second sheet, which on first glance looked almost the same. Except this one was written in English.

Audrey read through the formal language, discovering she held in her hands a deed dated August 17, 1873, transferring the ownership of the ranch to the people of La Huerta. She lifted her face to the cleansing breeze preceding the storm. Excitement replaced her fear. Gently, she tucked the fragile papers back inside the cradle board, then hurried away from her hiding spot. The sooner she found someone from the pueblo, the better.

She had found proof that Mary's theory was right. Her great-grandmother had held the keys to the pueblo's independence and prosperity.

Audrey's excitement over the find competed with her worry that Howard would find her. She forced herself to keep walking away from the tunnel, though the urge to look back was overwhelming. The terrain surrounding the hacienda was deserted, and Audrey felt terribly alone, terribly exposed as she walked briskly across the valley. The storm clouds lowered, dark, ominous, their bellies beginning to show gray streamers of rain. However worried about Howard she might be, a more immediate concern was getting back to the pueblo before she got caught in a storm.

She hadn't gone much more than a half mile before she heard someone shout her name. Turning around, she saw Howard standing in his Jeep, a high-powered rifle cradled in his arms.

Gray dismounted from a big sorrel while Hawk closed the wide corral gate after the last horse trotted through. Horses milled around, but because of the recent rains, didn't kick up much dust. Their scent permeated the air, a good earthy smell. Since coming to Puma's Lair, Gray most enjoyed assisting Hawk with his herd when he wanted a break from sculpting. For a while this morning, the work had given him something to focus on besides the pain he had caused Audrey.

He looped the reins of his mount over the top rail of the fence. This enclosure wasn't the usual one Hawk used, and though Gray had ridden past it numerous times, he had never understood until this morning the value of having a corral in the middle of the valley. They would have had their work cut out to keep the herd together another couple of miles to the enclosure closer to Hawk's house. About two miles away, to the southeast, the roof of the hacienda was barely visible, and to the northeast, he could see the top floor of the pueblo.

The two young men who had ridden with Hawk and Gray pulled up, dismounted and, like Gray, tied their mounts to the fence.

"Thanks for your help rounding up the herd," Hawk said to Gray. "It was touch and go there for a while. Don't think I could have gotten them settled down and back here without your help."

"No problem," Gray answered.

By the time he and José caught up with the herd, Hawk had them circled, and Gray knew his efforts toward calming the animals didn't warrant any thanks.

"What set them off?" he asked.

"Probably a cougar," Hawk replied. "I haven't seen any this far from the mesa in months, though. So, maybe it was lightning."

Gray glanced at the sky, which again showed the promise of rain. If there had been any lightning today, he hadn't noticed. He shook away the fleeting suspicion that chased through his mind—one in which Audrey's boss had something to do with the stampede. With the weather so unsettled, nearly anything could have set the horses off.

Hawk ducked into the corral, moving through his horses, touching them, talking low, reassuring nonsense to them. Gradually, they settled down, giving evidence to the rapport between man and beast. A mare nudging Hawk's shoulder in an unmistakable request for attention imprinted itself on Gray's mind—an image he wanted to sculpt.

His gaze drifted across the valley toward the ranch and his workshop, where his nearly completed puma beckoned. It was work he wanted to do, but he admitted even thinking about it was an avoidance tactic. He'd made the decision to go back and talk to Audrey before Rafe arrived.

Gray knew how badly he had hurt her, and one part of

him wouldn't blame her a bit if she sent him packing. Another part, a part that scared him spitless, would die if she didn't give him another chance to explain why they had no future together. There had to be a way to do it without hurting her.

I have enough trust for both of us. If ever a man had been given a blessing and a curse, it was him. Her faith was both, a tantalizing promise he dared not explore.

I knew you couldn't hit me. Would he ever have that kind of faith? He wanted nothing more than to ride back to Mary's, scoop Audrey up on the sorrel and take her back to the secluded shelf on the mesa and show her what he had so vehemently denied—that he was falling in love with her.

Each time he remembered the moment she had turned away from him, it was a punch in the gut. He didn't want to feel that way again, and he didn't want ever again to be responsible for hurting her.

He shouldn't have touched her. But he had.

He shouldn't have given in to his own temptations. But he had.

She was a song in his blood, and he knew he would never stop wanting her.

He wanted to believe she loved him.

He wanted to believe in the future she foresaw.

He wanted to believe he would never raise a hand against her.

And he was scared to death he couldn't live up to her expectations. *I have enough faith for both of us.*

Gray looked at the clouds. If he waited much longer, he'd be making the ride across the valley in the rain. The storm clouds had settled low on the far side of the valley, their first curtains of rain sweeping toward the ground.

"Hawk!"

Gray turned around and saw Francie running toward them. Behind her, far behind, Mary followed at a slower pace. Even so, both women looked as if they had run most of the way across the valley.

"Hawk!" Francie called again, waving. "Thank God you're back."

He came out of the corral, his arms catching Francie when she collapsed against him.

"I've been looking everywhere for you," she said between gasps.

"What's wrong? What happened?" he asked.

She looked past Hawk and met Gray's eyes. "Howard Lambert came a couple of hours ago."

Ice formed in Gray's veins.

"Audrey left with him," she added. "It was the darnedest thing. One minute we were talking, and the next, she acted like she couldn't wait to leave."

"Did she go willingly?" Gray's mind raced, estimating the time to catch up with them, knowing as soon as the rains came again, the back way out would be impassable.

"Leaving was her idea," Francie said.

Gray shook his head in disbelief. He'd known she was trusting, but he also thought she was smarter than to have gone off with Howard Lambert alone.

"They could be miles from here," Gray said tightly. "Two hours is a damned big head start."

Mary shook her head. "They are still at the ranch."

"How the hell would you know that?" Gray demanded.

"I looked with the binoculars. His Jeep is still there."

"And you just let her leave with him?" A band of pure dread tightened around his chest. Unthinkable possibilities threatened his control.

Francie shrugged. "She was a guest, Gray, not a prisoner. Of course, I let her leave—"

"You just signed her death warrant," Gray shouted. "That bastard killed Richard, and he tried to kill her. Us." He raked his hands through his hair, wanting to punch someone, something. "She was supposed to be safe with you."

Francie advanced on him, her own temper at the surface. "If you had trusted me enough to tell me—" she poked him in the chest "—I would have been able to get help. But no, you keep your secrets to yourself."

That truth struck him with the force of a gunshot.

Impotent fury rolled through him, and he stared at Francie, knowing she was right, knowing his actions, not hers, were ultimately responsible. If anything happened to Audrey, the blame lay squarely at his feet.

Turning from the three of them, Gray ran toward the corral where his horse was tied. Only one thing mattered: getting to Audrey before Lambert could— Gray broke off that line of thought. He would get to her in time. Anything else was unacceptable.

Before he mounted the horse, Hawk had caught up with him and grabbed him by the arm. "You can't go off half-cocked like this."

Gray shook off Hawk's hand. "I know exactly what I'm doing!"

He vaulted into the saddle without touching the stirrup. The horse shied, as if sensing his pent-up energy. Ignoring Hawk, Gray pulled his weapon from the waistband at the small of his back. He removed the clip, double-checked the ammunition and reloaded the gun.

Why in hell, he wondered, hadn't he told anyone else that he believed Howard had killed Richard? He turned the horse away from the corral and lightly touched his heels to its sides, flicked the reins across its flanks.

The horse leaped forward, its gait lengthening into a dead run.

Beneath the anger, fear spread through Gray like a cancer. He knew all the shades of fear, but this was new. Intense. Consuming. Suffocating.

Seconds later, he heard the cannonade of other galloping

horses, and out of the side of his eye saw that Hawk and José and the other young man, Sam, had caught up with him.

A breeze from the impending storm overtook them, carrying the scent of rain and the pungent aroma of raindrops hitting dry earth.

Above the rumble of the horses' hooves drumming over the earth, Gray heard thunder.

Or was it a gunshot?

Racing over the flats, guiding the horse through rabbit-brush, sage and yucca, Gray focused on the ranch buildings, which were getting closer. Not fast enough to suit him, though.

He couldn't shake the feeling that he was too late.

Off to his left, a sudden streak of blood red appeared, then disappeared. He searched, looking for the color again.

A splintered bolt of lightning flashed, illuminating the bleak landscape. And the color appeared again.

Audrey's sweater.

He pressed the horse into a harder gallop.

She ran toward him as though chased by the hounds of hell, her hair streaming behind her in a dark cloud, something clutched in her arms. She glanced over her shoulder, and though he couldn't hear her, he knew she had cried out.

A shot rang out, muffled by the roll of thunder and the beat of hooves against packed earth. In the distance, he saw the muzzle-flash from a high-powered rifle. Gray finally spotted the Jeep.

Howard Lambert stood in the vehicle, bracing his arm against the frame of the windshield, aiming a rifle at Audrey.

Too much distance still separated Gray from Audrey; there was no way to put himself between her and Lambert.

As Gray drew closer, he could see her face had no more color than the white curtains of rain that would soon be upon them. At a distant corner of his mind, he noted she was carrying a cradle board—looking exactly like the one he had seen with the ghost of Puma's Lair.

That day, he had been helpless.

Not so today.

Audrey ran faster, her lack of coordination mute testimony to her fear.

Another shot rang out, and she screamed.

''No!'' Gray roared. He pulled his gun and fired at Lambert, knowing the distance was too far, knowing he had zero chance of hitting anything, knowing he had nothing more precious in this life than Audrey.

A bolt of lightning split open the sky. The crack of thunder that followed rumbled across the valley, intense and deafening. The first drops of rain fell, icy against Gray's heated skin.

Lambert fired again.

Audrey suddenly swerved.

Gray saw a spray of dirt, the bullet striking where she would have been had she not changed direction.

He had only one thought. Reach Lambert before he killed her.

Yards separated him from her.

''Get down!'' he shouted. ''Audrey, lie down!''

Instantly, she obeyed.

Galloping past her, he turned in his saddle to make sure she presented less of a target for Lambert. She lay flat against the ground, only partially shielded by the sagebrush. Gray had pulled his mount to a halt, putting himself and his horse between Audrey and Lambert. Gray refocused his attention on Lambert and raced forward.

Lambert pointed the rifle toward him, and Gray lifted his own weapon. Close enough that he could hit the man if he had a steady aim, Gray fleetingly realized there was no chance Lambert would miss. Gray trained the gun on Lambert and squeezed the trigger.

Gray saw the muzzle-flash of Lambert's rifle.

Gray fired again.

An instant later, an impact against his shoulder knocked him out of his saddle.

In the next moment, a tremendous explosion sent a huge fireball into the sky.

Gray hit the ground hard, and rolled to his back. Pain, hot as a poker, speared through his shoulder.

Screams and the searing smell of hot metal and burning gasoline and cold splashes of rain against his face filled his awareness. He touched a hand to his shoulder. It came away bright red.

"Damn," he muttered, aware he was on the verge of losing consciousness. This was bad.

Clear as a bell, he heard his mother's voice. *A man who lives by the gun, dies by the gun.* He had broken his promise. Abruptly, tears filled his eyes.

Chapter 16

"Oh, God. Oh, God," another feminine voice cried out, repeating those words again and again. Audrey's.

Cool hands touched his face, his neck, his chest.

"Don't you dare die on me," she cried, her voice choked.

Gray clamped a hand around one of her wrists and, with immense effort, opened his eyes. Tears streamed down her face.

He released her wrist to touch her tears, which hurt him more than the searing pain in his shoulder. "It's...okay."

"It's *not* okay." She shook her head. "I love you."

His own eyes burned. Hers was too generous a gift, especially after the way he had treated her. He longed to think he was worthy of it, longed to be the man she seemed to think he was. But he wasn't. No matter how much he wanted to tell her that he loved her. She became blurry, and he couldn't imagine why. Then, he felt her soft fingers against his cheek...brushing away tears he hadn't shed since he was a child.

Beyond her, he could see the burning wreckage of Lambert's vehicle and knew the bastard was dead. Audrey was safe. She would be okay. And that was what mattered. Relief swept through him. He loved her, and he had never beaten her. She'd be safe. He looked back at her, her beautiful face etched into his soul for all time. The effort to keep his eyes open became too much.

"No. Gray, don't leave me." She bent over him, her lips touching his cheek. Soft. Her tears touching his skin. Hot. "Help him. Oh, God, please help him."

It's okay, love.

His instincts had been right after all, he thought, memorizing her features. He'd leave her before hurting her any further.

In the distance, beyond the edge of the storm, he could see the Indian woman. Her arms opened wide, her face filled with concern and worry. Then somehow, he was there…with her. She clasped him fiercely, her arms holding him as though she would never let him go, her cheek pressed against his. Within her embrace, the overwhelming pain faded, and his arms came around her. She felt like peace.

She pulled out of his embrace, then shook him. Slivers of pain sliced through him.

You don't belong here. You must go back.

He shook his head.

Yes. She turned him around and made him face the scene behind him. Audrey crying as though her heart was broken. Hawk and Francie working frantically over his body.

She is your future. Not I.

He turned back to her.

She glanced at Audrey, then smiled. *Go home. Go. Trust your heart.*

Beyond her, Gray sensed another presence. A tall man wearing only leggings and a breechclout. She turned to face him, and the joy on her face told it all. She ran toward him, and he lifted her into his arms, whirling her around.

Arm in arm, they walked across the valley and disappeared into the mist.

Gray watched, unbearable pain consuming him.

Fourteen weeks later, those moments on the valley floor when Gray hovered between life and death were as vivid as though they had happened an hour ago. Seared in Audrey's memory were the panicked efforts to stop his bleeding, Francie's competent care of him while they waited for a helicopter to take him to Albuquerque, the endless vigil at the hospital over the next days, wondering if he would die or if he would live. During bouts of delirium, he relived those last moments before he lost consciousness, muttering a protest against going home.

Worse…far worse…was the finality of his voice after he was better. "Nothing's changed, Audrey," he told her. "I don't want you here. Go home."

And she had. Not that she had much to go home to. Federal and state agencies were investigating Howard Lambert's business dealings. The offices had been closed, and she had no job. The assets belonging to Lambert Enterprises had been frozen except for one. Puma's Lair. The old deed Audrey had found took precedence, and the ranch was being returned to the people of La Huerta. The property's transfer reinforced one of the beliefs Francie had shared with Audrey—good comes from all things.

Strangely, that belief provided the encouragement Audrey needed to follow her brother's suggestion from months ago—use her mother's life-insurance proceeds to do something for herself. Go to Hawaii if she wanted, buy jewels if she wanted. What she wanted was a house in a small town, complete with friendly neighbors and a big tree in the backyard from which a swing could be hung.

With the return of the property to La Huerta, Mary

treated Audrey as though she were a long-lost and honored daughter, telling anyone who would listen about her vision and Audrey's connection to her grandmother. Francie encouraged her to stay, even suggesting she might be a suitable manager for Puma's Lair. Now that the pueblo owned the property, they would continue the operation of the guest ranch. Audrey couldn't imagine being there, and she certainly couldn't bear the idea of being so close to Gray knowing that he didn't want her at all. She had somehow resisted asking where he had gone. For all she knew, he'd left the ranch.

With Lambert Enterprises closed down, nothing held her in Denver, and she began exploring small communities. Some impulse she chose not to question too closely led her south. Part of it, much of it—if she was totally truthful with herself—was rooted in wanting to be closer to Gray. She found several small towns in southern Colorado she liked, but the one that drew her most was La Veta. Nestled at the base of the Spanish Peaks, the town was charming, and Audrey found a house that was her dream home come to life. Her brother had been pleased for her, promising to visit soon.

Audrey had last spoken with Francie a couple of weeks before to let her know she had moved. It was a chatty conversation on Francie's part, with no mention of Gray at all. Audrey wondered how he was doing, but she didn't have the courage to ask.

Every day since leaving the ranch, Audrey thought of Gray. Through her decision to leave Denver and her subsequent move. Through the chaos of packing and unpacking.

Through the discovery that she was pregnant.

Even though she was busy moving, she had time to think, to remember, to wish for things that could never be. Her mother had successfully raised two children alone, so Audrey knew she could raise this child. However much she wanted Gray's child, being a single mom wasn't a life she had envisioned for herself. She wished for a husband, a friend, a soul mate. In Gray, she had found the last two, if only briefly. Her mother's remembered advice was bitter-sweet: if you don't have a lifetime, be thankful for the time you do have.

The sorrow and the regret for all that might have been sometimes overwhelmed her. During those times, she thought about the Indian woman and hoped for a fraction of her courage. That woman had also been pregnant and without her man. Somehow, she had found the courage to go on. And Audrey would, as well, joyfully as her mother would have wanted.

Each day, Audrey thanked God for the pregnancy, and each day, she faced a dilemma for which she had no an-swer. Should she tell Gray he was going to be a father?

That thought, as always, made her stomach clench and brought on a surge of restlessness that took her to the open window. Outside, summer was in full force, heat waves shimmering above the roof of the house across the street and birds chirping in a tree outside her window. In the next yard, children played beneath a shady cottonwood tree, their laughter happy and carefree. A woman in shorts stood outside her house, watering her lawn, chatting with her neighbor, an elderly woman wearing a broad-brimmed straw hat and holding gardening tools.

These were reminders of all the reasons Audrey had de-cided to leave Denver. The idyllic scene made her feel lonely today. She knew from experience that time healed. Even so, she doubted the hole Gray had left behind would ever be filled.

The quiet was interrupted by the rumble of a freight truck as it slowly made its way up the street. To her surprise, the vehicle stopped in front of her house, and the driver got out, coming to her door.

"Delivery for you, ma'am," he said, meeting her at the open screen door and handing her a manifest to sign.

"I haven't ordered anything," she said.

He shrugged. "I just deliver what they put in the truck."

Beyond him, she could see his helper open the back door and lower the ramp. Seemingly assured that she wanted whatever had been shipped to her, the driver went back down the sidewalk, leaving Audrey with his clipboard in her hand. They loaded a huge crate onto a dolly and headed up the sidewalk and into the living room.

The crate's cardboard walls were reinforced with pine boards on the top and bottom. The box, well over seven feet tall and nearly as wide as the door, made a refrigerator crate look small. Plastered all over the container were stickers labeled Fragile and This Side Up and Do Not Drop.

"Where do you want this?" he asked, looking around.

"I don't even know what it is," she said. "So how can I know where I want it?"

"Can't help you there." They guided the crate-laden dolly toward an empty spot in the middle of the room. Efficiently, they unstrapped the box, and the helper headed back outside. The driver held out his hand for the clipboard, then gave it back to her with a pen. "Your signature?"

Audrey signed her name, then walked around the carton after the men left. There wasn't a marking on the box to tell her where it had come from or what was inside.

She discovered opening the crate would be no easy task, since it was nailed shut. From the kitchen, she retrieved a step stool and a claw hammer to pry up the boards. Climbing the step stool, she went to work on the lid. Once it was off, straw packing met her bewildered gaze. Another trip to the kitchen, this time for plastic bags to hold the packing.

Deciding there was no way she was going to stand on her head to pull the packing out of a seven-foot-tall box, she pried away one of the sides. As soon as it was loose, and she pulled it off, she leaned it against the wall. The packing spilled onto the floor.

And within the crate stood a magnificent puma.

Its front paws stretched into the air, and its hind feet flexed for the instant it would leave the ground. Sanded smooth and polished, the wood gleamed in the afternoon sun. In disbelief, Audrey touched the mountain lion. Sleek, cool and more perfect than she could have ever imagined. Numbly, she backed up and plopped onto one of the dining-room chairs behind her.

She sat there for a long time, watching the light slide across the puma's lustrous body, illuminating each muscle, each nuance of its expression in turn. Like the man who carved it, the puma was intense, powerful, graceful. Perfect. The work was fit for the finest galleries; instead, it was here in her small, modest living room.

And she could not fathom why he had sent it.

"Oh, Gray, why?" she asked on an anguished whisper, her throat clogged, her eyes sandpapery from the tears that would not fall.

"Because you made me believe in possibilities."

The baritone voice, familiar now only in her dreams, echoed her deepest wish for him. Her imagination had tormented her before, and each time she had glanced up, hoping to see him, she realized all she heard was the longing within her heart. This time, she refused to look, her attention remaining focused on the puma.

"Audrey?"

Slowly, her gaze left the sculpture. Her heart pounding, she finally looked at the front door. Shadowed by the screen door, a man stood on the porch. A tall man with broad shoulders.

She rose from the chair and moved toward the door with all the care of a demolition expert approaching a bomb.

A man with intense eyes.

She swallowed, not daring to believe he was actually here.

He opened the screen door and stood there watching her. He was thinner, the creases in his cheeks more pronounced, his eyes more shadowed than she remembered.

Too scared to hope he was really here, she couldn't say a word.

"Ah, damn, this was a mistake," he finally said, letting go of the door. It slammed closed, and he took a step toward the edge of the porch.

"No! Wait."

Slowly, he turned around. She opened the door and held out her hand.

"Please. Come in."

Stiffly, he walked into the house, not stopping until he came face-to-face with the puma. Feeling more awkward than she ever had in her life, Audrey followed Gray. His hair was tousled as though he had driven with the windows rolled down. A teal-green golf shirt stretched over his back, emphasizing the breadth of his shoulders.

"You're okay?" she asked. "You're all recovered from the gunshot…?"

He rolled his shoulder and turned around to face her. "Yeah. You?"

"Fine." She met his eyes briefly before looking again at the sculpture.

"You moved."

"Yeah." The word came out as though she had run a long way and was out of breath. She glanced around the room where boxes still needed to be unpacked. She wanted to look her fill at him, but his intense stare made it impossible to do so without his detection. "Can I get you anything? Iced tea? Lemonade?"

"That would be nice."

She fled to the kitchen, bright compared to the dimness

of the living room. Filling a pair of glasses with ice cubes, she was acutely aware that Gray had followed her.

"How did you find me?" she asked.

"Francie gave me your address." Joining her at the counter, he reached out and touched the leaf of one of the African violets in the window. "I hope that was okay."

Such a simple gesture shouldn't have reminded her what his hands felt like touching her. But it did.

"Fine." Deciding she sounded like an idiot, she poured the lemonade, unaware her hands were shaking until Gray took the pitcher from her. His remembered heat surrounded her, inviting as summer sunshine.

Setting the container on the counter, he took both of her hands within his. "I'll leave if I'm making you this nervous."

She stared at his clasped hands a moment before meeting his eyes. "I don't want you to go," she said, her voice husky.

He expelled a huge sigh. "This isn't easy, is it?"

She shook her head.

The corner of his mouth lifted. "Then maybe I should just lay all my cards on the table."

Not knowing what to say, she simply watched him. He squeezed her hands and let them go.

Wandering toward the back of the house, he stopped at the screen door and stared into the backyard, which was dominated by a big apple tree.

His back to her, he said, "I want you to have the puma. But it comes with a price."

"Can I afford it?" she asked. Her voice sounded strangled to her.

"I don't know." He turned to face her. "It's a package deal." He paused, held her eyes with his own when she finally looked at him. "I come with it."

Some of the awful constriction around her heart eased.

"If I take the puma, it's forever," she whispered.

"That's what I hoped."

One second, she was separated from him by six feet of kitchen floor. The next, she was caught in his arms in an embrace so fierce she couldn't breathe. She didn't care. She held him close, finding within his arms that sense of belonging she had associated with him from the beginning.

Suddenly, he lifted her up and returned to the living room, where he sat down on the couch, cradling her on his lap.

"I've missed you so much," she said, tracing the line of his jaw with her fingertips.

"Me, too." He clasped one of her hands within his and brought her palm to his mouth. The touch of his lips against her sensitive skin made her shiver.

"What made you change your mind?" she asked.

Easing his hands into her loose hair, he encouraged her to rest her head on his shoulder. Inhaling his aroma, she waited, sensing he was searching for the right words.

"I damned near got you killed because I didn't trust anyone else to take care of you," he said, his voice a deep rumble against her ear.

Though she didn't wholly agree with that statement, she remained silent.

"And I didn't trust myself to be the kind of man you deserve."

She tipped her head back so she could look at him.

"It's one of the things I most admire about you," he said. "Your willingness to trust. Do you know how rare that is?"

"Do you trust yourself now?" she asked softly.

He looked down at her, his hazel eyes dark. "I don't know, love. But I want to try."

She put her hands against his neck. "I love you."

"Ah, Audrey, I love you, too." His lips touched her mouth in a shimmering caress. "I love you more than I've ever loved anyone or anything."

Then he gave her the kiss she had been waiting for. So deep it sparked her desire for more, so tender it brought tears to her eyes.

"I have something to tell you," she said when the kiss ended.

"Whatever it is, it doesn't matter." His lips roamed over her face as he pressed kisses against her skin. "Nothing matters except being together."

"I'm going to have a baby," she said.

The kisses stilled.

"Your baby."

He lifted his head, his eyes dark and unreadable as they met hers. His gaze fell to her stomach.

"My baby?" Gently, he placed his palm against her belly. "How the hell did that happen?"

His tone was gruff, but she heard the note of happiness underneath. The last bands of apprehension loosened, and she dared a smile.

"Must have been something in the water," she teased. "That night in the pool." She touched the etching of Kokopelli on her bracelet. "Or Indian fertility symbols."

"You think so?" The corners of his eyes crinkled. "You, and this little one in here. You're a package deal, too?"

"'Fraid so."

"Our baby?" His somber expression eased into the smile she loved so much.

She nodded.

"Are you okay? No wonder you were so scared when I showed up." The smile abruptly left his face. "If I hadn't come to my senses, would you have told me?"

Cupping his cheek with her hand, she said, "I honestly don't know. I'm glad I won't have to find out."

Gathering her close, he whispered in her ear, "I'm glad, too. And I'm glad you're pregnant. I'll be a good father, I promise."

"I already know you will."

He brushed his cheek against hers. "And I'll be a good husband to you, love. I promise."

Emotion clogged her throat. "I know."

"We can still make love, can't we?"

"We'd better be able to."

He looked down at her, and she felt her face heat.

"Right now?" he asked.

She nodded, feeling the heat spread.

He laughed, cupping her face with his hand. "I love it when you go all shy on me."

She smiled, reveling in his laughter, realizing what a precious gift it was.

"Except, I know there is a brazen woman hiding in there." He kissed her deeply.

"Only with you," she murmured.

He stood up, holding her effortlessly in his arms, then carried her into the hallway off the living room, finding the bedroom.

When he set her down, she put her arms around him, gazing up at him with all the love in her heart.

"Oh, Gray, my love. You've come home to me," she whispered.

Cupping her face with his hands, he bent to her lips. "It's where I belong. To you. Forever."

* * * * *

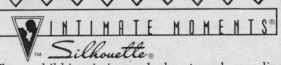

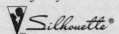

If you enjoyed what you just read,
then we've got an offer you can't resist!

Take 2 bestselling love stories FREE!

Plus get a FREE surprise gift!

Clip this page and mail it to Silhouette Reader Service™

IN U.S.A.	**IN CANADA**
3010 Walden Ave.	P.O. Box 609
P.O. Box 1867	Fort Erie, Ontario
Buffalo, N.Y. 14240-1867	L2A 5X3

YES! Please send me 2 free Silhouette Intimate Moments® novels and my free surprise gift. Then send me 6 brand-new novels every month, which I will receive months before they're available in stores. In the U.S.A., bill me at the bargain price of $3.57 plus 25¢ delivery per book and applicable sales tax, if any*. In Canada, bill me at the bargain price of $3.96 plus 25¢ delivery per book and applicable taxes**. That's the complete price and a savings of over 10% off the cover prices—what a great deal! I understand that accepting the 2 free books and gift places me under no obligation ever to buy any books. I can always return a shipment and cancel at any time. Even if I never buy another book from Silhouette, the 2 free books and gift are mine to keep forever. So why not take us up on our invitation. You'll be glad you did!

245 SEN CNFF
345 SEN CNFG

Name	(PLEASE PRINT)	
Address	Apt.#	
City	State/Prov.	Zip/Postal Code

* Terms and prices subject to change without notice. Sales tax applicable in N.Y.
** Canadian residents will be charged applicable provincial taxes and GST.
   All orders subject to approval. Offer limited to one per household.
   ® are registered trademarks of Harlequin Enterprises Limited.

INMOM99   ©1998 Harlequin Enterprises Limited

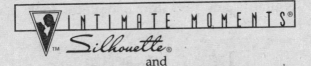

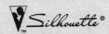

Available July 1999 from Silhouette Books...

AGENT OF THE BLACK WATCH
by BJ JAMES

The World's Most Eligible Bachelor:
Secret-agent lover Kieran O'Hara was on a desperate mission.
His objective: Anything but marriage!

Kieran's mission pitted him against a crafty killer...and
the prime suspect's beautiful sister. For the first time in his
career, Kieran's instincts as a man overwhelmed his lawman's
control...and he claimed Beau Anna Cahill as his lover. But
would this innocent remain in his bed once she learned his
secret agenda?

Each month, Silhouette Books brings you an
irresistible bachelor in these all-new, original
stories. Find out how the sexiest, most-sought-after men
are finally caught....

Available at your favorite retail outlet.

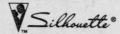

PSWMEB11

THE MACGREGORS OF OLD...

#1 *New York Times* bestselling author

NORA ROBERTS

has won readers' hearts with her enormously popular
MacGregor family saga. Now read about the MacGregors'
proud and passionate Scottish forebears in this
romantic, tempestuous tale set against the bloody
background of the historic battle of Culloden.

Coming in July 1999

REBELLION

One look at the ravishing red-haired beauty and Brigham
Langston was captivated. But though Serena MacGregor
had the face of an angel, she was a wildcat who spurned
his advances with a rapier-sharp tongue. To hot-tempered
Serena, Brigham was just another Englishman to be
despised. But in the arms of the dashing and dangerous
English lord, the proud Scottish beauty felt her hatred
melting with the heat of their passion.

Available at your favorite retail outlet.

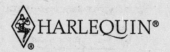

This August 1999, the legend
continues in Jacobsville

DIANA PALMER

LOVE WITH A
LONG, TALL TEXAN

A trio of brand-new short stories featuring
three irresistible Long, Tall Texans

GUY FENTON, LUKE CRAIG
and CHRISTOPHER DEVERELL...

This August 1999, Silhouette brings readers an
extra-special collection for Diana Palmer's legions
of fans. Diana spins three unforgettable stories of
love—Texas-style! Featuring the men you can't get
enough of from the wonderful town of Jacobsville,
this collection is a treasure for all fans!

They grow 'em tall in the saddle in Jacobsville—and
they're the best-looking, sweetest-talking men to be
found in the entire Lone Star state. They are proud,
hardworking men of steel and it will take
the perfect woman to melt their hearts!

**Don't miss this collection of original
Long, Tall Texans stories...available in
August 1999 at your favorite retail outlet.**

Silhouette®

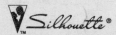